SOLDIER FOR THE STARLING

SAFE HAVEN SECURITY BOOK 1

BREANNA LYNN

ISBN: 978-1-955359-46-7 (ebook)

ISBN: 978-1-955359-47-4 (paperback)

Cover Design by: Lori Jackson Design

Edited by: Happily Editing Anns & VB Proofreads

Printed in United States of America

https://breannalynnauthor.com

There's safety in the light, but security is found in the dark.

Protecting Evie should be my mission—nothing more. But the longer I'm near her, the harder it is to remember where the job ends and obsession begins.

Her honey-colored eyes strip me bare. One look, and every instinct I've spent years sharpening is thrown into chaos. I've faced warzones, walked through fire—but nothing compares to the storm she brings just by standing too close.

She's on the run from something brutal. Something that wants her silenced. And I've made it my job to stand in the way. But with every touch, every breathless moment between us, the risk grows.

I was trained to protect. Not to fall.

But I've already crossed the line—and now I'm not sure I can pull myself back.

Can I keep her safe from the danger hunting her... or will my need for her be the one thing that finally breaks us both?

For Dennis...
For showing me that there are more chapters in my story and that book boyfriends do exist.

FROM THE AUTHOR

The prologue in this book is not necessary to understand the rest of the story. It features graphic, on page sexual assault and may be triggering for some readers. It is included only for those who wish to know what Evie's life was like before Sawyer.

Should you choose to skip it, please begin with Chapter 1 in the story.

PROLOGUE

EVIE

$\mathcal{I}$ hate this place.

And not because I'm tired from my "show" at the dive bar next door. The one Brad insists is a strong venue. The four songs I sang tonight aren't nearly enough to wear me out, but I tried that excuse anyway when we left the bar and Brad dragged me to the strip club he likes to visit when my set is done.

The stripper on stage finishes her dance to wolf whistles and applause, then disappears behind the curtain. Brad's attention turns back to the table just in time for another topless woman to drop off three shots—one for him, one for me, and one for the owner who sits with us when we're here.

"Shots?" The skeevy owner gestures to the glasses of clear liquid on the sticky table.

Brad grabs for his greedily before tossing it back.

I keep my hands in my lap, unwilling to dull my awareness in this situation. The way the owner looks at me makes my skin crawl and anxiety cramp my stomach.

"You don't want one?"

There's darkness in the way his focus lingers on the shot before it moves to my breasts. He never looks me in the eye. I squirm, and my hands itch to tug my top up higher to cover my exposed cleavage—not that there's much fabric, given the halter-style bikini cut top that Brad insisted I wear tonight.

"No, thank you," I say quietly.

"Come on, songbird. Have a drink." Brad lifts the glass in my direction, and liquid sloshes out and onto my bare thighs.

I cringe and shake my head.

"Your loss." He turns it in the direction of the owner, who lifts his own glass, then they toss back the shots.

The slam of the glasses on the table startles me, and I jump a little. The owner's smile at my response is a twist of his lips that looks more like a snarl.

"When can we convince you to get up there, *songbird*?" he asks and nods toward the stage.

Bile rises in my throat, and I look at Brad for confirmation that it'll never happen. I should know better after five years. Instead of reassurance, his face is full of consideration as he appraises me.

"You think she'd be good up there?" he asks.

The owner hums in response. "Never know until we see firsthand."

Oh god.

For the last five years I've done everything to make my dream of becoming a singer/songwriter a reality. *Everything.* I've given up so much of myself that I hardly recognize the person in the mirror anymore. But getting up there—doing what the women in this club do—that won't help me achieve my dream.

Brad's slimy gaze drags down my barely covered body. He licks his lips and palms himself through his slacks. Shit. He's visibly hard. I have to fight the shudder that wants to work its way down my body.

"Come on."

He pulls me from the chair and yanks me toward the back room.

"W-where are we going?"

Despite my attempts to stand still, he drags me behind him until we come to a scarred door in a dark hallway. With a flick of his wrist, he twists the knob, then he shoves me into the room. It's not as dark as the hallway, but I wish it was. Dim lights line the ceiling along the perimeter of the space, but the majority of the light filters in through the window that looks out into the club itself and casts a red hue on the single chair set up in the middle of the floor. The room smells of stale beer, cigarettes, and desperation.

Behind me, the door slams shut, making me jump. I whirl around in time to watch Brad flip the lock. Then he's palming himself again as he stalks toward me. It takes everything in me not to retreat against the wall.

A scream claws at my throat. I don't want to be here.

You have no choice.

"We need to work on your sex appeal. You're too stiff on stage."

It's obvious that he's had too much to drink tonight. The words are slurred, and his steps are unsteady as he bypasses me and slings himself into the chair in the middle of the room. It wobbles under his weight before settling against the concrete floor.

"Strip," he demands, unbuttoning his pants.

"S-s-strip?"

Panic locks a rough hand around my throat and tightens its grip as I stutter the word.

"Now."

Malice hardens his voice, and fear joins the panic.

"But the window—everyone can see."

"It's a mirror." He spits it like I'm a simple-minded idiot. "I don't like to repeat myself."

No, he doesn't. It's a lesson I've learned many times over. My fingers tremble when I lift them to the button on the skirt that barely covers my ass. Closing my eyes, I unsnap the button, and the skirt falls to my feet, leaving me clad in only a pair of small panties and my top.

"Dance for me, songbird."

I open my eyes to find his hand wrapped around his dick, stroking it as he waits for me to obey.

"Like what we just watched," he clarifies, tipping his chin up.

I'm frozen. Glued to the grimy floor beneath me.

He narrows his eyes but doesn't stop stroking. "You want your deal, right? Reverb has invested a lot of money in you. It would be a shame for us to sue you for breach of contract."

I swallow around the lump of shame in my throat. I've given up every other aspect of my identity. What will I have to show for it if I refuse now?

Tears burn behind my eyes, but I bite the inside of my cheek to stem them and breathe through the wave of panic while I focus on the beat of the song that pounds through the room. Once I've found the rhythm, I move.

"That's it. Now closer."

My feet move on autopilot until I'm between his spread legs.

"Turn around and keep moving."

His heat presses against my back as he stands and yanks the ties of my shirt. He pulls my hair in the process, and I cry out in pain.

His responding chuckle is dark. Depraved. "I know what you want, songbird."

He has no idea. I want to run, to erase the last five years, to forget I ever wanted to leave home.

My shirt flutters to the floor, then his hands find the sides of my underwear and wrench at the flimsy strings until they snap. But I keep moving, blocking out the sheer humiliation that floods my body and begs me to run.

"Such a good girl," he crows, dropping into his seat again.

He grips my hips painfully and changes the rhythm of my body, forcing me back toward him.

"I don't know why I didn't think of this before. Usually you can't touch the girls in this room. But you're mine to do with as I please."

He loops an arm around me and grips my breast to pinch my nipple viciously.

"Face me."

He doesn't give me the chance to respond. With his rough hands on my hips again, he spins my body. His pants and boxers are around his ankles now. His shirt has been unbuttoned, and his hard dick points toward the ceiling.

He grins at me and pinches my other breast.

"If I thought we could make money, you'd be on that stage," he says.

No. Ice-cold panic clenches like a vise around my stomach.

"But your tits are too small. Maybe after a boob job. We'll call a plastic surgeon friend of mine tomorrow."

This has never been about what I want. He constantly reminds me that these are the things I have to do to *make it*. But I don't want the fame if it comes at this price.

"For now, I want you on your knees, songbird."

Stomach plummeting and tears threatening, I sink slowly to the cold, dirty floor.

He wraps my ponytail around his fist and yanks me toward his lap. "You know what to do."

I pull back, desperate for the nightmare to end, but he tugs harder in response, his cock now brushing against my lips.

"Open."

Over and over for five years, I've thought things couldn't get worse. But tonight is rock bottom. From the show that no one bothered to attend to the disgusting experience in the back of the seedy strip club.

Hours later, it still feels like dirt covers my skin. Even after the hot shower I took when we got back to the apartment. Probably because even as I scrubbed my body raw, I wasn't allowed to be alone. I didn't have to endure Brad's touch again. No, he stood in the bathroom during what should have been a moment of relief and masturbated, forcing me to watch.

You can't do this anymore. It's not worth it.

Tears trail into my pillow, but I'm careful not to make a sound, terrified to wake up Brad, who is sprawled next to me. Something in me died tonight. It's been coming on for a while, but this was it.

The death of my dream.

What else is keeping me here?

Nothing.

But Brad won't let me go, not willingly.

I can't go home. He knows where my parents live. And he'd only manipulate me until I came back.

So I lie in the dark and create a plan. I'll leave. Change my identity. Hide so he can't find me.

He lets out a stuttered snore and flops onto his side. He snakes an arm around me and yanks me against him. I tense, expecting something more, and sigh in relief when his snore continues to drone in my ear.

Because there's a pinprick of light in the distance of this darkness, and for the first time in almost five years, a spark of something long extinguished ignites inside me.

Hope.

CHAPTER 1

EVIE

TWO YEARS LATER

The baby's belly laugh carries across the reception room and tugs at my ovaries. Or maybe it's the brawny man inspiring the sound. When my boss, Mia, insisted I tag along to her best friend Michaela's wedding after filming wrapped, I should have declined. I should have gone home.

But I didn't want to give up the chance to ogle Michaela's older brother Sawyer—even if it's from a distance. Because as much as I love to admire him, he knows too much about me. About my past.

Deep blue eyes meet mine, and warmth floods my cheeks. I've been caught staring. I glance away from Sawyer and his nephew quickly, focusing instead on the couples swaying on the dance floor—Michaela and her new husband, West, are there, and so are Mia and her husband, Garrett.

Seven years ago, I dreamed of being part of one of those kinds of couples. Happy, in love. I'd be famous, with a handful of chart-topping albums, and my husband would be supportive and kind. But reality crushed that dream and stomped on it for good measure.

Stop wishing for something that will never happen.

Standing, I grab my small purse and turn my back on the vision, then make my way quickly to the restroom. Two years ago, after I ran away from Brad, I made the decision. I can't let anyone get close enough to ask questions.

Because there would be questions. Ones I had no desire to answer.

At least now, when I look in the mirror, I see a little of myself in the nondescript brown hair and the baggier clothes. I'm... content with being Mia's assistant. She's my friend. And when I'm not at her house or on location with her, I'm at home in my cheerful apartment. I don't venture out except for errands and the occasional trip to a coffee shop she and I found.

My life is predictable. I've curated it that way. Except when Sawyer is close.

"No," I tell my reflection. "There are no feelings there. There can't be."

Taking a deep breath, I wash my hands and stand a little straighter. I'll find Mia and let her know I'm headed back to my room.

Only the first person I see when I open the bathroom door is the one person I was hoping to avoid.

Sawyer King.

Looking sexier than he should in the remnants of his tuxedo —dress pants, white shirt with the top button undone, and a loose bowtie.

"W-what are you doing here?" I swallow to steel the tremor in my voice.

"Looking for you."

"Oh," I breathe out, caught off guard. Immediately, fear settles in my stomach.

I don't want to talk about my history. Especially here. And there's no other reason he'd want to talk to me.

"Why?" I croak out.

"Mia asked me to come find you and let you know she and Garrett were heading back to their room."

I barely hold back a groan. Of course my matchmaking boss would ask the hunky single guy to deliver her message. She could have texted me since my phone is in my bag. But her tactics no longer surprise me. She tried to set me up with Garrett before she realized she was in love with him.

I. Am. Not. Interested. In. Dating.

It may be time to remind her of that. Even if she doesn't understand why.

"Thank you. For letting me know."

I turn and head for the exit, shuffling as quickly as I can in heels.

"You're going to need a ride back to your hotel."

I freeze and spin around. He knows where I'm staying? "H-how—"

"I know where everyone is staying. Curse of the job." He shrugs like that explains it all.

I guess it should, given that he owns a security company.

"Can I give you a lift?" he asks.

My choices are to walk back to the hotel in the dark, grab an Uber or Lyft, driven by a stranger, of course—are there even ride share options available here?—or confine myself in a small space with the only man I've found attractive in years.

Dammit. Is there really a choice?

"Um, okay."

"Are you ready?" His question is a murmur as he steps closer.

Why does the low timbre of his voice affect me the way it does?

"Y-yeah. Yes."

He reaches out to guide me toward the exit, and I shift out of the way. His hand drops, and he puts some additional distance between us.

"My car is this way."

The leather and vanilla scent that clings to him is even stronger in the small space of his rental as he pulls out of the parking lot. The hum of the road is the only sound. No small talk, and no radio.

I brace myself for his questions, dreading the moment he brings up my past.

Only he doesn't.

He drives the car like he does everything else—confidently. With his left hand, he grips the steering wheel easily, while his right arm is propped on the console between us. He doesn't take his eyes off the road, and he doesn't try to fill the silence, like he's content to ride in absolute quiet. I envy that quiet confidence. That assuredness of who he is and the space he inhabits.

Meanwhile, I'm constantly fixated on where I am and who I'm with. Like right now. I've got my attention trained on what's ahead, but when the fingers on his right hand stretch forward, I can feel them. And he's not even touching me. This desire to be closer buffets me like waves crashing on the shore.

The hotel isn't far from the venue, but for my sanity, the ride can't be over soon enough.

"Thank you," I tell him as we pull into the hotel's lot, my fingers already gripping the door handle.

"Can I walk you to your room?"

A small part of me knows I should decline, but the bigger part wins before I can harness my response.

"Okay."

Why did you do that?

Though I hate to admit it, his presence calms all the anxiety that normally filters through my blood. I'm attracted to him, but there's something more. Something I'm afraid to think about too much but loathe to distance myself from the way I normally would.

Without giving me time to rescind my response, he rounds the car, each of his strides precise and purposeful, and opens my door.

Inside, the lobby lights are dim, and the sound of a TV comes from the office, but we're alone as we make our way to the elevator. The silence continues as I press the button for the third floor. The chime sounds, and then the elevators open to the empty floor.

I don't look at him again until I'm in front of my door and have swiped my key and gripped the handle. All the lights I left on still blaze brightly, and I breathe a sigh of relief. I don't like the dark.

"Thank you." I meet his gaze, then quickly drop my focus to the shiny button near his throat.

"You're welcome."

"Good night, Sawyer." I take a step back to retreat to my room.

"Evie?"

The way he says my name—like he can't help himself—pulls my attention back to his face. Only this time, I can't look away. The deep blue of his irises is magnetic, the color like light filtering through the ocean. And just like the ocean, I could so easily drown in them.

"Evie." This time my name is a whisper on his lips. He lifts his index finger and drags it along my jaw.

For the first time in years, I don't pull away from physical contact—I can't. I want that light touch too much.

"Hmm?"

"You looked beautiful today," he murmurs.

Mia begged me to let her pick my dress, so it's more fitted than usual but still loose around my curves.

"I did?"

13

"Mm-hmm."

"Thank you."

It's hard to get my words out. My lips tingle with curiosity, almost silencing them. What would it be like to kiss Sawyer? I've kissed guys before. Before Brad. High school boys who had no idea what they were doing. But something tells me Sawyer knows exactly what to do.

We've gone silent again, and his finger continues to drag back and forth along my jaw. The sensation is hypnotic, sending that question—what would it be like to kiss a man like Sawyer?—pulsing through my body until all the anxiety is gone. All the walls I've kept in place are down.

Just once.

Standing on my tiptoes, I cup the back of his neck and tug him down until our lips meet. He sucks in a surprised breath, but it doesn't take him long to take masterful control of the kiss. It's a slow slide of his mouth over mine, small kisses pressed from one side to the other, then he settles them fully into place.

He licks along the seam, requesting entry, and I open for his tongue to tangle with mine. Cupping my face, he brushes his thumb over my cheekbone, as if I'm the most precious thing in his universe.

My fingers flex against his shoulders. I want more than anything to take this further. To be worthy of him. To leave my past behind and stay lost in his kiss.

I allow myself one more heartbeat, then I break the kiss. His eyes flutter open, and the desire in them is nearly crippling. I step back again, shivering at the cool air that rushes between us.

"Evie?" The desire in his eyes turns to confusion, and a frown mars his handsome face.

"Good night, Sawyer." I retreat fully and close the door quickly.

"Good night." His voice is clear on the other side of the door.

Lifting my fingers to my swollen lips, I try to memorize the way his mouth felt pressed against mine.

It's the closest thing to normal I'll ever allow myself to have.

Because Brad is still out there, and my baggage is heavy. I'd never allow myself to burden someone else with it. I may dream about that shared kiss with Sawyer, but my reality is haunted by a very real boogeyman.

CHAPTER 2

EVIE

TWO AND A HALF YEARS LATER

*C*ouples. Romance. Love.

It's everywhere.

It's Valentine's Day. It's supposed *to be everywhere.*

The holiday doesn't make the lovey-dovey scenes any more palatable, though. February fourteenth comes and goes every year, and I avoid it at all costs. But somehow, this year, I let myself forget. One would think Mia and Garrett would tip me off, but every day looks like Valentine's Day in their presence.

They still act like newlyweds. All romance and twitterpated looks all the time. With Mia's filming schedule since her award-winning best actress performance in *The Queen's Consort* and Garrett's busy schedule running Arabesque Productions US, I suppose their extended honeymoon phase makes sense.

And now that Mia is expecting a baby, they're even more touchy-feely. I don't see any of this changing anytime soon.

"Ev-Evelyn?" The barista holding my dirty chai latte stumbles over the simple name.

My blood runs cold. It's been years since I've used my real name. Two to be exact. Now I go by Evie. Rushing forward, I snatch the cup and inspect the mess scrawled on the side of it. An *E* and a *v* are the only discernible letters. I groan at the smudges after them. No wonder the worker donning a green apron screwed it up.

Ten years ago, I would have laughed off the situation and accepted my drink. Maybe flirted with the cute guy over my old-fashioned name. Six years ago, I wouldn't have been in the coffee shop. I wasn't allowed to frequent places like this. Right now, I just want to run back to the safety of my apartment.

When I left this morning, it was so I could avoid the loneliness waiting for me at home.

But loneliness is better than how exposed I feel right now.

"That's me," I mumble, still clutching the cup in front of me.

He studies me for an awkward moment. Or maybe it only feels awkward for me. Like he can see through the brown hair dye from a box and the baggy beige sweater. Like any moment now he'll ask me if he knows me or if I realize I look like a woman who was once almost famous.

Instead he gives me a small smile. "Have a good night."

I shrink into myself, hunching my shoulders while he walks back to the espresso machine. Only someone crazy, stupid, or forgetful would risk coming here on a night dedicated to couples. Every one of the cozy couches I normally curl up on is occupied by a couple in love. The place is packed.

Not one person here even realized I almost had a panic attack that almost sent me running from the shop screaming. It's fine. I'm still as unnoticeable as I was when I walked in. No one recognizes me. And they haven't in almost five years. With a sigh, I drop my shoulders.

Stop being stupid. No one here cares enough to bother giving you a second glance.

This is LA. Where a real famous person could walk into this

coffee shop at any time. Not an almost was. With a hand on the door handle, I let out a breath, ready to push out into the bustling LA twilight. I'm fortified with caffeine for my rush hour fight of a drive, then I can settle in for a quiet evening at home. It's my pattern. It's predictable. It's safe. The three things I require in my life.

A balmy breeze pushes against me, but that's not what has all the fine hairs at the nape of my neck standing on end. It's the sensation of being watched. And at the same time, I can just make out the melody to "Good Obsession"—one of the last songs I recorded—under the coffee house jazz that buzzes pleasantly through the speakers. The shiver that works its way down my spine is full of adrenaline-spiked fear. On instinct, I squeeze the cup in my hand, then gasp as hot liquid sloshes out of the lid and splashes onto my hand and wrist.

The door wrenches from my grasp, and I bobble the cup, almost upending it in my clumsiness. The last few days have been long. I've spent countless hours working Mia's schedule for projects around her maternity leave. I wanted to treat myself, and this place makes the best dirty chais I've ever had. Only now I wish I hadn't stopped at all.

"Oh. Sorry. After you." The woman on the other side of the door waves me through.

"Th-thanks."

The door shuts behind her, and I'm alone on the street. The flight-or-fight response still buzzes through me, and I spend most of my drive home checking the rearview mirror. But all I see are a bunch of headlights, just like I would on any normal night in LA. It's not until I'm in my apartment with my door locked behind me and my now-cold drink still clutched in my hand like a security blanket that the tension eases from my shoulders.

"Well, there goes that."

Grimacing, I pour the contents down the drain, breathing in

the scent of cinnamon and cloves as the creamy liquid disappears.

The scent brings thoughts of a certain someone to mind. Cinnamon and vanilla, but a hint of leather too. When I finally let go and kissed Sawyer at his sister's wedding two and a half years ago. A mistake. One I'll avoid making again at all costs. And whether by his design or mine, I haven't seen him since that night. It's given me plenty of time to bolster my determination to keep my hands, and my lips, off the brooding, broad-shouldered hunk of man muscle. Even if I do crave him like a junkie craves his next fix.

Nothing can come of that.

Not anymore.

Tossing the empty disposable cup in the trash, I flip on all the lights as I shuffle to my bedroom, not bothering to turn anything off when I lie down.

There's safety in the light.

By the next afternoon, I've convinced myself that the anxiety that pulled at me like an undertow was nothing more than my imagination. A caffeine-induced panic.

And if the only caffeine I consumed was the one cup of coffee yesterday morning?

There are a hundred other ways I can excuse the panic. Over-stimulation. Stress. Whatever.

My powers of self-persuasion are so strong I manage to delude myself into limiting my caffeine for the day. Herbal tea with honey. Like half the plastic bear worth. The half-empty bastard judges me from his spot in Mia's cupboard, and I add a note to my grocery list on my phone to pick up another bottle for her.

"Stop looking at me like that," I say and slam the cupboard door.

Great, Evie, just great. You're talking to an inanimate object.

Correction. I'm lecturing the inanimate object. Like the distinction makes me feel better.

Mia went to lunch with Michaela and her son, Benji, while I stayed behind to respond to emails about schedules. Ten years ago, if I'd been offered a position as an assistant, I would have responded with "hell, no." From the time I was a little girl watching *American Idol*, my dream was to be a singer. As I got older, I amended that to singer/songwriter.

But that dream was why I came to LA after high school, despite my parents' insistence I stay close to home. If it were up to them, I would have enrolled at Michigan State and gotten my teaching degree, just like they did.

But my dream involved something neither of them could understand, though they tried. They love our hometown. So does my brother, Austin. I'm the odd one. And even after I failed, I didn't want to admit that to them. I was ashamed. For more reasons than I wanted to admit. It was easier, still is, to call them once in a while and keep the conversations short than to tell them what happened.

A breeze rustles the papers on the counter, and the goose-bumps I got rid of last night push back to the surface.

"Mia and Garrett's property is gated," I remind myself.

Despite the reassurance, I check the lock on the front door, and I breathe a sigh of relief when the deadbolt is still in the locked position.

"See? Quit being crazy. Finish the emails."

I have several episodes of *The Bachelor* to binge watch tonight, and I want to get home sooner rather than later.

Thank god Mia isn't here to see me talking to myself. I may have caught her mid-monologue several times over the four years I've worked for her, but that's different. She's a creative type.

What about you?

No. I used to be. Now I'm firmly ensconced in my role as her assistant and, as such, I need to act like it.

"Which means you can't forget the tea you took a break to make," I say with a roll of my eyes.

Because I did.

Steam still rises from the cup sitting on the counter as I pick it up and take a sip of the lemongrass and mint flavored tea. I close my eyes, rolling my shoulders back as I take a deep breath in through my nose and release it through my mouth. The focused breathing is yet another attempt to clear the residual anxiety that crops up if I think about it for too long. Busy. I need to stay busy. Back to work.

Spinning from the counter, I keep my eye on the rim of the teacup so I don't spill. But that goal is negated when it goes flying across the kitchen and shatters on the floor. A strangled scream gargles from my throat and my heart pounds in my chest.

"Ev, you okay? I thought you heard me say hello when I got home." Garrett's easygoing smile morphs to a frown as he steps forward and lifts his hands in concern.

I wave him away before he can cup my shoulders. Even that soothing gesture is too much touching for me to handle right now.

"Garrett, oh my god. You scared the crap out of me." I slide back a step, then another until the counter is between us.

I try to laugh off my ridiculousness, but it sticks in my dry throat and comes out more like a sob.

"Did something happen? Where's Mia?" He pivots, scanning the room for his wife.

"No, everything's fine. Mia's at lunch with Michaela."

His shoulders ease slightly, but he studies me way more closely than I'd like.

"You're white as a ghost. What's going on?"

"Nothing. I was just grabbing a cup of tea before I finish up a few emails. I guess I didn't hear you." My voice comes out high and squeaky. Dammit. I want to wince at the overly chipper sound.

But I'm trying to maintain the *everything is fine* façade. Which means ignoring the chipmunk-like sound in favor of denial.

"Coming and going from the house like we do, Ev, I've startled you before. But never enough to make you throw your cup across the room."

He holds out a hand, gesturing to the shattered mug and puddle of rapidly cooling liquid beneath it.

"Shit." I start forward, but he waves me toward the chair at the bar where I set up my workstation when I got here this morning.

"I'll get it. It was my fault for startling you. Do you want to sit? Talk about it?"

One thing I've learned about Garrett? He's a really nice guy. The best match for Mia, although it took her a while to figure it out. I count both of them as friends, and a part of me wants to take him up on his offer, to unload all my anxiety and worry. But I can't.

Nobody knows. If they did, what would they think of me?

Sawyer knows.

Not that I told him. He discovered my previous identity through his own digging. But he promised to keep the information a secret. As far as I know he has. What does he think of me?

He kissed you, right?

And I haven't spoken to him since. But I don't care about that. The only thing I want from him is his discretion.

Yeah, sure.

So what if I still think about the kiss? That hottest-experience-of-my-life-lip-lock. It can't be repeated. Ever.

With Garrett distracted by the mess on the floor, I pack up my things. The rest of my work can wait.

"No, I'm okay. Probably just more tired than I realize. Lots of emails today," I lie.

There were a handful. Manageable in the grand scheme of things.

"I'm going to head out. See you guys tomorrow," I tell him.

I want nothing more than to run to my bags as fast as I can. One is my purse and the other is a bag I never leave behind. It holds everything I would need for a few days in case...in case I need it.

But instead of running, I take in a deep breath and force myself to wait until he responds before I move.

"See you tomorrow, Evie."

My drive from Mia's is long enough for me to indulge in a lengthy lecture about calming down. Because if I keep behaving like I did today, Mia and Garrett will ask questions. Ones I don't have answers for. Or, at least, not ones I want to provide. Because they'd mean not working for Mia. She's as close to a best friend as I've had since high school, and it may be selfish, but I don't want to give up the few friends I have.

Once I've pulled into my assigned parking spot, I flip down the visor and scrutinize myself in the mirror. I'm almost unrecognizable anymore. Dark brown hair instead of my auburn tones. Dark circles instead of bright, naive eyes. I don't sleep well. Not anymore. Haven't for a long time. And if I sleep deep enough to dream, I don't remember them. But that's nothing new. From the time I gave up on my goal of being a singer/songwriter, I haven't remembered. It's like my mind decided that if I can't have that dream, I don't deserve any.

Probably a good thing.

"No." I shake my head. "Enough. Stop thinking about before. Focus on now."

Now is a job I enjoy, working for a woman who is more of a friend than a boss. Now is a quiet apartment in a nice neighborhood with neighbors I wave to when we run into each other. Not the small-town, question-asking busybodies who infested my hometown.

The seat belt slides off with a click, and I open the door to the quiet afternoon.

No one recognizes me. I need to focus on that. I've done it really well. Except for the one lapse in judgment. Kissing Sawyer. It was a mistake because there's no future there. Not for us. Not for me.

I lean into the back seat to grab my bags. "Because that's not focusing on the no—*Ow*." A weight presses me further into the little hatchback, and my heart lurches.

"Hello, my little songbird."

That voice. And that smell. Instantly, nausea roils in my stomach, and sweat pops between my shoulder blades with the shiver that skates down my spine.

Songbird. The smell of stale alcohol with too much Axe body spray to cover it up. Unwashed clothes and fried food.

Brad Russell. My former label rep. The man who crushed my dream and took everything from me. My self-esteem. My body. My identity. My future.

No.

A whimper escapes before I can bite it back, and I shudder at his touch as he digs his fingers into my hips.

"There, there, little bird. No need to cry. I've found you again."

He grinds his erection against my ass, and bile climbs to my throat. My stomach churns as I scramble, looking for something to defend myself with, a way of escaping him. But all I find is the strap to my safety bag he pushed me on top of.

The safety bag that's supposed to help me run.

His grip tightens against my hips, and I gasp for breath as pain overrides all rational thought.

"I don't like to be ignored."

Oh, I remember.

"I-I'm sorry. It's hard to talk like this."

It's hard to breathe like this, but I don't dare say that. It gives him more power over me than he already has in this moment. Power he loves to wield.

"Maybe we should go into your apartment. No need to tell me which one, songbird. I watched it all night long."

Panic rushes through my body at his confession, restricting my lungs further.

"Come on." He releases my hips and wraps his fingers around my wrist with a bruising strength, then yanks me back toward him. "We have a lot of catching up to do."

The movement causes spots to dance in my vision, but I blink them away. He hasn't changed. Dirty blond hair with leftover product, dull brown eyes, and a fake-and-bake tan.

But as I catalog him, he does the same to me.

"What the fuck did you do to your hair?" He rips his fingers through the strands.

Tears spring to my eyes, but I bite the inside of my cheek to keep them from falling.

Give me your tears, songbird.

"N-nothing."

"What's with the baggy ass clothes? Did you get fat since the last time I saw you?" He jerks the hem of my sweater up, exposing my stomach. "No, huh. I was sure you were hiding some extra pounds under there."

My reflexes kick in, and I bend as far away from him as I can get. But in return, he tightens his hold on my wrist and drags me toward my apartment. I barely get my car door shut before I'm forced to follow him.

No. No. Please no. Not now. I've successfully hidden from him for almost five years.

"H-how..." It's the only word I manage to get out of my closed off throat.

"How did I find you?" he asks, though he doesn't wait for a response before he continues. "Imagine my surprise when I was in a coffee shop last night and heard the name Evelyn. It's a classic name. Not very common anymore, though. I watched, figured it was an eighty-year-old woman. Turns out it was you. And it was easy to follow you home, you little rule follower. Turn signals and speed limit the whole way."

He *was* there. At the coffee house.

"Good Obsession," I whisper.

"Always was one of my favorites. "

The song was out of character for me. He insisted I record it. No wonder it's one of his favorites.

"Yeah, when no one else showed up here last night, I knew you were alone. I figured I could wait for our little reunion."

Twenty feet or so from my door, I stumble, tripping toward the ground, but he yanks me harder to keep me moving.

"Hurry up."

I can't. Not again.

For five years I survived, desperate enough to stomach his touch because I wanted so badly to achieve my dream. In the beginning, I could pretend I'd willingly chosen to date someone like him. Pretended I wasn't being manipulated to keep a record contract. But as the years ticked by, his touch, his voice, made me more and more ill.

At the front door, he turns to me. "Well?"

With shaky hands, I pull the keys from my pocket. What happens when he gets inside?

I don't want to think about it.

Because it'll be the same thing that happened when I lived it.

For five years.

"Are we going inside or what?" Brad's temper is fraying. Shit.

"I—"

"Open the fucking door. Now!"

It's muscle memory. A defense mechanism to avoid unnecessary pain. My body does what he demands without question. So I find the right key and slide it closer to the door. All the while, my mind screams at me to run.

Run where?

"Babe? Are you okay?"

I nearly collapse in relief at the sound of my neighbor's voice. I can't remember his name, but he's dressed in a reflective orange vest and beat-up jeans and a T-shirt. Construction. He's told me that before.

"She's fine," Brad answers for me, twisting his fingers around my wrist.

My neighbor looks at Brad for a long moment before he turns back to me.

"Babe?"

This is the universe providing a rescue. And I jump at it.

"Hi, honey," I say with a smile that no doubt looks more like a grimace, but if he notices, he doesn't say anything.

I yank at my wrist, surprised when Brad releases it. On shaky legs, I step closer to my savior and wrap my arms around him, popping up to kiss him on the cheek. He doesn't act as if anything is amiss. No, he curls his arm around me and holds me close to his side, being sure to tug me back just a little so he's subtly shielding me.

"How was work, sweetheart?" he asks.

"Okay. Glad I got home early, though. Couldn't wait to see you."

Thank god he was here. What would have happened if I'd come home when I normally do?

"Friend of yours?" he asks, nodding at Brad.

The glare Brad shoots me sends ice through my veins.

"An old acquaintance from the label."

"Hey, man, good to meet you." My neighbor extends his hand toward Brad, who sneers at him and levels a look of rage at me.

"I'll be back, songbird. And you better be alone."

He stomps off, and the instant he's out of sight, my knees

buckle beneath me. The only thing that saves me from hitting the ground is the strong arm still wrapped around me.

"Are you okay?"

"I—I don't even know your name." We've been neighbors for the last couple of years, and I don't know his name.

"Dennis. You?" He makes sure I'm steady, then takes a step back.

"I'm Evie."

Dennis nods and sticks his hands in his pockets. "Nice to meet you, Evie."

"Nice to meet you too," I say, twisting my fingers in front of me, my heart rate finally slowing.

It's absurd. The man just rescued me from Brad, and we're talking like we've just bumped into each other.

"I—thank you," I tell him.

"Of course. I could tell something was off when I walked up. You should call the police."

The police can't help. He hasn't done anything wrong. Even if I'll have bruises around my wrist and on my hips tomorrow, it won't matter. I shake my head and grab my keys out of the lock. I'm not going in there. Not right now.

"Can I ask you for a favor?"

Another one.

"Of course."

"Can you walk me to my car?"

There's only one place I can go.

I just hope I'm still welcome there after I tell them the truth.

CHAPTER 3

SAWYER

"*U*ncow?"

The little voice from the back seat of my Jeep is barely discernible above the road noise. Maybe I should have kept the doors on, but since I'm heading out to camp tonight, I removed them. It's a process, so I started this morning, only leaving the back doors on so I could take Benji to the zoo first. Despite what my sister thinks, I'm a responsible uncle, and I freaking love bonding with my little buddy. Gotta do it now before he's too grown up to spend time with *Uncow Sawyer.*

"Yeah, buddy?"

"We going home now?" he asks just as I pull into Michaela and West's driveway.

I point to the house. "Sure are, bud. See?"

He crows and claps his hands. "That's my house."

"Sure is."

With a click of the button, the gate opens, and I pull through.

Just inside, I stop and wait for it to clang firmly shut, then I continue the several hundred feet to the house. My sister and my best friend don't live in some enormous house, but it's safe and big enough for several more siblings for Benji in the future.

"No ice cream?" he asks, the sadness evident in his voice.

Guilt swamps me. I glimpse into the rearview mirror and meet green eyes on the verge of a pout.

"We had ice cream at the zoo, remember? Right after we saw the giraffes."

And if I got him two servings of ice cream? Michaela would kick my ass.

"They have long tongues." He sticks out his tongue.

Distraction successful, I chuckle as he tries to pull said tongue out farther with his fingers. Cranking off the ignition, I unbuckle my seat belt.

"Sawyer Branson King! What in the hell are you doing driving around with my baby like that?" Michaela storms out of the house, hands on her hips.

She may be my baby sister, but she's no longer the dandelion-fluff-headed kid who used to follow me everywhere. And it wasn't just me. She trailed my best friend, West, just as often. Until she married him almost two and a half years ago.

"You look like Mom," I tell her.

Ten years ago, she might have risen to the bait, but now she just laughs.

"I am one, so I take that as a compliment."

With her blond hair pulled into a messy bun, she's in cut-off shorts and an oversized Temple T-shirt that probably belonged to West. She doesn't look twenty-four. Every day, it blows my mind that my baby sister married my best friend. And they have a toddler who is closer to three than two these days.

"Mama!"

"Hi, baby. Did you have fun with Uncow today?" She kisses the fingers he's got peeking out above the window.

"We saw snakes," he says proudly, popping up a little straighter in his car seat.

Michaela shudders. She never was a fan of the reptile house at the zoo.

"Better you than me, little man. And I didn't forget my question. Sawyer, what happened to your doors?"

"Benji's door is right there," I point out.

Since she's already opening said door, all she does is huff and roll her eyes.

"I left the ones I needed."

"Where are the rest?"

"I'm heading out of town tonight. Camping trip."

"And you can't have doors?" she asks, glancing at me over her shoulder as she leans in to greet her son. Obviously, she doesn't get my reasoning.

"Why do I need them?"

We're in the hills surrounding Los Angeles, far from any kind of danger behind that gate. I've been in more dangerous locations than I care to count. Not that I'll offer up that tidbit of information anytime soon.

"Whatever. West didn't mention anything about camping."

"West isn't going."

My best friend and I will spend a night or two out in the woods, drinking beer and reminiscing about the shenanigans of our high school days. The innocence of youth that died somewhere during my first deployment and ended up with him falling in love with and marrying my sister.

But sometimes—like now—the rat race of the city gets to be too much, and I take a few days for myself.

"I'm not going where?" West steps out the front door and stops next to me.

Michaela is busy getting Benji out of the car seat I keep for our adventures.

"Camping," I tell him.

Green eyes that match his son's study me intently for several beats. He gets it. When he's not invited, it's because I need time to decompress. And lately, there's an urgency—a frenetic energy—that's pushing at me. While LA is ordinarily a fantastic distraction from memories that won't ever leave me alone, it's time to recharge.

And now is as good a time as any since Sentinel doesn't have any big jobs on the calendar.

"Daddy!" Benji's legs are pumping before Michaela sets him down. Once free, he tears toward West like the little running back he's going to be someday.

"Hi, buddy." West kneels and scoops his little carbon copy into a hold he releases as soon as Benji is at chest level.

The midair giggle that erupts from Benji is pure joy as he drops a foot or so before being caught by his dad again.

"Weston James."

West meets my eye at Michaela's scolding. His lips twitch first, and then we both crack up. Benji joins in, although the furrowed brow and the way his eyes dart from me to his dad and back give away his confusion. He has no idea why the two of us are laughing.

"Men," Michaela says before stomping into the house.

"Down," Benji demands.

West complies, and Benji beelines after his mom.

"Bye, Benj," I call after him.

"Bye, Uncow."

"God, I hope he never outgrows that," I tell West after the door shuts.

"What?"

"I'm Uncow," I say with a smile.

I'm proud to be Benji's Uncow, and I enjoy the hell out of my nickname.

"It's pretty fucking cute."

"You and my sister make cute kids, Abbott. Feel free to give me another niece or nephew anytime," I joke.

"One toddler at a time on tour."

I can't imagine trying to entertain a baby on the road like that, but he and Michaela did it last summer when she toured with Jax

Bryant and Dylan Graves, two other artists at the record label she's signed with.

"You guys touring again soon?"

West shrugs. "Not sure. We've talked about it. But nothing's decided yet."

I grunt and leave it at that.

"Everything okay?" he asks.

He may be Michaela's husband, but he's been my best friend for over twenty years, so when West fixes his firm attention on me, I know he's seeing more than I want him to.

I shrug. "It will be."

My last client was a woman who was trying to leave her abusive husband. And, fuck, I'm done with those kinds of cases. I'll turn those over to Cole or subcontract them if I need to. It happens too often around here. Trophy wife fed up with the cheating and the verbal abuse and the bruises that come after the verbal shit escalates.

Enough is enough. I promised myself a month ago that I wouldn't take on any more. But I couldn't say no when faced with two little girls who cowered behind their mother, afraid of their own shadows. All thanks to a bastard of a sperm donor who loved how his family looked on his arm but wasn't man enough to be a real husband or father.

That was it. Now that she's been moved to an undisclosed location, she and those little girls are safe. And before I succumb to the belief that all humanity is done for, I need to recharge.

"You need anything?" West asks, interrupting my miserable walk down memory lane.

"Nah, man. My bag's in the back. I'll be back in a couple days."

"You'll drop your coordinates?"

That's always our deal. He doesn't push to come when I want to be alone, but he knows how to find me if need be.

"Yeah. I've been there before, so it'll look familiar."

He nods. "You want to come over for dinner this week?"

35

Will a few days gone be enough? This damn case has taken me right to my breaking point. To memories of a woman I couldn't save.

Amani.

No, a few days probably won't be enough to stuff all the darkness back into the box I keep it locked up in.

"I'll—uh—I'll let you know."

"West, is—oh, you're still here." Michaela steps back outside. She's got Benji on her hip and she's clutching her phone.

There's a tension around her eyes that wasn't there a few minutes ago, and while she's trying to play it cool in front of her little guy, all my senses are tingling.

"What's the matter?"

"Mia just called. Evie showed up at her house after being attacked—"

"Call her back. I'll be at her place in ten." I don't bother to say goodbye.

Firing up the engine, I buckle my seat belt, then gun it down the driveway.

"I thought you were going camping?" she calls after me.

In response, I wave half-heartedly as West ushers his family inside.

The memory of Evie McBride has lived in my brain rent free for the last two and a half years. No, if I'm honest with myself, longer than that. Our kiss may have been two and a half years ago, but thoughts of Evie have occupied my mind a lot longer than that.

Camping can wait.

In my high school history classes, the wars we studied—Revolutionary, Civil, World Wars I and II—were written in epic tale fashion, and I soaked up the stories while picturing myself as a great hero on a battlefield. A man who would live forever in history books for future high school students to learn about.

My time in the Army was nothing like that. Days spent in basic training were riddled with hunger, exhaustion, and so many push-ups I'm still surprised my arms didn't fall off. And when I was recruited into special forces, it was worse. The things I witnessed had me craving the darkness I used to my advantage. But none of it prepared me for the file I compiled almost four years ago.

Evelyn McBride's file ate at me in a way I couldn't explain. The young girl who had succumbed to the same asshole who attacked my baby sister got under my skin. Evie, Mia's assistant, didn't even resemble that woman. The one who haunted my dreams. It's one thing to read a file and learn about what a person has been through, but it's another entirely to listen to every word as they recount the experience. It's the difference between reading about battles in books and fighting in the trenches. Evie is a survivor, and rage at what she endured simmers just below the surface.

"Ev, why didn't you say anything sooner?" Mia scoots forward, her knees bumping Evie's while she clasps her shaking hand.

"I—I didn't want anyone to know. I'm ashamed..."

I ball my hands into fists and squeeze. She has nothing to be ashamed of. If I ever find the asshole who preyed on Evie and my sister—and several other women—there won't be enough left to bury. Guaranteed.

"Why should you be ashamed?" Mia surges off the couch.

Garrett holds tight to her hand and pulls her back down. "Ames."

Mia's given name is Amelia Hudson. Garrett has been calling her Ames since childhood.

She looks at him, rage that matches mine written across her face. "What?"

"Let her finish."

"She doesn't have to. I've heard enough. He's a predator, Garrett. And Evie's been hiding for five years because he wouldn't leave her alone. Now he's found her again—"

"I'm glad he has," I say from the doorway where I've been standing.

"What?" Mia's attention whips to me, as if she's surprised I'm here.

It's what makes me good at my job. My ability to blend, to be forgotten.

"Until now, he's been an unknown entity. We didn't know when he was going to crawl out of his hole again. Especially after Reverb canned his ass."

"He got fired?" Evie asks, her eyes wide in surprise.

I nod. "They could no longer ignore his behavior after what happened with Mikey."

Especially when Michaela's lawyer and I both threatened legal action if they didn't do something.

"Good. That's...good." Evie ducks her chin and clasps her hands in her lap.

She hasn't made eye contact since I walked through the door. Is it because of Brad or because of our history? We kissed. One time. At Michaela and West's wedding. She was attractive and...skittish. Understandably so. But while I would have happily moved at the speed she was comfortable with, she's the one who walked away— more liked ran, with the finality of that door closing between us.

Will it ever be the right time? That's the million-dollar question. I've known her real identity since I investigated my sister's attack. It didn't take me long to piece together that Evelyn McBride had changed her hairstyle and had taken on a new identity. Evie Holt, Mia Maddox's assistant. But the emotion that flared in her eyes when I told her I knew who she really was?

It wasn't anger. That I could accept.

It was shame.

And like Mia said, Evie has nothing to be ashamed of.

She survived hell.

And now I'll make sure she never has to deal with Brad Fucking Russell again.

Evie stands, drawing my attention back to her. I've seen pictures, but what would she look like up close with her natural auburn hair color? With the soft smile and smattering of freckles visible up close. Does that woman still exist beneath the persona she's adopted for her own safety?

"Where are you going?" Mia asks and stands, ignoring her husband's attempts to keep her calm.

Good luck, bro.

Evie shrugs.

"A hotel, I guess."

Her strength would be admirable if she wasn't so fucking clueless.

"The fuck you are." I move to the middle of the doorway as Mia echoes my words.

"You can stay with us," she offers.

"I won't put you two in danger. It's bad enough you won't accept my resignation."

Yeah, according to Garrett, she tried that before I got here.

"No way in hell. Evie, he stole your dream from you. He doesn't get to take anything else," Mia argues.

I agree but keep my mouth shut. Evie's got enough backbone that telling her to do something might result in the exact opposite.

I don't want her to run. I want her to fight.

"Mia." Evie's sigh is full of resignation.

"No buts," Mia says.

"It isn't safe for me to be here."

I have to admire her argument, her desire to keep the people she loves safe. But she doesn't have to fight this battle alone anymore.

"That's why I called Michaela looking for him." Mia points to me like that's enough of an answer.

It is, but Evie is still fighting that point.

"I don't need a bodyguard. I'll disappear again. I did it once—"

"When he wasn't looking," I interrupt the broken record of Evie's reasoning.

"So?" she asks.

She shoots me a look, and I can't decide whether I want to kiss her or shake her for it. Maybe both. And fuck if I'm used to the conflict. Crossing my arms, I level her with a stare I've used on countless soldiers who needed to use *actual* reasoning and not just the bullshit they've made up in their heads.

"Chances are, he followed you here."

Her mouth snaps shut, and her eyes go wide at the realization.

"He'll wait until you leave. Then he'll follow you wherever you go."

Shit. Her color pales further.

"He may not come out of the darkness yet. He may wait until you stop looking for him around every corner. But when he does come at you again, he won't stop just because other people are around. Watching for him won't be enough. Planning on your own won't be enough. That's where I come in."

She fidgets with the hem of her too long sweater—a frequent habit judging from all the frayed edges. She may know how to school her expression when she needs to, but the condition of her sweater gives her away. She's never moved beyond this. Not entirely.

"I don't know what else to do." Her hazel eyes are more green than brown, fear ringing the irises.

Dropping my arms, I approach slowly and kneel in front of her.

"Trust me. I do this for a living."

This close to her, the dark red of her lashes is caught by the light that filters in the windows. Even without the pictures of her from her early days with Reverb, those lashes, along with the almost translucent tone of her fair coloring, tell me she's a natural redhead. Another way for her to hide. I have to admire her strength. Despite her fidgeting, she holds herself upright. But she can't go on like this forever. She can't continue facing an enemy she can't predict and, therefore, can't defend herself against. She's fucking tiny—almost a foot shorter than I am—and all my instincts are screaming at me to protect her.

"What do I do?" she whispers.

"Let me help. We'll go back to your apartment to grab your stuff and lock everything up. Then you'll come stay with me."

"I can't stay with you—"

"This is what we have to do to make sure he never bothers you again."

"I can't live with you indefinitely!" She surges up and brushes past me to pace the living room.

I try—and fail—to ignore my body's response to the brief contact. There's something about her I connect with on a primal level. I want to kiss her again.

Bad idea.

My first and only focus has to be keeping her safe from Brad Russell. Forever.

"It'll only be until we deal with Brad."

"*Oh,* are we taking a hit out on him?" Mia asks with an evil grin.

"Christ, Ames. You're violent." Garrett hugs his wife to him. "I love you, but violence isn't going to solve this problem."

"It would. But no one I know looks good in orange," she muses.

"You do." Garrett's words are low, but I still pick them up. Based on the blush that overtakes Mia's features, there's more to the story there.

"Give me and my team some time. We'll handle Brad. Nonvi-olently."

Probably. Although I wouldn't mind punching the fucker a time or two. But that's not something Evie needs to know right now.

My mission when I met her was to keep her secret. Then it was to fight the attraction that simmered between us. The newest one is something I've been desperate to do all along—keep her safe.

I've never failed at a mission before. And I don't intend to start now.

CHAPTER 4

SAWYER

"You want me to get in that?" Evie waves at the Jeep with exaggerated movements as she stops suddenly, her brows in her hairline and her eyes as big as saucers. "There are no doors!"

"There are doors," I correct. "In the back."

"Where did the front ones go?"

We've been standing in Mia and Garrett's driveway for five minutes. All the while, Evie has argued that she should just drive her own vehicle back to her apartment.

She has a car here, after all. That argument was simple.

She conceded when I pointed out that Brad could easily follow her again, since he knows what her car looks like.

Her next argument centered on her need to get back and forth to work.

My first argument still applied, and I added that since I was now her bodyguard, she would be riding with me. Maybe not in this vehicle, given her response to the lack of doors, but at least in one I control.

Now she's arguing about the state of my Jeep. One I hadn't planned on having passengers in after dropping Benji off.

But plans changed.

"Does it matter?" I ask.

"Yes! What if I fall out?" Her question ends in a squeak.

I can't help the smirk that tugs at my lips when the truth comes out.

"Do you really think I would let you fall?" My voice drops to a husky whisper and my feet propel me into Evie's orbit.

Good thing Garrett and Mia said goodbye at the door when we walked outside, since I can't explain my compulsion to move closer to the one woman I shouldn't want.

She jumps and whirls around, backing up to add some much-needed space between us. Maybe now I can take a breath without the combination of lavender and chocolate invading my olfactory senses and making me temporarily insane.

"There are seat belts," I say, pushing away the need that fights to take over every time I'm close to her.

Her teeth sink into her lower lip, pulling my attention to the plump flesh caught between them.

Focus on the situation, not her mouth, dammit.

I blink and drag my eyes away from her and back to the vehicle in front of us.

The deep breath she releases is audible.

"Fine. Let's just go before I rethink all of this."

She casts a longing look at her sensible hatchback. It's obvious why she picked it. It's allowed her to blend in perfectly over the last five years. But now that Brad knows what to look for? It's a neon sign pointing straight at her.

I shift to the side and gesture to the doorway.

She approaches it like a death row inmate being led to the electric chair. "How am I—oh." She turns around, surprised at my proximity.

"Allow me?" I ask.

My hands are inches from her hips, but I might as well be touching her. The electric arc is just as strong as it would be if we were skin to skin. But I'll be damned if I put my hands on her without her permission.

Not after everything she's been through.

"Umm, okay?"

Slowly, I settle my palms on her hips, and she lifts her hands to cover mine. I try to ignore the cool touch of her fingers and the smooth skin that trembles slightly at the connection. Her chest rises and falls rapidly, making it hard to keep my attention on her face and not her breasts. Closing my eyes, I lift her into the passenger seat, surprised at how slight she is. Even seated in my lifted Jeep, she's barely taller than I am.

From here, I could easily close the distance to claim her lips. It's been two and a half goddamn years, but I still remember how they felt under mine. How she tasted. The soft little sigh that escaped the moment I deepened the kiss. Before she broke the connection and walked away without a second glance.

"Is—is everything okay?" She swipes her bottom lip with her tongue.

I'm mesmerized by the move, by the shine left behind.

Fuck. What the hell is wrong with me?

She probably thinks I'm insane. Fuck, I'm staring at her like *I'm* the creeper.

Embarrassment burns the tips of my ears, and I grunt in affirmation.

"Can you work the seat belt?"

The five-point harness is an aftermarket installation since I like to drive without the doors on when I can.

She studies it for several moments, a curtain of brown hair hiding her features from me before she glances back up.

"I can do it." The determination in her hazel eyes is just one of the things I find inconveniently attractive.

No, not find. Found. She's off limits.

This kind of uncontrollable attraction has only happened

once before. This situation is nothing like that one, but the lessons I learned from that first experience run soul deep.

With one more grunt, I round the hood.

Time to work.

And time to put my attraction to the woman gripping the console next to me out of my mind so I can focus on my mission. The gate whirs open once I'm close enough, but I pause in the driveway, doing a sweep of the street to look for any signs of Brad.

I almost wish he was here, waiting in the open so I could deal with the bottom dweller once and for all. But I'm not that lucky, so I pull out and head toward Evie's apartment. With the road noise and traffic, attempting conversation is pointless, and Evie is silent until we're almost to her place.

"You know where I live?"

I nod a little reluctantly.

"How?"

I glance at her from the corner of my eye to gauge her reaction.

"Back when I investigated Brad, I found addresses for all five of the women before..."

I don't have to finish my sentence. She flinches, the move so fast I might have missed it if I wasn't looking at her.

"That was a couple of years ago."

I shrug, unwilling to admit that while Evie's address has been burned into my brain, I don't remember where any of the other four women live.

"It's my job. To know things about the people my sister interacts with."

It's plausible. And I *do* know where everyone in Michaela's inner circle lives. But Evie is peripheral enough that if she were anyone else, I wouldn't have bothered with that information.

"Your job?" She turns to me and tilts her head in confusion.

"Not like that. As her big brother. You have a brother, right?"

46

"Let me guess, that's in my file too?"

I fidget and twist my grip on the steering wheel.

"Yeah." The file I compiled isn't news to her, but this feels more invasive than the other information—including knowing where she lives.

Her sigh is one of resignation.

"Yes, I have a brother. Austin."

"I'm sure Austin is the same way with you."

"He's younger."

"That doesn't matter."

"He...doesn't know. Any of this. I don't really talk to my family anymore."

"Why?"

"My parents were perfectly content to only leave our hometown for college. They didn't understand my dream of moving to LA."

"What about Austin?" I ask.

"When I left, he was still in middle school."

"They would still want to know what's happening in your life."

Evie turns away, watching the scenery fly by us. "It's my problem."

"You don't have to tackle it alone. I'd never let Mikey deal with something like this by herself."

"What if you didn't know?" she asks, turning back to me.

"I know everything." The corner of my lips twitch in a smile. "Don't tell Mikey."

"Hmm." She sits back in the seat, but the heat of her gaze still has all my nerves on high alert.

I want to ask what that little sound means. What is it about her that has me ready to talk for hours when I often go days without saying a word? I swallow my question, fidgeting in my seat as we pull into her apartment complex.

The closer we get to her building, the more palpable the tension radiating from her is.

I squeeze her thigh. "I'm right here. You're safe."

The bigger part of me wants to tell her we can forget it. We can make do with what she's got in the bag I tossed in the back of my Jeep for now and buy anything else she needs later. But before I can open my mouth to say it, she takes a deep breath and releases it, easing some of the tension that crackles around her.

She wants to do this. To reclaim this piece of her life. And I'm going to help her.

"Stay there," I remind her. "I'll come around to your side when it's clear."

"Okay." Her voice is strong, but her white knuckles are a visible reminder that this isn't just a normal drive home for her.

The parking lot is quiet. It's long past the time commuters come home for the night. I study each car around us methodically, moving one by one until I've cataloged them all. Unlike during my deployments, I'm not searching for IEDs or a foreign enemy. I'm looking for an asshole I'd love to get my hands on. One who preys on women he thinks are weaker than he is. Only once I confirm there's no sign of him or anyone else in the parking lot do I move to the passenger side of the car. Evie's seat belt is off, and she's poised on the edge of the seat, waiting for me.

"Let's go. Stay close," I tell her.

We walk side by side, my head on a swivel as I survey every shadow, relying on my instincts to sense danger when I might not otherwise be aware of it.

"Fuck." The word is out before I can stop it when I catch a glimpse of her front door.

Despite the dim light, the black lettering is easy to see.

"Wha—oh my god." She rushes forward, but I catch up in less than three steps.

"Wait." I move in front of her, one arm curled behind me and around her without touching. "Was he still here when you left?"

"I...uh...I don't know. I just asked Dennis—"

"Who's Dennis?" And why am I fucking jealous?

"My neighbor. He was here when Brad tried to...when he..." A swallow locks partway down her throat, trapping the rest of her words with it.

When he tried to force her into her apartment.

"Did he walk away, or did you?"

"He—he did."

I stare at the words written in black Sharpie on her door.

Songbird,

I'll be back to visit soon.

"Songbird?" I ask.

"It's what he used to call me. Before." A shiver works its way down her spine.

I move my arm closer. If we were touching, it would almost be a hug.

But I maintain an inch of space. It's a slippery slope I can't let myself slide down.

I try the knob, relieved when it doesn't turn, even though the flimsy locks might as well be made from cardboard.

"Do you have your keys?"

She digs in her pocket and hands them to me without a word. Her attention is still focused on her door, her lower lip caught between her teeth.

"Stay behind me."

I wait until she meets my gaze and nods.

"Okay."

Her warm breath soaks through my T-shirt between my shoulder blades. It's another reminder of how small she is.

Evie has been in hiding for almost five years, blending in by wearing drab colors and shapeless clothing. But her apartment is where her truest self exists. It's an explosion of color. An eggplant-colored couch with a rainbow of throw pillows. A trio of fat pillar candles on her coffee table, hardened wax dripped down the sides.

A TV on a corner stand, with a stack of DVDs on one side and a stack of books on the other. I leave her in the cozy living room while I check the spotless kitchen and bedroom with the messily made bed. After a quick check of the bathroom, I rejoin her.

"Pack enough for two weeks." My words are more directive than request.

"Two weeks?" She crosses her arms over her chest like she's gearing up to argue.

"It'll take a few days for my team to track him and study his movements. Then we'll need to figure out the best way to shut him down. He needs to leave you alone. For good."

I understand her sigh. This apartment is her sanctuary. It's where she can freely be herself. And I'm telling her she has to leave.

But she doesn't argue.

"Do you know how to get rid of permanent marker?" She tosses the question over her shoulder at her bedroom door.

I'm so hyperaware of every small noise that it takes me a minute to process.

"No idea."

"I'll have to google it." Her voice is muffled.

Her door is not my first priority. It's her safety. That should be her focus too.

I follow her and prop myself up against the doorframe. "First, you need to pack."

"No need to bark orders." Her hands are perched on her hips as she glares at me.

"I didn't."

Did I?

"You did. This is hard enough without your attitude thrown into the mix."

"What attitude?"

"Whatever stick you have up your ass. If you don't want to help, just say so. I'll figure it out."

Her arms are crossed again, and I'm halfway prepared for her foot to start tapping.

A chuckle breaks free of my chest. "Christ, woman. You'd try the patience of a saint. I want to help."

"I—thank you." She dips her chin. "All I'm saying is a 'please' wouldn't hurt."

This is the feistiest I've ever seen her. Is this who she used to be? Regardless of the why, I fucking love it. And I can't help but humor her.

"Would you please pack your stuff?"

"For two weeks?" she asks, obviously still not thrilled.

"Two," I confirm. I wasn't lying earlier when I told her we needed time.

Without another word, she pulls an empty duffel bag out of her closet.

Giving her some space to pack, I head back to her living room and settle on the purple monstrosity known as her couch. A quick text message to my new IT guru—who happens to still be in college—and I have the contact info for Evie's apartment complex.

I leave the office a voicemail, requesting they fix the door ASAP, then google ways to remove permanent marker.

"Do you have nail polish remover?" I ask.

"Yeah, why?"

"Supposedly it removes marker."

"It's in the bathroom. I'll grab it."

"No. I'll get it. Keep packing."

"Sir, yes, sir."

I don't know what's a bigger turn-on—her sassy words or the message they hold.

Ignoring my hardening dick and my increasing need to repeat

the kiss from Mikey and West's wedding, I grab the nail polish remover and a rag. I have no idea how many people have seen the message, but I'll be damned if I leave it there until the maintenance staff can come clean it. They can repaint the door or replace it.

I'll call back during business hours and request more security. The little deadbolt wouldn't stop anyone who wanted to put in the effort to get to her.

"Sawyer?"

I'm nearly finished—the black now smears of gray over the turquoise door—when she tentatively calls my name.

I rise from my crouched position next to her door.

"Here."

The tense lines on her face ease when she spots me. Did she think I left?

Her teeth sink into her lower lip. "I was...worried."

"Worried? He's not going to get to you with me here."

"No, that's not what I was worried about. What if..."

She doesn't finish the question, even after several moments of silence.

"What if what?" I close the door and take several steps closer.

She knits her fingers together and frowns. The worry on her face is so obvious, but I don't understand it.

"What if something happens—"

"Nothing is going to happen." That's a promise I can make with confidence.

I'll keep her safe.

"To you. What if Brad does something to you?"

I snort a laugh. Brad Russell is a coward. He gets off on hurting people who can't fight back. Women like my sister, who, fortunately, was able to get away. Women like Evie, who was trapped with that douche for years.

He won't do anything to me.

But the fear in her eyes doesn't diminish.

My snort fades to silence as I watch her. "You're serious?"

She nods. "You're helping me. I don't want him to come after you."

"Evie." I move closer. Bringing my hands up to cup her biceps, I lock my eyes on hers. "He's not going to do anything to me. If he comes close enough to try, I'll be more than glad to get my hands on him. He doesn't scare me."

Her eyes search mine, and I let her see the truth of my words. I've faced things far more dangerous than the likes of Brad Russell.

"I'm packed. Maybe I should just go to a hotel—"

"Your car is at Mia's," I remind her.

"I can order an Uber."

"We've talked about this." I huff.

"I don't want anyone else to get caught up in this."

"I'm not going to get caught up in this."

She opens her mouth to argue, but I keep going.

"I'm going to get in front of all this. You'll never have to worry about him again."

"That sounds like a promise."

"Sweetheart, it's a goddamn guarantee."

CHAPTER 5

SAWYER

For more than two years, I've relegated the stolen kiss with Evie to the back of my mind. But in the last two maddening weeks, I've thought about our kiss almost nonstop. Thought about more than the semi-chaste connection of our lips. I've moved into dangerous territory, boundaries I shouldn't cross. Like how her skin would feel against mine, how she would sound if I worshipped her body with mine.

In short, the last two weeks have been a test of my self-control in a way I haven't been challenged in years.

Not since Amani.

But other than her slight stature, Evie is nothing like the woman who captured my heart during my last deployment.

With dancing brown eyes and a smile that lit the darkest of nights, Amani took over my dreams. The kinds that included a wedding and children. And introducing her to my parents. With the rose-colored glasses of youth, I convinced both of us I could do my job while also finding a way to rescue her from her impending arranged marriage to a man twenty years her senior. A future she was terrified of. I was so short-sighted. It never crossed my mind that there were other dangers out there, ready to attack our relationship.

Dangers the universe had no problem reminding me of.

I've thought about Amani more in the last two weeks than I have for the last several years, and that's a big fucking red flag. I'm on the brink of insanity.

All because of the petite human being whose physical presence doesn't hold a candle to the way she overwhelmingly occupies every corner of my condo. Nowhere is safe while she quietly waits, day after day, for word that we've found Brad. She's settled in, resigned. Because we still haven't found him. And now two weeks is getting dangerously close to becoming three.

And I'm losing my motherfucking mind.

"Looks like he moved out last month," Sydney tells me over the phone. The clack of her keyboard is a telltale sign that she's still searching for the asshole, who clearly has the disappearing skills of Houdini.

The shower pipes in the hall bathroom creak behind my headboard, and my dick hardens predictably, despite my attempts at ignoring both it and the image of Evie in the bathroom. Naked.

Fuuuck.

"What about credit cards? Debit cards? Anything? He's not a goddamned ghost," I say through gritted teeth.

The shower curtain swishes across the rod once and then a second time, sending me into another level of hell.

"Sawyer, I've run it all again and again. I'm doing the best I can. He pulled this trick once before—"

He did. After Reverb fired him, he vanished. Every attempt I made to find him was a dead end.

That was the tipping point for me. I'm okay with technology, but I needed an employee dedicated to that side of the business. After a long search, I found Sydney. At seventeen, she was the only one who passed a test one of my old intelligence contacts created for me. In the last year, she's done some impressive stuff with her computer. But now I need her to do the impossible—find Brad.

Eighteen or not, she's a damn computer genius. Usually.

"That was before I hired you. Shouldn't this be child's play for you?"

My favorite thing about Sydney? She might be young, but she doesn't take shit from anyone. Including me. Anyone working for me needs to know that I might sound like a drill sergeant, but I trust them to do their jobs without having to look over their shoulder. Sydney is no exception. In this instance, I'm frustrated with the situation—and the continued presence of my kryptonite in my condo—not her efforts.

"I *can* do it. When I know what I'm up against. But I think we're underestimating his skills."

"He doesn't have any skills. Other than being a dick."

"What if someone is helping him hide?" she asks. "It would explain why you couldn't find him before. Evie said that he found her by pure coincidence."

"That was his story. We don't know that for sure."

The humming on the other side of the wall starts, and my attention goes to shit. Because I know what comes next. This is the only time Evie sings. It starts off as a gentle hum, followed by a word here or there, and then the entire song escapes her while she's under the water—a sweet whisper of sound that has my ears straining against the headboard where I'm propped.

"Sawyer, did you hear me?" Sydney's voice breaks through my concentration. Judging by her tone, it isn't the first time she's asked that question.

Pay attention, dumbass.

"I'm sorry, what?"

"Are you okay if I reach out to a few of my contacts and see if they can help me track Brad down?"

I don't like outsourcing work. But what I usually do isn't working.

"Yeah. Go ahead."

"Thanks, boss man. Hanging up now. I hear cold showers help in your situation."

"What situation?"

The only response I get is the phone beeping in my ear.

I drop my head back and focus on the song Evie's singing. The lyrics are about being porcelain. Eyes closed, I picture her on the other side of the wall, belting lyrics into the shower head as moisture turns her brown hair darker, redder, closer to her natural color. The hot water pinkens her fair skin and creates a rosy hue on her cheeks. It trickles down and over her beaded breasts. The tips are a deep red, the texture slippery and sweet as I tongue them. My hands slide over the slick skin of her hips to trace the curve until I reach the apex of her thighs.

My eyes spring open, and I jackknife up, disgusted, because I've got my palm curled around the sizable erection I'm sporting.

"Motherfucker."

I need to get out of this house. The walls are closing in on me. I'm surrounded by her voice, her scent, her...everything, and my fantasies are only growing stronger.

You can't leave her alone.

Cole is on another assignment. Otherwise, he'd be rotating in for protection duty far more than usual.

The water cranks off, which means I only have a few minutes to keep the door between us and hide my arousal. I stride from my bedroom to the hallway and rap sharply on the door once.

She yelps in response.

Dammit. I suck in a breath and tamp down on my frustration. No need to scare her. "We're leaving."

"We are?" Her voice is muffled through the door.

I shake my head to erase the image of her wrapped in a towel with steam surrounding her.

"Get dressed. We move out in twenty." So much for playing it cool.

"Twenty minutes?" Her voice is much closer than it was a moment ago.

Shit.

I move into my doorway and conceal my lower half as best as I can. The bathroom door swings open, and she pokes her head out, a towel wrapped around her hair like a turban. Her cheeks are the color I imagined. Shit. I have to swallow the groan that threatens when her bare shoulders become visible.

"Twenty minutes?" she repeats. "Where are we going?"

"West and Mikey's."

"Why?"

Fuck. Her question has me scrambling for a plausible excuse.

"I—uh—I made plans with West before I had this assignment," I stumble over the lie.

She doesn't need to know that when I'm on assignment, I almost always cancel my plans with him.

"So where am I going to be?"

"With Mikey and Benji."

"Is it safe?"

"You'll be perfectly safe," I assure her.

She presses her lips together, and concern glitters in her eyes.

"No, not me. Them. Is it safe for them if I'm there?"

God help me. This woman is one of the most caring people I've ever met. And she's going to bring me to my knees with her heart.

"I installed their security system myself. If Brad wants to get to you while you're in their house, I wish him all the luck in the world."

A shiver works its way down her body.

It's the cold air in the hallway.

I'm only imagining the heat in her gaze.

"Can I please have a little more than twenty minutes to get ready?" It's a reasonable request.

Reasonable sucks.

I grunt.

"Thirty minutes."

Thank god I have my own bathroom. Conversation finished, I all but slam my bedroom door and head for my bathroom and a cold-ass shower.

☆☆☆

"I didn't realize that agreeing to hike with you meant I was enlisting in a damn Marine-style marathon march," West huffs from behind me.

"I wasn't in the Marines."

"Didn't...fuck...didn't say you were. Can we slow down just a little?"

"What's the matter, old man? Out of shape?" I tease him.

"Fuck you. I'm only a month older than you are."

"But you're a family man now. Doesn't that mean a dad bod and slippers?"

"That's not what your sister thinks of my body," he retorts.

"Fine. Fuck, you win. No more talk of my sister like that."

This isn't the first time we've hiked Eagle Rock Canyon, but he's right. We usually do it at a much slower pace.

I stop, and he leans against a rock to catch his breath and guzzle water.

"I'm glad you told me to leave Benji with the girls," he says, pulling off his baseball cap to mop at the sweat that dots his forehead.

"Benji wasn't glad," I remind him.

My little buddy was pissed as hell at Uncow. *No* isn't a word he's used to hearing from me—or from anyone, for that matter.

"Think he'll forgive me?" I ask.

Fuck, just thinking about the way his lip trembled and his eyes welled with tears makes me second guess myself. But no way could he have dealt with the pace I set.

"He forgives Michaela and me all the time for telling him no," West reasons.

"But you're not Uncow."

"I'm sure you'll find a way to make it up to him," he says wryly.

I'm already making plans to do exactly that, so his comment startles me.

"What? You think you're the only one who can read people?" he asks.

I shrug and take a drink from my own water bottle. Turning away from his too astute gaze, I assess the rest of the trail in front of us.

"Okay, I think I can finally feel my lungs working again. Let's go." He quirks his head, motioning me forward, but this time our pace is slower—normal.

It's quiet up here, just the crunch of our boots and the occasional hum of a grasshopper nearby. Each breath is filled with the aroma of sun-drenched plants and dirt. I inhale deeply and release it, both happy and sad it doesn't have the same hints of lavender and chocolate that the rest of my life has taken on.

Despite the change of scenery, Evie isn't far from my thoughts.

"Why don't you tell me what—or should I say who—we're running from." West continues to watch the path ahead as we move to a shadier area of the trail.

He reads my responding grunt correctly. It's a big fucking no.

"Argue all you want, but right now, you're a man running away from something. I'd know. I did the same thing."

My stomach tightens at the reminder.

"I'm glad you eventually got your head out of your ass and married my sister," I tell him.

This time he's the one who huffs.

"Me too."

He's quiet for several moments. Long enough for me to ease into it and begin the process of clearing my mind. But it doesn't last.

"Want to talk about it?" he asks.

"What?"

"Whatever's upsetting you."

"Not upset," I deny.

Upset isn't really the right word.

West sighs. "Semantics. How about keyed-up? Is that more accurate?"

Yeah, but I choose not to admit it.

"I'm not."

He stops and scrutinizes me, the heat of his gaze burning the back of my neck until it feels like my ears are going to explode.

With a sigh, I stop too, then turn to face him.

"There's no sign of that jackass anywhere. It's like he fucking disappeared. Again."

I don't need to explain who "that jackass" is. West has a similar opinion of the man who assaulted Michaela.

A muscle ticks in his jaw. Yeah, we're on the same page. "I thought Sydney could find him?"

I shrug. "She's trying. He's a crafty son of a bitch."

"He'll turn up."

"Hmm." Except I need him found sooner rather than later. Before I lose what little sanity I have left.

"In the meantime, is Evie going to keep staying with you?"

I jerk my head once in a nod, and West grins like an idiot.

"What?" I growl.

"Is she that horrible? Didn't take her for a difficult roommate."

"What? No. She cleans up after herself. She doesn't talk my

ear off, and her cooking is better than my mom's—and don't go fucking telling my mom I said that, or I will make your death look like an accident." I point my finger at him, because he'd dime me out to Mom in a heartbeat if it meant being her favorite child.

He's done it to me plenty of times in the twenty-plus years we've been friends.

Instead, he holds his hands up in surrender.

"I didn't say anything."

"And you're not going to either."

The bastard laughs.

Asshole.

"Okay, she's the perfect roommate. So you don't mind her staying with you?"

Spinning on my heel, I continue our hike.

"You do mind?" he asks, falling into step beside me.

"I don't know."

Maybe that's the part that rankles more. It's not an either-or situation. It's fucking both.

"What do you mean you don't know? Haven't you lived with other people before?"

"In the Army, sure. But it's been a few years. I'm used to my own space. To coming and going as I please."

"Were you doing that a lot before she moved in? Seems to me you were always working."

"I wasn't *always* working. I'd take a night or two off occasionally."

"For what? Dates?"

I shake my head. "More like arrangements. A couple of women who want the same thing I do. A night of no-strings company. That lawyer friend who helped me with Mikey's legal stuff."

"If you're worried about leaving Evie alone, she could hang out with us so you can have the night off."

"I don't want a goddamned night off." The thought of being with any of those women doesn't appeal at all.

They were perfectly fine before. But *fine* isn't going to cut it anymore.

"So what do you want?" His question is so quiet, I almost don't hear it under the thunder of my own pulse.

"Sanity."

"What does sanity look like?" he asks.

"Finding Brad Russell so Evie is safe again."

"And not living with you anymore."

"Exactly."

"So you can have your own space again. To come and go as you please," he uses my words from earlier.

I can't help the way my molars grind together at the thought. "Yes."

Maybe.

Who knows?

"Because being attracted to her is making you crazy."

"Exa—wait a fucking minute. Who said anything about me being attracted to her?"

"It's obvious."

Fuck.

I grunt.

"That's a yes," he crows, throwing his head back.

The urge to punch him almost takes over. "How the fuck was that a yes?"

"Have you kissed her?"

I stumble over nothing on the trail, giving myself away, god dammit.

West halts and stares at me with his mouth open. "When?"

"When what?" The tips of my ears are hot with embarrassment. Maybe from tripping on nothing, or maybe because my best friend is far too observant.

He rolls his eyes. "When did you learn to walk? Asshole, I'm talking about Evie. When did you kiss her?"

"I haven't."

Lately.

"Tell that to someone who doesn't know your tell. You lean on your left foot when you lie." He points to my hiking boot.

"I fucking hate you."

"Love you too, bro. Out with it."

"You cannot tell Mikey."

He mimes zipping his lips and throwing away the key. It's so Michaela that I can't help but poke fun.

"God, you really are married to my sister."

"Don't change the subject," he says.

"Fine. Can we at least walk while we talk? We gotta get back to the car before dark."

And this way, I don't have to look at him and admit he was right. I'm seriously attracted to a woman I can't have.

"After you." He gestures to the trail with a bow.

We continue down the path. West doesn't push. He knows me well enough to give me time to collect my thoughts.

"I kissed her at your wedding."

Outside of Evie and me, he's the first person to know. The only other person to know.

"Fuck. When?"

"You and Mikey had already left. I offered to give her a lift to the hotel."

"I thought Evie came with Mia."

"She did. But when Mia headed back to her hotel room, she asked me to let Evie know."

"So you gave her a ride back?"

I nod, remembering the way Evie's pulse had visibly fluttered at the base of her neck. The way she smelled of something exotic and sexy but gave off this air of innocence. The contrast was impossible to ignore.

"I walked her to her room, and when she turned around to say goodnight, it was like we couldn't help ourselves."

We'd come together as if magnetized. It was more than the shy brush of the lips of a first kiss. It was sizzle. It was heat. It was the promise of something more.

Until she pulled back, metaphorically running away with the snick of the door between us.

"And nothing in over two years? What the fuck is wrong with you?"

The punch he throws against my arm catches me off guard, and I stumble again.

"She's a client," I say and rub my arm.

"She wasn't until two weeks ago."

He's correct.

"I just...I can't."

"Can't or won't?" he asks.

Both.

I won't risk letting emotion cloud my judgment again.

"Can't," I say.

"Why not? You're both adults. Maybe she doesn't realize you're still attracted to her. Maybe if you told her—"

"She's one of the five," I blurt out.

"Five—oh. Shit." The realization slams into him. "How didn't I put it together sooner?"

"Neither she nor I said anything. She's changed her appearance. Not that you were looking closely at the time."

I started my investigation right after Michaela told him she was pregnant.

"But Brad—"

"Yeah, I know."

Sometimes it's easier to hide in plain sight. No one put the pieces together. No one linked Evie and Brad, because they never had a reason to. I didn't say anything because she asked me not to.

"Sawyer?"

"Yeah?"

"Was she..." He trails off.

But he doesn't have to finish that sentence. He's my best friend. He doesn't have to ask.

Was she the one who spent five years with Brad, working to get her music career off the ground?

"Yeah. She was."

CHAPTER 6

EVIE

"*I* don't think this is a good idea." Mia chews on her lip while rubbing her softly rounded stomach.

I'm still over the moon that she and Garrett are going to have a baby. I love helping her pick out all the little nursery items she's obsessed with. I'm so happy that my friends are in love.

For me, though? I'm okay being alone. Why would I place someone else—someone I love, at that—in jeopardy?

I've come to terms with that decision. I'll be alone and enjoy my friends' children. I'll snuggle happy babies and give fussy babies back to their parents. God knows I'll have plenty of opportunity hanging out with Garrett and Mia. I swear every one of their friends has a child. And some, like Benji, are cute toddlers who soak up everything around them like little sponges.

But right now, I'm on edge. I've been this way since I moved in with Sawyer. And I don't know why.

Liar. You know why.

Having the hots for my bodyguard is a bad idea. I worked so hard to distance myself from him after our kiss, and it was all in vain. Because my libido doesn't seem to remember my vow to stay away. From him.

And on top of it all, I spend half my time with Mia, who's gotten herself wrapped up in her perfect marriage. I need to remind myself that being alone is what I want.

"It's fine," I urge.

I've been arguing with her for the last ten minutes. I plan to take my car, which has been here since I moved in with Sawyer, and visit my apartment, but she's adamant that I stay here.

Sawyer is off doing whatever he does when he isn't watching me like a hawk.

His attention is constantly laced with a strange combination of safety and lust. And after two weeks of fighting that combination, I'm at a breaking point. I worry that if I don't go home, I'll end up kissing the ever-loving shit out of him, consequences be damned.

If I were stronger, I could almost ignore the way the timbre of his voice makes my core pulse. But given how seldomly he speaks, I haven't had a chance to build my resolve. To learn how to ignore the response he evokes in me with just a word.

Maybe then I could ignore the steel blue gaze he keeps trained on me when we're in the same room.

Regardless of all that, what really drives me to my only place of refuge, a.k.a. the bathroom, is his smell. His cologne calls to me like an all-you-can-eat buffet tempting a starving person. The spicy, citrusy bergamot blend is intoxicating and tempting, and I act like a damn drug addict constantly sniffing for my next fix.

Showers are my safe haven. For those small snatches of time, I purge the hypnotizing scent from my olfactory senses. But as soon as I step out of the bathroom, *bam*, I'm back under its spell. So naturally, I've taken more showers than normal. A lot more. He probably thinks I'm crazy. And maybe I am. But he's the one driving me that way.

I can't afford to let my walls down. I let my defenses crumble once before—when I kissed him. And I knew who he was before that night. Was already aware of my visceral reaction to him. It was hard to ignore once Michaela moved into Mia and Garrett's pool house. But I fought the good fight. I ignored my attraction to him as best as I could. Until the night he dropped me off at my hotel room. Until my gaze locked with his and I saw my own darkness reflected back at me. I was powerless to deny what came next, to avoid the kiss I hurtled toward like a falling star plummeting to earth.

Back then, we were two magnets that called to each other, and our connection hasn't fizzled with time. It's only gotten stronger. And I need to figure out how to avoid his orbit and keep him out of mine. Hence my own space and the sanity it offers. So I don't have to see, hear, or smell the man I can't let myself want. It's a good plan, despite Mia's arguments.

"If it was fine, wouldn't Sawyer have suggested it by now?" she asks.

"There's been no sign of Brad in weeks. Sawyer was on the phone with Sydney the other day. I guess neither she nor her friends can find any trace of him. Looks like Brad gave up."

At least that's what I'm telling myself. Because Brad is lazy. I should know. I spent five years with him. He always did the minimum he had to in order to stay under the radar.

He also has the attention span of a cracked-out squirrel, distracted by one shiny object after another. Luckily for me, my plan to go into hiding coincided with a new assignment for him. A new artist Reverb was in negotiations with. It wasn't Michaela —the timing didn't line up.

In the five years since, I doubt he's changed. If anything, based on our brief encounter, he's more erratic than ever.

Is he involved with someone now who is too scared to run the way I did? I ran, and Michaela fought back. Maybe if I had said something—done something—when the abuse started, I could have stopped him. But I was too naive. I believed him.

This is how it goes in the industry. It's just one of the things you have to do to get ahead.

God, I was so stupid. It took me so long to understand how manipulative he was. How he played on my insecurities to get what he wanted. And by then, I was too ashamed to say anything.

"Mi, I love you, but it's time I took charge of my life. I'm not a little girl. I don't want someone else making my decisions for me."

Not anymore.

"I still think you should wait until Sawyer comes back."

He said he'd be back in an hour, and it's been almost that long now. If he does show up before I can get out of here, I'll have to argue with him too. And he's harder to convince than Mia.

"It's fine," I repeat. "I'll see you tomorrow. Garrett should be home soon too."

I'm gone before she can say anything else. Once outside, I thread my keys between my fingers—a trick from a self-defense class I took a few years ago. Despite what Sawyer thinks, I do have some self-preservation skills. Brad surprised me before, but now I'm ready for him. And I've learned a lot from watching Sawyer these last few weeks. How he pulled out of Mia and Garrett's driveway, how he scanned his surroundings, looking for anything out of place.

"It's fine," I tell myself.

It's too quiet.

I turn the radio on low. The background noise helps to drown out the sound of my pounding heart and the voice of my conscience that may or may not be screaming about how this isn't a good idea.

There don't appear to be any cars following me when I check my rearview mirror, but I still alter my normal route—another trick of Sawyer's. Fifteen minutes and a little more peace of mind later, I pull into the parking lot. It's early afternoon, and the almost empty lot isn't what I hoped for. Most people are at work.

"It's fine. It's daylight."

Daylight didn't help before.

I quiet the doubts that niggle at my brain and stay in my car with the doors locked until I scan the few cars around me for any sign of Brad.

Nothing.

Releasing the breath I'm holding, I crank off the ignition and steady my shaking hand so I can unlock the car doors.

"There's nothing to be afraid of."

But the wobble in my voice says otherwise. My fight-or-flight instincts have kicked in—mainly flight, since the urge to turn around and head back to Mia's to wait for Sawyer overwhelms me. I breathe through the nerves that twist my stomach in the distance from my car to the front door of my apartment. Any sign of the vandalism is gone, including the dingy gray left behind when Sawyer scrubbed off most of the permanent marker. The door is back to its regular brilliant turquoise. But the words from that night are like a phantom pain despite the fresh coat of paint.

Songbird. I'll be back.

My front door was one of the things I loved most about my home. The bright color never failed to make me happy. But the magic is gone. Anxiety makes my palms clammy, and I almost lose my keys with the shudder that works through my body.

"He's not here. He hasn't been back. Not for two weeks," I remind myself.

Sawyer had this place under surveillance. They would have seen him.

The apartment is the same as it was when I left. Physically, at least. But the goosebumps that cover my arms and the alarms that blare in my head are worse than they'd be if Brad *had* ransacked the apartment.

"Stop being a scaredy-cat. You're home."

Double-checking that the lock is engaged, I drop my purse on the table and shuffle to the bedroom. I'm desperate to find the peace this apartment has always brought me. But it's glaringly absent.

"It's fine. Calm down. He doesn't deserve to take up head space." My voice is loud in the empty room, but it does the trick.

Deep breath in, hold, and release. The book I left behind sits innocently on the nightstand, ready to transport me to a world where Brad doesn't exist.

It's upside down. Even if I read until I can't keep my eyes open, I always put the book down with the cover up and the pages facing my side of the bed.

"You were more tired than you thought. Maybe you just don't remember."

Exhaustion pulls at me now, the long rush of adrenaline and nerves taking its toll. But that isn't all. Two weeks of fighting my attraction to Sawyer, of waiting for Brad the Boogeyman to pop back up, of pretending all of this is fine when it's not, have worn me down.

"It's been two weeks. Time to relax, Ev."

Not many apartments in LA—hell, not many houses in LA—sport anything like the deep soaking tub I fell in love with the second I laid eyes on it. The cheery front door may have been the first selling point for the apartment, but my bathtub clinched the deal. I've surrounded the ceramic paradise with fat candles of all different heights and scents.

Today calls for relaxation—jasmine and vanilla. For the first time since I left Mia's, my heart thumps in anticipation instead of fear.

"Pajamas."

In my hasty pilgrimage to my oasis, I'd forgotten to pick out a set. Easily remedied. I left a few pairs of panties in the top drawer of my dresser when I packed my bag. Sexier ones I wouldn't need while I stayed with Sawyer but still love to wear because of the way they make me feel.

A scream sticks in my throat at the empty expanse of black

felt where my panties should be. Only it's not completely empty. The glossy back of a photo stares blankly up at me. One I didn't put there. I don't want to see what's on the other side, but my hand is already moving to flip over the four-by-six image that could have fallen out of any one of my photo albums.

If I had any.

I wouldn't have saved a picture like this, though.

It's me. But it isn't.

The picture is at least six or seven years old. It was taken when I still thought I could have my dream. Brad had convinced me that every artist took pictures like the one I'm holding now. The pit that cramps my stomach feels exactly like it did the day of the shoot—the one where Brad and the photographer convinced me that being photographed naked, covered only by a strategically placed guitar, was tasteful, artistic.

The slimy sensation of all those eyes that watched me when the guitar wasn't in place slides along my skin.

A small piece of paper flutters along the black felt now that the picture is gone. It's a page from a book. No doubt the one that now mocks me from the top of the dresser.

See you soon.

My heart drops to my stomach, and fear rushes through my blood with every pound of my heartbeat. My fingers go numb, and my grip loosens on the glossy photo—the physical remains of my nightmare. It flutters back down to the drawer and covers the words Brad scrawled across the paper, but it does nothing to stem the scream lodged in my throat.

Run.

That word unlocks my body. I need to escape. Rushing from the bedroom, I don't look back. I'm at my front door before I can process anything else. I throw it open, my only focus getting back to Mia's. To safety. To Sawyer.

Large hands stop my progress, the past and present colliding into my worst nightmare. Every impulse in my body shifts from flight to fight, and I lash out. Based on the grunts, I land a few punches and kicks, though I'm too panicked to see past the arms holding me. Strong fingers wrap around my wrist and subdue me, stopping my attempts to escape.

"Evie, stop. It's me. You're okay. You're safe." It's the cadence of Sawyer's voice as much as the words he says that reaches me.

The adrenaline drains from my body, and I sag against him. Safe. I'm safe. It's okay. The large hands that had been so terrifying now sweep up and down my back in comfort. I heave a sigh and look up to meet his concerned gaze.

"What happened?"

He directs us back into my apartment and closes the door, but the space isn't as terrifying with him in it.

I drop my head against his chest, focusing on the steady thump of his heartbeat. "He was here," I whisper.

Sawyer's body tenses, and I tighten my grip, not ready for him to let go just yet.

"When you got here?"

I shake my head. "No. I'm not sure when. But...he left me a message."

"Show me."

Reluctantly, I release my grip on him. Cool air rushes between us, and I wrap my arms around my body in an effort to maintain the warmth and security of his embrace while I lead him into the bedroom.

The drawer is still open, the picture face down once more, but Sawyer doesn't grab it right away.

"He was in here?" The words are barely discernible as they grind out from the thin line of his lips.

A muscle ticks in his jaw, and my attention zeros in on the flutter.

Closing my eyes, I take a deep breath and release it.

"I...nothing was wrong at first. Except for my book. It was upside down." I wave toward the innocent-looking paperback.

It sounds ridiculous saying it out loud, but his face remains serious.

"What else?"

"I just figured I left it that way, but then I decided to take a bath and relax—"

I've taken thousands of baths in my life. But suddenly, hot and cold simultaneously spread through my body, sending shivers through me at the thought.

"I—I opened my drawer to grab a change of clothes for after and...and..." My throat closes on the words, and I wave at the dresser.

Sawyer steps gingerly forward to study the open drawer.

Without flipping the picture over, he slides it to the side to reveal the message scrawled across the mutilated page of the book.

His attention shifts from the drawer to me, but he stays silent.

"That drawer has—had—some under...things I left behind. But they're gone. All of them. The only thing left was that note and the picture of..." The words rush from my lips, more breath than sound.

His observant eyes flick to the picture before coming back to study my face.

Hate is probably not a strong enough word for the sensation those pictures invoke. They're proof of how easily manipulated I was. Of what I was willing to sacrifice for my dream.

I have no doubt Sawyer saw these or something similar when he looked into Brad before. It makes my skin crawl with a dirty sensation, and all I want to do is scrub myself clean.

He carefully pushes the drawer closed, never bothering to flip over the picture.

"You didn't—"

"It's obviously a picture that bothers you. And I know what kind of asshole he is. I don't need to see it."

Relief and gratitude war for control over my body, the combination dizzying.

His expression shifts, and if possible, turns more serious. The silence while he studies me grows more and more awkward until I can't handle it anymore.

"What?" I finally ask.

"You left."

"I—"

I don't have an excuse for my behavior. Not a logical one anyway. We haven't heard from Brad in weeks. I've been going crazy. I don't want to be a burden. Any and all of the above. I used every one of those excuses to convince myself that this is okay.

It's not.

"You were in danger, and you left a place I *knew* was safe," he says.

My breath catches. "I—"

He takes a step closer. "I saw you as you left Mia's. Followed you—"

"I didn't see you!"

"I didn't want you to see me." Another step. "That's the fucking point, Evie."

"What is?"

Somehow, we're nose to nose in my bedroom, both of us breathing heavily.

"You could have been hurt. Fuck, he could have been waiting for you. Obviously, the apartment complex never fucking added more locks like I told them to. Which means I'm calling my guy in the morning."

"Why do you care? I'm the assistant to your sister's best friend. I'm nothing to you. I'm just a job—one you're not even being paid—"

My words are silenced as he yanks me against him and plants his lips on mine.

In all my life, I've only been kissed like this once before.

At Michaela and West's wedding.

But *kiss* doesn't do this justice. Not the masterful way Sawyer's lips mold to mine. How the steady pressure of his mouth against mine makes my knees weak. He deepens the kiss, his tongue finding mine, and I tighten my grip on his shirt while he cups my jaw like I'm fragile. Like I'm cherished.

This isn't a kiss. It's consumption. Sawyer is consuming me.

And for the first time in a long time, I don't think about how I'm damaged. I don't think about my past.

My only thought is him.

CHAPTER 7

SAWYER

"I don't understand how this is supposed to work," Evie says from the small seat next to mine, her elbow brushing against my arm.

Hard to find space cruising above the clouds on the way to Alaska. Every shift, every sigh, every everything is a reminder of her presence.

As if I can think about anything *but* her since the kiss we shared in her apartment. The one that still eats at me. It shouldn't have happened. Even if the urge had only grown over the two weeks we shared my condo.

I should have been better. I *know* how to be better.

But my self-control had been obliterated by the need to prove that she was safe. When she left Mia's, I could have cut her off at the driveway and strapped her into my car.

But I had to find out why.

Why would she leave the safety of Mia's? Why would she go somewhere and not tell me?

The longer I followed her, the more pissed I became. She had no idea I was following her through traffic. A few turns, and I knew her destination. Once I figured that out, I slowed further until I could park in the street and study her as she left the safety of her car.

And if I knew all that, so could someone else, if they were paying attention. Someone like Brad. Her safety was my top concern, but his only purpose would be getting her alone—I couldn't let that happen.

"He's staying hidden because we're looking for him. If he thinks we've stopped, he'll show himself again."

It's simple. So long as he does what I think he'll do. While I'm protecting Evie, Sydney and Cole will be searching relentlessly for the bastard.

"Why can't we stay in LA?" she asks.

"It's too close." For my sanity.

I need to put distance between Evie and Brad. I need to know she's safe. The fucking maintenance crew at her apartment dropped the ball and didn't add the extra locks I requested. Lesson learned. It's a reminder of why I have my own vendors.

"But Alaska?" Her hazel eyes bore into me.

I fight against their pull. Because if I surrender, I'll lose what little focus I have.

"I have a cabin in Alaska."

One I can guarantee is safe. One very few people know about.

My fortress of solitude.

Ironic. Evie is my kryptonite, and here I am, taking her to the place I go to recharge. Typically, the only woman on my mind when I'm at the cabin is Amani. Every time. I get lost in memories of her and of all the ways I failed her. She's been front and center every time—except once.

My trip a few weeks after Mikey and West's wedding. After the kiss I couldn't forget. I didn't want to.

If that first kiss had the power to do that, the second one in her apartment was even stronger.

I wish I could blame her. That I could excuse my actions as an automatic response to every question she asked me. Fuck. She wanted to know why I cared so much, why I wouldn't stop keeping her safe. I've never been great with words, and between one breath and the next, I went from trying to find the right ones to fusing my lips to hers.

To stop the questions.

Yeah, right. The truth was, I wanted to kiss her. Had wanted to kiss her until it was the only thing that occupied my attention.

As soon as my lips connected with hers, I knew I should step back and apologize. But Evie had other ideas. She pulled me closer and threaded her fingers through my hair to deepen the kiss until the only thing I could think about was her. Not her safety. But the flavor of her lips, the way her breath mingled with mine, the weight of her breasts where they pressed against my chest.

I needed her.

I was consumed by her.

And every part of me wanted to forget Brad Russell existed. To walk Evie to her bed and worship her the way I only allowed myself to imagine.

The way her fingers gripped me and her body pressed against mine was proof—she was on the same page. We matched each other with every step.

Thank god the universe stopped us when I didn't have the willpower to. Mia's call had been well-timed. She was worried when Evie hadn't answered her cell phone.

"Sawyer?"

Evie's light touch on my arm yanks me out of my head.

Fuck. Pay attention, asshole. You're supposed to be protecting her, not fantasizing about her.

Is it fantasizing if I'm lost in a memory?

Do you really want to know?

Clearing my throat, I push memories of her taste to the back of my mind.

"Sorry, what?"

"Is your cabin in Anchorage?"

Not many people know about the cabin—West and Michaela since they honeymooned there. My parents. Sydney and Cole know. That way they can get a hold of me while I'm there.

"We're not staying in Anchorage."

"We're not?" she asks.

"My place is just outside of Homer. On Kachemak Bay. We'll grab a connecting flight to Homer once we land in Anchorage. I keep an SUV there."

"Isn't that expensive? To just leave a vehicle at the airport all the time?"

I shrug. "I worked something out with one of the employees. It's cheaper and more reliable than renting a car."

Especially if snow is in the forecast. I'm not sure if getting snowed in with Evie would be heaven or hell. Being confined to four walls with a woman who's haunted my dreams for years? Dante missed a circle of hell.

Rather than dwell on that, I glance at my watch.

"We've got another hour or so until we land. Maybe you should try and get some sleep. We were up early this morning."

"I'm not tired," she says, her jaw set.

"Tell that to the dark circles under your eyes. We could have checked those with our suitcases," I joke.

Keep it light.

Right. It's been virtually impossible since the day she found out Brad had been inside her apartment. Those dark smudges appeared, and they've only gotten darker since. So the team and I created this plan. We need Brad to drop his guard. And I need those shadows—both under her eyes and in them—to disappear. More than I need to kiss her again. But no one would ever know that. Despite West hinting at it more than once when he found out we were leaving for Alaska.

Brad has stolen something from Evie. Again.

Her peace of mind.

I promised her he would never hurt her. Not with me here. But that day, at her apartment. I failed.

And it's in-fucking-excusable.

This mission takes precedence over all. Meaning I have to stop thinking about kissing Evie and focus on keeping her safe.

Warm breath penetrates the soft cotton of my shirt. She's asleep with her head resting against my arm. It's what she needs. But now that she's quiet, I miss the lyrical cadence of her voice. And her constant fidgeting. The way she questions me with those almost-too-wide-for-her-face hazel eyes. The ones that look at me like I'm invincible. It creates a vulnerability inside me I'm not used to. One I'm not exactly comfortable with.

What the fuck is wrong with me?

Unwilling to dig into the truth of it, I huff a frustrated breath and reach for my phone. Thank god our connecting flight from Seattle to Anchorage has Wi-Fi.

Status?

SYDNEY

Nothing has changed in the three hours since you last texted.

Surprised you were able to wait that long.

COLE

There's still no sign of him. I checked the apartment again.

Since I found Evie at her apartment, Cole has been patrolling the complex several times a day to keep an eye on things.

Nothing?

COLE

I didn't say that.

The new locks you wanted are in.

Before we left, I did the one thing I should have done in the beginning. I called my locksmith and had him add the additional security to Evie's door.

> It' about fucking time.

COLE

If Brad wants back in, he's going to need to ghost himself through the walls.

> He's not getting back into her apartment again.

> I'll check back in when we land.

SYDNEY

Why? Because something will have changed in an hour?

This is what I get for hiring a goddamned teenager. Sydney's primary language is sarcasm. Some days it almost makes me regret hiring her. But despite her young age, she's the best hacker I've ever met. Military or otherwise. Today is one of those days that her sarcasm grates more than normal.

I tighten my grip on my phone, ready to reply, but Cole beats me to it.

COLE

I've seen situations go sideways a lot faster than sixty minutes.

More like sixty seconds.

We both have. Cole was the new kid during my final deployment. But kids don't stay that way long in war zones. Even as young as he was, I recognized how much of an asset he would be. First him and now Sydney. Fuck. The more time I spend around them, the older I feel.

COLE

Besides, he signs our paychecks. If he wants to
micromanage us like a pageant mom, what do
we care?

I huff a laugh at his comparison. Guy's from Mistletoe Creek, Tennessee, and he knows more about pageants than he ever wanted to. Or so he says. But since he has a pageant comparison for any situation—usually scarily accurate based on the few episodes of *Toddlers and Tiaras* I got stuck watching with Mikey— I rarely question him.

Evie shifts in her sleep, a frown wrinkling the smooth skin between her eyebrows. The dark shade stands out against the pale skin, hinting at the more auburn tone of her natural hair color. But it's the frown that has guilt pricking at me again.

"Shh, little starling. You're safe," I murmur.

The frown smooths out after a moment, her body relaxing against mine once again. Confident her dreams are peaceful, I lift my phone to find Sydney and Cole have carried on with the conversation.

SYDNEY

For a security guard, you sure do talk a lot about
pageants.

COLE

And for a kid, you sure don't respect your elders.

SYDNEY

So you're telling me you're old?

COLE

No, I'm telling you that Sawyer and I are your
superiors.

SYDNEY

Yeah, yeah. Tell me that if I ever join the military.

If I dig deep enough, will I find pictures of baby
Cole in beauty contests?

COLE

First of all, I'm not a security guard. I'm a security
threat analyst.

SYDNEY

::cough:: Security guard. ::cough::

COLE

Two, before you go trolling the internet or
whatever the fuck it is you do to look for
blackmail material, hell no, I was never in a
pageant.

Finally, if anything like that ever shows up—real
or photoshopped—I can make your death look
like an accident.

I guess he still hasn't forgiven her for the time she photoshopped him as an extra band member for One Direction after
one of our clients had him escort his daughter to a concert.

SYDNEY

Touchy.

Would you two give it a rest?

Sydney, please tell me you deleted Photoshop.

SYDNEY

Of course I did.

...

SYDNEY

Duh.

And Cole, stop picking on Sydney like she's your
baby sister.

COLE

Baby is an accurate statement.

SYDNEY

Whatever. 😏

You're both fired.

Get back to work.

Sydney and Cole both send what I think is supposed to be a thumbs-up emoji. Coincidentally, though, they mistakenly send the middle finger emoji instead.

CHAPTER 8

EVIE

*C*abin. Sawyer said cabin. I guess I expected something a little more rustic. A bare bones sort of shelter with log furniture. A bed. Maybe two. A table and chairs. Basic. Secure. A bit rough around the edges—all attributes I could use to describe the owner.

All my expectations scatter under the magic of the waves in the bay against a backdrop of snow-covered mountains. Everything is encased in sparkling white except for the blue of the water as it shifts against itself.

"Ready?" Sawyer asks.

"Hmm?" I tear my attention away from the peaceful scene to face him.

The SUV is in park, and he's already unbuckled his seat belt. He motions to the house, and I follow the path, my jaw popping open at the sight in front of me.

When will I learn to not be surprised by this man?

He shouldn't be this hard to predict. The car he left parked at the airport was what I expected. A large black SUV with a pristine interior and every tech imaginable that took the snow-bordered roads with ease.

But *cabin?*

"I thought you said cabin."

"What were you expecting? A one-bedroom shack?"

"Well…" That's not far off from my assumption. "How big is this place?" The question pops out before I can stop it.

But seriously, though. There's a large wooden deck along the front side of the main floor and a smaller balcony on the next level. And the garage and driveway appear to be part of a walk-out basement.

"Four bedrooms, three bathrooms."

His succinct descriptions continue as he gives me a tour of all three stories. It's nothing but clean lines and natural light.

He points out the wooden deck I noticed from outside.

"Wow."

If it weren't the middle of winter, I could spend hours in one of the comfortable chairs set up on the wooden boards.

"I'll show you your room."

I trail Sawyer up the next flight of stairs and into the master bedroom. Two of the walls hold large picture windows over-looking the bay. There is a door that leads out to the small balcony on a third wall.

"This is your room," I say.

It's a statement instead of a question, but he nods anyway.

Even without his confirmation, I would know. The space is all dark colors and darker wood—a stunning contrast to the brilliance outside.

"I'm going to take one of the room downstairs."

"But this is your room."

He shrugs.

"You'll be more comfortable up here."

"What about you?"

"I'll be fine downstairs. There's a guest room—"

"Then I'll stay there."

He shakes his head.

"Negative. I want you up here. It's safer."

Safer. Well, hell. There go all my arguments.

"Are you sure?" I ask, but my question lacks any conviction.

His smile is soft around the edges. Broody Sawyer is hot. But Smiling Sawyer? He takes the heat up another notch.

Maybe I should sleep outside—the cold might help.

I've found my new favorite spot in Sawyer's cabin. The little nook by the back door off the living room is more like an over-sized window seat than anything else. While it should be cold, the steadily burning fire and plush blanket Sawyer left out for me makes it perfectly cozy.

A flash of movement catches my eye, distracting me from my book. Thank god for my e-reader, since Sawyer's limited library trended more toward Tom Clancy and Stephen Ambrose than Nora Roberts or Julia Quinn.

Sawyer's back from wherever he's gone every day for the last four days—according to him, it's warm enough to cross-country ski.

Warm enough or not, that's a hard pass for me.

Which is what I told him on our first full day, when he asked if I wanted to join him. My exercise involves lifting a book or running after Mia. In addition to the cross-country skiing, the cabin has a gym in one of the bedrooms. I've yet to see him use it, but every morning, he glides off into the trees that border the cabin and emerges two hours later.

Even when he's gone, I'm not scared.

Safe? Protected? Without question.

There's no doubt in my mind he's coming back. That I'm anything less than safe even in his absence.

I consider the two hours without him as a reprieve. Without fail, the need to kiss him again wanes for the hundred and twenty minutes he's gone. Fighting the attraction while living with him at his condo in LA was one thing. Our kiss before that had been years before. Easy to forget. Or fool myself into thinking I'd forgotten.

But the one in my apartment? The one where all that attraction over those two weeks coalesced into one earth-shattering connection of lips? Just remembering it makes my mouth—and other body parts—tingle in anticipation of more.

There will be no more.

"What are you reading?"

Sawyer's deep voice startles me, and my e-reader slides to the floor. Despite the flash of movement that briefly caught my attention, I didn't hear the basement door open or the sound of him coming up the stairs. In the last few weeks, he's transformed little by little from the harsh military man to something softer. His dark blond hair is longer, mussed from a combination of wind and the knit cap he wears outside. A dark blue Henley deepens the color of his eyes and molds to every one of his mouthwatering muscles before tapering into his ski pants.

The cartoon socks on his feet are in sharp contrast to the honey-hued color of the wood. He follows my gaze, half of his mouth lifting in a smile.

"Benji," he explains.

I'm still in full ogle mode when he picks up my forgotten e-reader from where it landed at his feet. A burst of heat floods my cheeks. I was in the middle of a particularly steamy part of *Thinking 'Bout You*. He scans the screen quickly, then looks up at me over the device, his eyes glittering with an emotion I refuse to name, despite the throb in my core that demands I acknowledge it.

"Here." He holds it out without another word.

Electricity arcs where our fingers brush. My breath catches, and the heat in my face travels through my body.

"Th-thank you." I stumble over the words, my suddenly dry lips being uncooperative.

He fixates on my mouth, his blue eyes igniting. Nervous and turned on, despite my best efforts, I drag my tongue along my lips to moisten them.

He sways toward me, and I lean forward, two magnets that shift inexorably closer to the other. My eyelids flutter closed as my entire body readies itself for another fireworks-inducing kiss.

"I'm going to shower," he says, shifting back and thumbing over his shoulder. He's gone before I can respond, a vapor trail practically streaming after him.

Did I imagine that initial reaction?

No. No way. He's kissed me not once but twice. And the last time, he definitely initiated. So what the hell was that?

For the first time since we arrived, the day takes an awkward turn. I want to ask him what's happened, but do I really want to know the answer?

Hours later, I jolt upright in bed. The only sound in the room is my harsh breathing. Goosebumps cover my skin, and my heart races.

"You're fine. Everything's okay. Just a nightmare," I whisper, hugging my chest while a shudder travels along my spine.

When I was a kid, my nightmares were filled with monsters and boogeymen. It was easy to find comfort from Mom. She'd whisper soothingly, reminding me that they didn't exist. For so long, I believed her. But one day, long after the last time she comforted me like that, I learned they were real. They preyed on a person's dreams and ground them to dust until all that was left was a pile of ash and rubble.

Brad was my boogeyman. And the only way to escape my nightmare was to walk away from my dream. Now he's back. I have no idea where he is or when he'll come for me, but he will.

His lack of visibility still frustrates Sawyer. Coming to Alaska was supposed to draw him out, but so far, no luck. Earlier this evening, he paced the length of the living room and back, on a call with his team. And afterward, when his eyes clashed with mine? They were full of misery.

His plan isn't working. Brad still has the upper hand.

"Explains my bad dream," I mumble to myself and swing my legs to the side.

3:09 AM.

A light breeze rattles against the panes of the door and window. I don't want to be up here. And sleep?

Not happening.

The wood floor is surprisingly warm as I move through the quiet house. I don't bother with lights until I reach the kitchen. Once there, I flip the switch and blink against the sudden brightness, then bring the kettle to the sink. I'm hoping the orange cinnamon tea Sawyer ordered specifically for me will settle the adrenaline that still pulses through my system.

The thoughtfulness he exudes effortlessly still surprises me, though it shouldn't. He had the cabin stocked with food before we arrived and made sure to include things I like. I've never had someone consider what I needed or wanted like this before, let alone take care of things without making a big deal out of it.

"Couldn't sleep?"

For the second time in twenty-four hours, Sawyer sneaks up on me. How is that possible given his size?

I spin around, a hand pressed to my heart. "God. Don't do that."

He shrugs, looking sheepish. "Sorry."

I wave off the apology and turn back to the stove, where the kettle is heating.

"Couldn't sleep?" he asks again.

"No."

"Why not?"

I study the tea bag, considering whether I want to answer his question. But the physical awareness I have of him is so acute I can sense his movement as he steps just inside the kitchen entryway.

"Bad dream." I lift a shoulder, feigning nonchalance.

"About what?"

What's with twenty questions all of a sudden? This is the most he's spoken to me since he disappeared to take a shower earlier. Quite possibly, it's the most he's said to me the entire time I've known him.

Finished making my tea, I have no reason to avoid turning to look at him. Mug in hand, I rotate, gripping the handle tighter.

Holy sweet baby Jesus.

Despite practically living with Sawyer for a month, I've only ever seen him fully clothed.

Now, though? Flannel pajama pants hang low on his hips, revealing a set of chiseled abs that taper down to twin brackets along his hips. Those mouthwatering lines disappear into the soft fabric of his pants. Now I understand why those grooves can make a girl stupid. And I might have stood a chance at coherent thought if that was the only temptation I was faced with.

But no.

His well-defined chest is just as tempting. It's covered in a smattering of light hair that obscures the ink decorating his skin just a little. I want to move closer. I want to identify each piece of art, feel his heat, discover whether the hair is soft or springy beneath my fingertips.

Maybe I should be embarrassed when my gaze meets his. But I'm not. Heartbeats pound out the seconds while we stare at each other.

Finally, he breaks the silence. "Evie?"

"Hmm?" I blink, finally released from the spell his body cast over me.

"What was your bad dream about?"

Ice water wouldn't be any more effective at bringing me back to reality.

"I—I don't remember," I say and beeline past him to the spot by the window I've claimed.

"You don't?" he asks, squinting at me like he doesn't quite believe me.

Not that I blame him.

Every part of the dream is still as vivid as the day it happened. That's the way it goes when memories become nightmares. I keep them buried deep, but they sneak out from time to time when I can't actively fight them off.

The dream was of my first time with Brad—my first time ever, actually. Even now, the phantom pressure of his fingers remains. Everywhere. A slimy sensation that crawls along my skin like oil on top of water. Invisible, but just as toxic.

The scalding liquid of my tea cascades down my throat, but the pain pushes the awful memory back into the box it escaped from.

"I don't remember bad dreams," I explain.

"Lucky."

The word is so quiet, I almost miss it.

"What?" I set my tea down carefully and wrap a fluffy blanket around me.

"Nothing."

The silence stretches between us once more. But Sawyer doesn't leave. He doesn't retreat to his room or office. Instead, he moves one of the living room chairs so it's facing me and drops into it.

"Can I ask you something?"

His fidgeting leaves me leery.

What could he possibly ask that would make him so nervous?

"Umm...sure?"

"Is there anything you can think of that could help us find Brad? Did he ever talk about family? Or friends?"

My stomach cramps. I'd rather think of anything but Brad—my nightmare tonight was more than enough. But I want to help.

So I force myself to sift through memories I'd rather leave forgotten. Sawyer stays silent while I relive each one.

Songbird.

Mine.

Do as I say.

I squeeze my eyes shut, but the voice in my head is as clear as day and circles around me like a twisted merry-go-round.

"I…"

I don't want to remember.

You have to. Maybe you can help.

With a deep breath, I open my eyes.

"If he did have any friends or family, he never shared that with me. We didn't talk a lot."

He wasn't interested in what I had to say. Or in speaking to me in general. Especially once he realized how easily he could keep me under his control. But even before that, he was never much for conversation.

Criticism? Yes.

Innuendo? Definitely.

I wasn't the first woman he manipulated. I also wasn't the last. But I stayed the longest. Maybe it makes me the stupidest. Or the most gullible.

But I did eventually walk away.

"Can you tell me about the places he'd take you?" Sawyer asks.

I shrug. "Dive bars mostly. For gigs."

Anywhere we went fit his agenda. He never intended to help make my dream come true.

"Was there a specific one you frequented?" he presses.

"No, usually one and done…Wait. There was one bar I played at a few times. Guy's."

"Guy's?"

I swallow around a lump that builds in my throat and nod.

"It was next door to a strip club."

He would drag me there when I finished my gigs. Every time,

I was mistaken for an employee because of the way Brad insisted I dress. He thought it was hysterical. The third, the last time, was the night he dragged me to a back room and forced me to my knees.

That was my breaking point. I found it in a dirty room that smelled of cigarettes and stale alcohol while music thumped and girls danced for money on the other side of a one-way mirror.

Bile rises to my throat, and I desperately crawl out of the memory.

"I—I think he and the owner were buddies," I choke out.

"Why do you think that?"

"I—I saw the same guy there a few times. We would...sit with him."

The image of a smoke-ring leer in a sunken face surfaces. Some protective mechanism kicks in, and a wall in my mind slams shut. With a shiver, I tug the blanket tighter around me and squirm under the steady attention of the man trying to help me.

"What?" I ask when he doesn't look away.

"Do you know how brave you are?"

"What?" I blink, stunned by the question.

"Do you know how incredibly brave you are?"

I shake my head.

"I'm not brave. I was stupid, naive, gullible. Take your pick, but it isn't brave." I was a fool, so intent on achieving my dream that I gave up who I was in the process. Gave away parts of myself I can never get back.

He kneels before me and rests his hands on the seat on either side of my legs. He doesn't touch me, but the warmth of his body drives out the cold that radiates from within me.

"Brave," he corrects. "So brave."

The moment stretches from one heartbeat to the next.

I open my mouth, the truth locked in my mind pushing to be released, freedom from the cage of my own making within reach for the first time in forever.

"Sawyer."

He moves his hands to my legs, and with his thumbs, rubs a soothing pattern along my calves.

"What?"

"Can I tell you something?" I whisper.

He's watching me with the most earnest expression I've seen from him. "Anything."

"It won't change, right?" I couldn't bear it if it did.

"What won't change?" He scoots just a little closer.

I clear my throat. "What you think of me."

"Not possible."

The genuineness of that statement is written in the lines of his face.

With another deep breath, I open my mouth, ready to confess everything.

"I—"

His ringtone interrupts my confession.

Fumbling in his pocket, he pulls his phone out and glances at the screen.

"Sydney." He looks up at me. "She wouldn't call this late unless she had something."

He still doesn't answer the call, despite its importance. And he doesn't take his eyes off me.

"Go ahead," I tell him.

It's the only approval he needs. He unfurls from his position and steps away, bringing his phone to his ear.

A dose of clarity hits me along with the cool air that rushes in. I got so caught up that I almost told him everything.

It *would* change how he looks at me.

My decision to confess was impulsive. Fed by the scattered memories swarming me. But I have to remember one thing: no one can know.

I can't drop my guard. Obviously, the universe agrees.

CHAPTER 9

SAWYER

*T*he temperature is several degrees below crisp, and the frozen air stings my lungs as I ski up to the cabin next door. Smoke curls lazily from the chimney, and a golden retriever bounds over to me, nearly taking me off my feet.

"Hello, Watson." I give him a good scratch behind his ears.

"You're late." The voice sounds like it belongs to a two-pack-a-day smoker but is still warm and welcoming.

From what I've gleaned, Ed Bailey *was* a two-pack-a-day smoker when he was a psychological profiler for the FBI.

"Didn't realize I was that predictable," I mutter, setting my skis off to the side of the deck.

He barks a laugh and hands me a hot cup of coffee once I reach the top of the stairs. For the last week, I've made daily trips over here. At first it was to catch up, but over the last few days, I've been picking his brain in hopes of coming up with something I can use to find Brad.

"I can set my watch by it."

I take a drink of the thick brew and grimace. The heat of it is a shock to my system.

"I was on a call with my team," I tell him.

"Obviously, it wasn't a good one."

I long ago stopped questioning how easily he reads me. It was his job for over thirty years. One he was really fucking good at.

He holds an arm out, motioning to the door. With a dip of my chin, I lead the way. Watson, named for Sherlock Holmes's associate, of course, shakes the melting snow from his fur, then wanders to his pillow by the crackling fireplace.

"You could say that."

Beside the hearth, Watson stretches with a groan. If only I could channel such a relaxed mindset. I've been wrapped in a tight ball since Brad first resurfaced.

"Did the call have anything to do with the questions you've been asking me the last few days?" he inquires, sitting back in his chair.

To most, he's the picture of relaxation. But his eyes are too serious, too steady. He's cataloging every detail about me, from the way I sit in my seat to the grip I have on the coffee mug.

"I have a case..."

He interlaces his fingers and brings them to his lips.

"Tell me."

Those two words are all it takes to unlock every detail. From the investigation I did after Michaela's assault to my frustration with how Brad hasn't only evaded me, but my team members as well. By the time I'm done, my mug is empty and it's time to head back.

"Thanks for the coffee," I tell Ed as I stand and stretch.

"Anytime. See you tomorrow?"

"Probably." I huff a laugh.

"I'll think about your case. See if Brad hits any of the standard profiles."

"I appreciate it."

I've tried everything I can think of.

Hopefully Ed can see something I don't.

☆☆☆

Evie's different.

The dark circles that prompted our trip to Alaska are gone. But so is everything else. Every emotion that had begun to emerge in the last few days has vanished, and she's even more withdrawn than she was that day at Mia's house, when Brad found her. Like she's been replaced by a pod person. The attractive exterior is still in place, but the vibrancy that drives her from within has disappeared.

And I can pinpoint the exact moment it happened.

The call from Sydney.

I hate—I fucking detest—my need to ask Evie more about Brad. She fought demons so dark I can't fathom them while she answered my questions and wrestled with God knows what. If I ever discover what memories drained all the color from her face like that, I may not be able to stop myself from beating Brad into the ground.

Her life with him was hell. I've seen it in the slew of pictures I found while I investigated him after what he did to Michaela. In them, her expression morphed from happy and hopeful in the early days to wan and demoralized. Between the first picture and the last, she became almost unrecognizable. And different still from the woman I know. The one hiding as an assistant to Mia Maddox, even though she has the talent to be so much more.

"I thought you said you found something," I tell Sydney.

She called me with more leads but doesn't have anything concrete.

When she called the other night and interrupted our conversation in the dark, it was to tell me that Brad's credit card had been used in Hollywood. Her systems had blown up with alerts when it was used at a seedy hourly rate hotel. But since then, he hasn't been spotted, and we haven't found evidence of him on any surveillance footage Sydney accessed.

"I have. I've found lots of somethings. But it's going to take me a while to sift through all the data."

She's been compiling photos and videos from social media posted within a small radius of where his credit card was charged.

"How long?"

"Fuck, Sawyer, I don't know. There are a lot of goddamn images to go through, even with the facial recognition program I'm using. A few days? Maybe three?"

Three days.

Can I handle staying here another three days, living with the one woman I want but can't have? Can I survive living with the ghost of her when I've seen the real her?

Do you have a choice?

Fuck. I promised to protect her. And this is the first solid lead we've had on Brad. Easy or not, I'll let Sydney work her magic for three days. So long as it leads to removing Brad from Evie's life permanently.

He stole her past. I won't let him have her future too.

"Fine. Just...get it done. Keep me posted."

Static crackles across the signal, and Sydney's voice sounds more distorted when she answers.

"I will."

Hanging up, I drop my head back against my desk chair and rub my tired eyes. I've been staring at my computer screen for hours, reviewing progress on this case as well as drafting responses to requests for future work from new and existing clients.

I need to hire more help. It's a good problem to have, even if it exhausts me just thinking about it. Hiring Cole was a no-brainer. Same with Sydney. But this time around, the choice isn't so obvious.

My phone chimes with a message, and I crack one eye to read it.

WEST

Heard a storm's headed your way.

How did he know before me?

Probably because you haven't looked.

True. Normally, I check the weather daily. Storms mean my cell service goes to shit, and most of the time, my landlines go down too. Three years ago, a storm knocked the power out for a few days. After that, I installed a generator, though it's not powerful enough to keep me on full power.

Are you texting me to rub it in?

What's the temp there?

I pull up the weather app on my phone.

Fuck.

72 for the next week?

You poor baby. However will you handle it?

It wasn't my idea to buy a house in Alaska.

You could have bought something in a more tropical location.

Only I had my fill of tropical locations while in the Army.

No thanks. Too many bugs.

It also wasn't my idea for you to leave LA. I offered to help you find that bastard.

If anyone hates Brad as much as I do, it's my best friend. Michaela's ability to fight him off was probably the only thing that saved him from a major ass-whooping. From me. My best friend is a different story. Brad terrorized his wife, and that's not something he'll forget anytime soon.

> It's the middle of the semester.
>
> I can do my job.

Never said you couldn't.

Just that I can help.

> We have it covered. Sydney is working some leads now.

You may want to let her know about the storm.

And Evie.

> And Evie what?

Tell her about the storm.

I need to mention the storm and its potential impacts to her. But until I have something more concrete on Brad, I'll keep the credit card charge between Sydney and myself.

> Thanks for the heads-up on the storm.
>
> If you don't hear from me in a few days, at least you'll know why.

Yep. Anytime. Stay safe.

It's the way he always ends a call or text with me. And my reply is just as constant.

> Safety is my middle name.

I find Evie where I expect to—the little nook that overlooks the bay and part of the forest. I'm glad I gave her the fluffy white blanket. She spends half her day here, and though the house is well-insulated, the chill from outside still seeps through the window. And it'll only get worse with the storm coming.

She's curled up like she always is, but her e-reader sits dark and forgotten next to her. A small frown mars her face, and she's staring out the window blankly.

I stop on the other side of the room and clear my throat to announce my presence.

Evie barely spares me a glance before she turns back to the vista on the other side of the window, where the storm is rolling in and blocking the blue sky with gray clouds while lengthening the shadows in the room.

"There's a storm coming in," I say. Like she isn't watching it taking place in front of her.

"Oh."

One word. Two letters. And I've never hated two letters more. I want to rush across the room and demand she say more. Anything. I want her to drag her focus from the gloomy landscape and look at me. I've gotten used to the weight of her gaze on me, and now that it's gone, my life is like the weather outside—the sun has disappeared under the mounting pressure of a storm.

"We might lose power."

It's more than a might. Especially if the storm is as bad as they're predicting.

Finally, she turns her attention to me, and suddenly, I wish she hadn't. The shadows that had slowly disappeared from her eyes are back with a vengeance. The helplessness that fills me wars with guilt. Because I should have fixed this already. I should be capable of making her feel safe again.

"D-don't we need power for heat?"

I nod. "But the fireplace is wood-burning, and we have plenty of wood in the garage. But it might mean sleeping on the main level."

Fuck. Like a goddamn freight train, it hits me.

Sleeping on the main level. Together. In the same room. No escape.

"Has there been any word on Brad?" she asks.

"No."

I hate the way the small spark of hope in her eyes is snuffed out like a candle in the wind.

This is your fault.

Fuck that. It's not. Although my inability to locate that bastard is a thorn in my side. But Evie wouldn't be here if it wasn't for him. If he didn't believe he could take what he wanted, including her happiness.

Do I regret bringing her here? No.

Do I wish it was for another reason? Hell yes.

Without another word, she turns back to the window and rests her head on her bent knees. The wave of absolute defeat that rolls off her travels along the floorboards until it's consuming me, hitting me in the solar plexus and stealing my breath.

Forcing the guilt back down, I clear my throat.

"I'm going to grab more wood."

She doesn't say anything or acknowledge my departure. But I can't resist. Pressing my hand to the doorjamb, I look over my shoulder.

"Evie?"

No answer.

Not that I expected one. She's locked so far inside herself I worry she'll never surface.

I've felt that hopelessness too. After my last deployment. Guilt over Amani weighed me down so much that I couldn't breathe through the crushing heaviness. That summer, I traveled through Alaska, camping, searching for peace. I didn't deserve it, but even then, I knew if I wanted to be a son, a brother, and a friend again, I needed to find it.

The search brought me here. But memories of Amani never left.

Tell her about me.

The voice in my head is one I haven't heard in a long damn time. It's just as melodic as it was the first time I heard it.

I shake my head and step into the garage.

"No," I say, my voice filling the otherwise quiet space.

My memories are my own.

The lights flicker, and I brace for the darkness, readying myself to welcome it again. Instead, they pulse again, dimming slightly, then they brighten to full strength again.

You can't stay in the dark forever.

To hell with that.

By the time I've brought enough firewood into the living room to last the night, Evie is gone. The only sign that she was here is the rumpled blanket in the window seat and the half-empty teacup on the table next to it. I stack the last of the wood next to the fireplace and toss another log into the fire. The flames dance and lick along the fresh piece.

Satisfied it will continue to burn and ready to change into a pair of flannel pants, I head back to my room, then shuffle to my office. My computer sits on my desk, and I crack my neck as I consider the dark screen.

I'm tempted to check on the status of Sydney's investigating, but I can already hear her response.

What could have changed so soon?

Tracking men like Brad takes time. But my unflagging ability to wait it out is vanishing faster than a snowman in June. I need answers. Two steps toward my computer, I stop. There's a need that's calling to me more than my drive to work. An itch along my fingers and a heaviness in my heart that hasn't tugged at me in two and a half years.

The beaten-up case still leans haphazardly against the wall of the closet, exactly where I put it when I purchased the cabin. I grip the handle, muscle memory making it an almost automatic movement. I back out of the closet and rest the case gently on the bed, then catch either latch with my thumbs and unclip them.

Smooth, polished wood gleams in the light from the lamp on the nightstand, the strings glittering like figments of my imagination against the light wood.

How has it been so long since I played?

Michaela may be the professional, but she's not the only one of us who knows how.

My fingers itch to glide along the strings, and my heart demands I pick up the instrument I inherited from my grandfather and learned to play in high school. Gripping the neck, I lift it reverently, my hands shifting to position easily.

"Hello, old friend."

CHAPTER 10

EVIE

I'd like to say I feel something watching the storm roll in and blot out the colors of the forest.

Fear. Sadness.

Something.

But honestly, most colors have long since drained from my world. The few that remained after those five years with Brad leached with the realization that I was in this weird sort of purgatory. Waiting for Brad to show up. Or slip up. My own personal nightmare is waiting in the wings to snatch me back.

Now all I feel is resignation. A fear that the storm will force us to leave. Force me to face the reality that life isn't as simple as I've been pretending it is since I've been here.

I could feel Sawyer's gaze roving over me from the door to the garage, where he stopped and turned back. It was powerful, questioning. Too much so. I wanted to run to him, to admit the truths that fester and eat at me. But I was paralyzed. Frozen by the fear that once those words are out, the emotion that glitters in his stormy blue eyes will fade to pity and all that will be left between us will be obligation.

That's all that can exist between the two of you.

Ten years ago, maybe it could have been more. Maybe I could have flirted with the handsome soldier. I could have agreed to go to dinner with him. Could have entertained the prospect of a relationship. But I am not that person. And I won't allow myself to let him get close. Let anyone get close. To put them at risk.

Sighing, I unfold from my seat near the window and trudge up the stairs, my legs heavier with each step. Sawyer said there's a generator, but I don't want to risk not having hot water if we lose power.

The bedroom is colder than the living room, where the fire is roaring.

Outside, the brilliant blue of the sky has shifted to a soft gray light that filters into the windows. The dim light makes it seem later than it is.

Too dark.

I flip on the lights in an effort to drive back the darkness, then I do the same in the bathroom. Avoiding my reflection, I crank the hot water on. I don't strip until the steam builds and fogs the mirror. Dark reminders of other showers in other times push at the flimsy boundaries built between memories and sanity. I pull in a deep breath of the humid air and exhale slowly. Instead of falling into those memories, I consciously focus on each step as I complete it—wet my hair, grab the shampoo bottle. I focus on the slick, cool plastic beneath my fingers and the weight of the shampoo where it pools in my other palm.

I'm almost finished with my shower when the lights flicker out. The darkness lasts for several racing heartbeats before they hum back to life.

"Just in time," I say, twisting the water off.

I wrap a large towel around my body and another around my hair turban style.

The bedroom is even colder after the heat of the shower, so I rush to my bag for fresh clothes. The storm is in full effect now, and snow batters against the bedroom windows. In the twenty minutes or so since I walked into the bathroom, the gray light has shifted to small white fragments that collide against the windows, the trees, each other—they obliterate the visibility of all but the opaque outline of the dark waters of the bay.

A shiver works its way down my spine, a reminder that I'm still in a damp towel with wet hair while chaos ensues outside. Shaking my head, I grab my flannel pajama pants and an over-sized sweater, donning both before rubbing the moisture from my hair as best as I can with my towel.

The knock on the door startles me, and I drop the terry cloth with a squeak.

"Y-yes?"

"The generator kicked on a few minutes ago. I just wanted to check on you."

Sawyer's voice is muffled through the door, but the gravel's still there. The vibrations and pulses tug at me on a different level. If only—

"Evie?"

Caught drifting into a daydream, I'm suddenly grateful for the presence of the door between us.

"I'm okay. Figured I would take a shower before we lost power," I say.

When I open the door, his body takes up most of the width of the doorframe. Standing before the imposing backdrop of the dark hallway, he looks dangerous. Except he doesn't scare me. No, he's an avenging angel with blond hair and blue eyes.

Those mesmerizing orbs burn into mine for the span of a breath before they shift and the fire dims. I should appreciate the ability to control my own breathing.

So why don't I?

"I—" I lick my dry lips. "I wasn't sure if the generator would work the hot water heater."

He shrugs.

"It should, though I don't bring company here, so I've only

ever used it alone. We'll have to see if it can keep up with the two of us."

He's never been here with anyone else. Why does that create a fuzzy warmth?

"Oh."

"I'm not sure how long the power will be out, but..." He trails off, his eyes flicking to all the lights blazing in my room and the adjoining bathroom.

"Right." I flip off the closest switch, shrouding the room in shadows cast from the bathroom lights.

My awareness of his presence grows in the darkness and draws me closer—like a moon orbiting a planet. I want to lean in, to find safety and shelter in him. Give him some of the weight that has held me captive for years.

"Are you going to stay up here? Or come back downstairs?" he asks, his voice raspier than before, his eyes fixed on my face.

If I didn't know better, I'd swear he wants to kiss me. But since he's been avoiding me, I doubt it.

"Up here."

His eyes go wide, like he's surprised by my response—or maybe the speed of it.

But it's safer. I need to bottle the desire I have to spill my guts to him.

He nods.

"Okay, I'm going to follow your lead on the shower."

An image of his perfect form in the shower I just vacated takes center stage in my imagination. His large hands running over the sculpted muscles while he tilts his head back, his neck taut as the water cascades down and—

Oh my god, get a grip!

This is what I get for reading books with steamy scenes. And the one I'm reading now has all kinds of images floating through my mind.

"D-do you want me to make dinner?" I figure I should at least offer since he's made most of our meals.

"I'll pull something together."

"Okay."

We've reached the conclusion of our safe topics—weather and food. With nothing else to say, he retreats down the hall, and I close the door. I snag my e-reader from the nightstand and snuggle under the blankets in bed.

Sawyer's bed.

A fact I try to ignore as I attempt to lose myself in the story. I usually love a good second chance romance, but after rereading the same paragraph three times, I toss my device onto the bed with a huff. Leaning back against the pillow, I study the other side of the empty bed.

What side does Sawyer sleep on?

I've claimed the left side, my usual side, although more often than not, I migrate to the middle at some point in the night. But I could roll to the middle of this monstrosity and still have room on both sides to almost lie sideways too. Unsurprising—Sawyer isn't exactly small.

"Ugh."

Why can't I think of something *besides* my taciturn roommate? Flopping the pillow over my face, I breathe deeply and rack my brain for subjects that don't include Sawyer King or my fucked-up past. I miss Mia and her crazy schedule. The best part of my position as her assistant is that it has led to an incredible friendship. But a close second is that I never had time to think about the past. Not like I do now.

I don't even know whether she's having a boy or a girl. She had an ultrasound scheduled for the day after we left for Alaska. And it's not like I can text or call her. Sawyer had me leave my phone with Sydney. Apparently, she could use it somehow in her efforts to find Brad.

Since boarding that plane, I haven't spoken to anyone but

Sawyer. And so far, neither of us has had much to say. It's not abnormal for me, but Sawyer? Even though he doesn't have much to say to me, he seems to have no trouble talking to Sydney and Cole for hours.

About helping you.

I'm being ungrateful. I should be more than okay with this situation. Sawyer and his team are helping me. I'm not a prisoner.

The air under the pillow grows too thick, and I wiggle free with a sigh. What does it say about me that the two people I want to talk to are my brooding bodyguard and my bubbly boss?

Of the two, Mia is the safer choice. A few questions about the baby or Garrett, and she'd fill the silence. Pull me out of my dark thoughts, if only for a little while. And I don't have the urge to confess to her. Not like I want to spill my guts to my roommate.

"I can't do this."

I can't be alone with these thoughts. There's got to be a way for me to talk to Mia. I may not have my phone, but I bet Sawyer has her number.

"I'll go ask him."

Easy peasy.

Kicking off the blankets, I move fast—if I stop, I'll second-guess seeking out my attractive roommate. I don't have to. I haven't yet. But he's the means to an end—my sanity at the hands of a phone call with my boss/friend.

Is that the only reason? Mia's number?

A part of me recognizes the lie for what it is. It's the part that wants to forget about the darkness of my past and give in to the heat that simmers between Sawyer and me. But the other part, one that's just as demanding, reminds me to keep my distance. No one deserves the toxicity I have to deal with.

Torn between the two halves, I focus on my end goal—distraction. Also known as calling Mia.

The house is cooler than it was even an hour ago, the darkness a mix of the storm outside and the limited power from the generator. My fingers tingle with the urge to flip on light switches as I go.

This darkness can't hurt me.

"Sawyer?" I call his name as I descend the steps.

But he's not there. The living room is warm and brightly lit from the fire that crackles in the hearth, but it holds no sign of him.

"He's probably downstairs after his..."

Shower. The thought conjures images I pushed away earlier. Not that I mind said visual. Or won't be pulling it up again later. But not right now.

The stairs to the lower level are in the kitchen, behind a closed door. As I pull it open, I can just make out the faint notes from a guitar. They reach out, whispering, and beckon me further. I'm halfway down the stairs when a gravelly voice joins in, singing about Tennessee whiskey and strawberry wine.

It's one of Chris Stapleton's from the days when I thought about singing country music. Before Brad. Before Reverb.

The door to Sawyer's room is open. I approach quietly and peek inside. The man in question faces his window. Given the darkness outside, his reflection is so clear, it's as if he's looking in a mirror. His eyes are closed, his brow furrowed while the notes warble and his hands expertly lead the song where it needs to go. He finishes, and his fingers still on the vibrating strings.

"Hi," he rasps.

Without even opening his eyes, he knows I'm here.

"I didn't realize you played. Or sang."

His eyes flutter open and meet my gaze in the window.

"I don't. Michaela is the singer in our family." One corner of his mouth quirks up, the smile self-deprecating.

"So what was that?"

Whatever it was still has goosebumps dancing along my skin.

"That was me just playing around," he says.

"You're good for 'just playing around.'"

He shrugs.

"Michaela is the professional. And my older brother Lucas is crazy talented at the piano. He went to school on a music scholarship."

"What about you?"

He stands, lowering the well-loved guitar to the bed tenderly, like he's lowering a lover to the soft covers. I squeeze my thighs together as I imagine his hands on me the same way.

"What about me?" he asks.

He lifts his arms above his head, stretching, and the move reveals a line of muscular torso between the low hanging waistband of his pants and his T-shirt.

"You play," I argue, yanking my attention away from the exposed skin and back to the relative safety of his face.

He smirks.

"I play around. I learned in high school. Used to think it was a good way to impress girls."

A giggle bubbles up. "Was it?"

What was he like in high school? Was he always so serious? Or did the stoicism come later in life?

"I did okay with girls."

"Hmm. 'Okay'? I'm sure you did more than okay." The words are out of my mouth before I can stop them.

He lets out a low laugh and smirks.

Okay indeed.

"I figured between guitar and football and knowing a little about literature, it couldn't hurt."

"Literature?"

He moves closer. With every step, the air grows thick between us.

"She walks in beauty like the night," he murmurs.

Instantly, my knees turn to Jell-O. "What's that?" My voice is breathy, my attention zeroed in on his expression. On the fire that glitters in the depths of his eyes.

"Byron."

Another step closer, and the heat of him presses against my front.

"You remind me of a piece I read a long time ago." His voice is so quiet, it's hard to hear him above the thud of my heart.

"I do?"

"Mmm."

"What?"

"It's from a book called *A Sentimental Journey through France and Italy*." The words are so quick, so natural, it's as if he's been waiting to say it. Like he's rehearsed it. "There's a part called 'The Starling.'"

"What's it about?"

"A man finds a bird locked in a cage. And no matter how hard he tries, he can't set it free." He lifts his arm slowly, his palm resting against my cheek.

His warmth flows through me, and my eyes flutter shut. The sensation only intensifies as he caresses my cheek with a thumb.

"H-how does it remind you of me?"

"Nothing I do is working. I can't set you free."

His breath mingles with mine.

"Sawyer." His name is a whisper as my entire being drifts closer.

"Little starling. I'm trying. Trying and failing."

Starling. The nickname makes my chest tighten and makes tears prickle at the backs of my eyes.

"Failing what?" I open my eyes, finding a mix of agony and desire in his.

"You. I should be able to fix this. I should have no problem keeping my distance from you."

His words echo my thoughts from earlier. But right now, all I can focus on is the way his heat wraps around me.

"I-is that what you want?"

He squeezes his eyes shut. The battle within him is visible in every line of his face. "No."

"What do you want?" I ask.

It's like he's been waiting for the question. His answer tumbles from his lips effortlessly.

"To kiss you again."

I want him to. I want the pressure of his mouth, his possessive grip on my hips.

"I—"

He opens his eyes and studies me quietly. No doubt he sees me in a way no one else ever has. In a way no one has ever bothered to try.

"What do you want, starling?"

One word.

Three letters.

They push at my lips, begging to be set free.

Y.

O.

U.

"I—"

He watches me, his lips pressed together, waiting for the answer to untangle itself from my tongue. But no matter how much I want him. I can't.

I step back, and cool air rushes between us. I miss the heat of him, the warmth of his palm against my cheek. But I have to keep the distance.

"I—I was hoping I could get Mia's number from you."

The fire dims in his eyes until not even an ember remains. Clearing his throat, he unlocks his phone and hands it to me.

"She's programmed in."

He steps around me, giving me a wide berth.

"I'm going to see about dinner."

"Sawyer."

Phone call suddenly forgotten, I turn, ready to apologize. Ready to kiss him.

Ready for more.

Of what? I have no idea.

"I'm sorry," I tell him.

My voice is quiet, but based on the way his shoulders tense, it was loud enough for him.

It's the truth. I am sorry. I just no longer know what I'm sorry for.

CHAPTER 11

EVIE

*H*ours later, despite a marathon phone conversation with Mia that nearly drained Sawyer's phone battery, I can't sleep. I can, however, still feel the phantom pressure of his palm against my cheek, the way his breath brushed my lips as he told me about the story that reminded him of me.

Starling.

It's so close to songbird. But light years apart.

Brad's nickname represented a creature he wanted to cage. Sawyer's describes the one he wants to set free. And for the first time in years, thoughts of a man other than Brad are keeping me up at night. But not out of fear.

This is straight desire.

I never mentioned Sawyer to Mia. Not the kiss. Not the crush that has refused to die, despite my best efforts. But she still asked if I'd kissed him yet. How could I respond? By admitting I had almost kissed him stupid just before I called her? Yeah, no thanks. It might be an accurate representation, but I couldn't talk about it with her.

It's all I've thought about since she asked the question. And the thoughts have only multiplied since he decided it would be best for us to sleep near the heat of the fireplace. So I'm stretched out in my little nook while he's sprawled on the couch. The steady movement of his chest shows the ease with which he fell asleep while I'm still struggling.

"And whose fault is it you're like this?" I mutter under my breath and roll to face the window.

The snow is still coming down. It's like a blanket, covering everything in sight. It's less violent than before, and it's mesmerizing to watch one snowflake after another float quietly down. My eyelids grow heavy as I fix on one and then another. And another.

"Tell me." Sawyer's loud command has me rolling over so fast I almost fall off the bench.

"Tell you what?" I snap, irritated that he's chosen now to start this conversation.

Only I don't think he's awake. He's still lying prone on the couch with his eyes closed. But his breathing is labored, and his face is tense in the light of the crackling fire.

"Tell me." His voice is full of anguish.

Whatever he's dreaming about, he has the answer. But he wants someone to tell him it's not true.

"Sawyer?" I move cautiously, not sure if I'm more afraid of waking him or leaving him as he is.

Is he talking about me? Does he want me to tell him what I've been holding back? He knows most of my past. But not this. No one does.

"Amani." The word holds so much heartbreak that my own organ twinges in sympathy.

Kneeling next to him, I press one hand against his heart, surprised by how quickly it races under my fingers.

"Sawyer?"

"No! Bastard. Stay away from her." His hands fist at his sides as he fights with the demon holding him in his dream.

"Sawyer." I press gently on his chest, trying to wake him

gently.

"You can't. Not her too. Fuck. No. Evie!"

Before I even register the sound of my name, his eyes shoot open, and he yanks me down. He pulls me tightly against his side and tries to shift me behind him on the couch.

"Sawyer. It's okay. You were having a bad dream." My voice is muffled against his shoulder.

Some of the tension ebbs from his body as he blinks several times. But his hand stays intertwined with mine as he exhales deeply and tucks me further into the couch.

"Fuck." He groans, and the vibration transfers from his chest to mine.

"I—you were having a nightmare," I tell him.

Like he hasn't already figured that part out.

"Are you okay? I didn't hurt you, did I?"

I was surprised by the sudden move, but nothing hurts. With his body against mine, I'm more turned on than anything. One of my legs is wrapped around his waist while one of his is between mine. My core throbs, and I bite my lip to hold back the moan that threatens.

"Evie?"

I open my eyes to find him staring at my lip where it's locked between my teeth.

"You didn't hurt me," I assure him.

"I'm sorry I pulled you down."

I'm not.

I should be. But if I'm honest, I've craved this closeness.

"It's okay," I murmur. "Can I ask you a question?"

He nods.

"What is Amani?"

Immediately, his body goes rigid again.

I almost retract my question. Instead, I take a page from his book and wait silently for him to respond.

"Who." His voice rumbles under my cheek. "Amani is a who."

"Who is she?"

"That's a long story." He sighs and shifts, like he's going to lift me off him.

I squeeze his hand, stopping his movements.

"You sounded really upset. Maybe it would help to talk about it."

What would it look like for me to follow my own advice?

It's different.

He takes a deep breath and releases it, the air rushing against the top of my head.

"The woman I fell in love with."

"You don't sound happy about that."

"I wasn't supposed to."

"Why not?"

"I didn't know it when I met her, but her father was a loyal supporter of the Taliban."

"Where did you meet?"

"Afghanistan. I was at the markets, and someone was trying to cheat me on a price. My Farsi isn't as good as my Arabic, and she intervened."

"She rescued you." I can't help but smile—the gentle giant that surrounds me needed to be rescued.

The sound he huffs is a cross between a sigh and a laugh.

"She did."

"What happened?"

"We wandered the market. She had a few vendors to visit, and so did I. We started talking. I was surprised at how well she spoke English and by the modern clothing she wore. Most women I'd come into contact with while in Afghanistan wore burqas. She explained that her father had sent her to school in England. He didn't believe what the Taliban believed."

I can picture it. A young soldier, Sawyer, walking through a crowded market, maybe with a smile on his face back then, with a young Afghani woman.

"We met every day for a week before I was sent on a mission. For three weeks, I had no way of telling her I couldn't see her. When I returned, she was waiting at the market. She'd gone every day because she knew I would come back."

"Of course you would have."

"It was easy to fall for her. We'd even discussed the idea of her coming with me when I went home. She could stay with my parents until my enlistment was over."

"What happened?"

"Her father found out about me. Turns out, he did support Taliban beliefs when it came to his daughter falling in love with an American. I went to the market for weeks. Asked the vendors she frequented if they'd seen her or if they knew where I could find her. Nothing. It was like she had vanished. Finally, one of her friends found me there. He explained what happened and where I could find her. Told me I needed to move fast because her father had promised her to another man."

"Did you find her?"

His fingers tighten around mine.

"The town her father had taken her to had recently been destroyed in an effort to get to an al-Qaeda leader we had intelligence on. Turns out we had false intel—he wasn't there."

"What about Amani?"

"It took me weeks before I discovered the truth. She and her mother and younger sister were killed by a bomb that struck their house. Her father blamed me for their deaths. If Amani had never met me, they wouldn't have been there."

"What happened?"

"He strapped as much C-4 to his chest as he could and came to the market looking for me. Only I wasn't there. One of the younger guys was. I was coming off assignment and asked him to meet with one of my contacts for me. I got there shortly after Amani's father blew himself up. Jimmy was barely hanging on. He died while I was screaming for a medic."

"Sawyer." Tears burn my eyes. They drop faster than I can catch them and soak into his shirt, one after another.

We lay in a silence only broken by my sniffling and the pops and crackles of the weakening fire.

"You were dreaming of her?" I ask quietly.

"Not just of her." He rubs a hand over his face. "It was her, but Brad was there too."

Just the mention of his name sends a chill down my spine.

"Sounds like my nightmare joined yours."

"A little. But you were there too."

"I know."

"You do?" he asks.

"Mm-hmm. You said my name. Just before you woke up."

"Did I say anything else?"

"Amani's name. Something about not her."

"Sounds like I had a lot to say," he grumbles.

"Do you always talk in your sleep?"

He lets out a long breath. "Every once in a while. It's rare."

"It sounded like an awful dream."

"Worse than any other I've had," he says quietly.

I want to ask him more, but his face is drawn and his eyes swim with pain. Now isn't the time.

"You probably want to get back to sleep. I should get up." I wiggle and shift, trying to free myself from the little space my body is content to stay in.

Sawyer tugs, and with just that small pull, I pop free. Naturally, I land straddling his hips with one hand splayed across his chest.

His thick erection presses against the seam of my pajama pants, causing me to suck in a breath. With all the strength I possess, I hold my hips still instead of rotating them the way my body demands. Sinking my teeth into my lip, I try and fail to hold back a whimper at the feel of him where my body craves him most.

"S-sorry." I try to move my uncooperative legs, but the friction holds me in place, and my body looks for more.

He sits up, and we're nose to nose.

"You're killing me, starling."

"What?"

"The feel of you wiggling against me. Do you know how fucking badly I want to kiss you right now?"

"I—"

He pulses his hips, and I moan. I'm completely unprepared for the fireworks that spark behind my eyes, and I can't hide my reaction even if I wanted to.

"Do you want that?"

Consequences be damned, but I do.

"*Yes.*"

"Fuck it."

He cups my jaw with both hands, and his lips find mine effortlessly. He nibbles and licks until I open to the demand and allow myself to feel everything instead of denying what I want. Who I want. Our tongues tangle, and my fingers tunnel through his hair to hold him close to me and demand as much as he'll give me. More. Another mingle of tongues and breath. Another taste that drags me back under until all I feel, all I know, is the man whose heartbeat echoes mine.

I grind my hips against his erection, breaking our kiss, and tip my head back, exposing my throat to his focused attention. Hot, open-mouthed kisses are followed by tongue and teeth. A sharp nip at my collarbone presses me more firmly against his erection as need pushes out all other thought. His hands span my back, and he lowers them until his palms cup my ass, and he drags me forward, then back over him.

"*Fuck.*" His moan fills the air.

He shifts us until I'm pressed back into the couch, his body aligning with mine from hip to chest while one of his hands lifts my leg and wraps it around his waist again. His fingers flex into my hip and create more sparks while he drags his other hand along the skin at the waistband of my pants, further fanning the flames.

His mouth claims mine once more, his tongue consuming me as easily as the fires he sets in my body. With every thrust, he burns through the walls I've erected, eradicating every reason I came up with as to why this can't happen.

Why it shouldn't happen.

When he kisses me, the only thing I can think of is how much I want him to keep doing what he's doing.

How much more I need.

How much more I want.

CHAPTER 12

SAWYER

I should break the kiss. I should release the warm flesh beneath my fingers and ignore the heat that radiates from where Evie's leg wraps around my waist.

But I'm done with following those rules. The dream still holds me in its icy clutches. I need to prove that Evie is alive. I didn't fail her. Not like I failed Amani.

She's here. Touch her. Feel her.

I grip her tightly, as if she's going to disappear. Her moan vibrates between us, trapped by my lips as I continue to claim her.

She slides her hands up my chest and wraps her arms around my neck, dragging her nails along the short hair at my nape. It's fuel to an already raging fire building deep inside me. I press her back further against the couch, breaking the connection of our mouths so I can trace her neck with my lips. The pulse at the base of her throat vibrates like a hummingbird.

Hummingbird.

Starling.

Fuck.

What am I doing?

The haze of lust I've been lost in dissipates. I gentle the kiss before breaking it completely, then shift so her head rests against my racing heart. She relaxes in my arms, letting out a sigh. As her warm breath penetrates the fabric of my shirt, I tangle my fingers in the silk of her hair. It's a poor substitute for what I want to do—strip her naked and worship her body in ways I've only allowed myself to imagine—but it's all I'll allow.

"Sawyer?" Her voice is quiet, or maybe it just seems that way after the rush of sensations that rolled through me as we kissed.

"Mmm?"

"I—why did you stop?" She presses her chin against my chest and meets my eyes.

So many emotions ripple in her golden irises. I want to memorize each one as they swirl in the dim light.

Desire. Awareness. Apprehension.

My dick may not agree, but I made the right choice by stopping things now. That doesn't mean I don't want to claim her lips once more, though. To make the flesh more red and swollen than it already is.

Why don't you?

My impulses are hard to control tonight, but I don't want to rush things.

"I didn't want to," I admit.

I don't know whether to laugh or groan at her pout. She didn't want me to stop either.

"So why did you?"

"I need to ask you something." My voice is rusty and warbles over my question.

Because this question will bring up shit she doesn't want to think about, let alone talk about. But I still need to know.

"Okay," she says, pulling her bottom lip between her teeth and dropping her attention to my throat rather than my face.

Fuck. I don't want to hurt her. She's already been through so much. But I'm tired of fighting the attraction between us. Of reminding myself that she's a client and I shouldn't get involved.

It's too late.

"It's been a few years since…" I avoid using his name, but she flinches as if I did, her expression shuttering. "Have you…has there been anyone else?"

I hold my breath and search her face while I wait for her answer. With the small shake of her head, my stomach clenches.

"No. After, I—" Her painful swallow creates a responding ache in my throat. "No one deserves to deal with the mess that is my life."

"What about you?" I ask.

I can't stop my need to touch her, so I lift my finger to trace her jaw.

"What about me?" Tears form on her lashes, and one slips free.

"You don't deserve to have to deal with him or the havoc he wreaks either."

Her shrug is pure resignation. Like she's convinced herself that she'll have to deal with him, at least on some level, forever. And I fucking hate it.

"It was my choice. I could have said no. Michaela did. The other women did. But I wanted to sing so desperately, I was willing to…to…it was my fault."

Oh, fuck no.

"Is that what you think?"

Her eyes are closed, cheeks glossy with the tears she refuses to acknowledge but I can't ignore. Using the pads of my thumbs, I stop two errant drops before they reach her chin.

"Open your eyes, baby," I whisper.

She shakes her head.

"Open your eyes," I say again.

After several moments, her lashes flutter and lift. There's a new emotion there. One I've seen only glimpses of.

Shame.

And I can't have that.

"Evie, he used you. He manipulated you."

God, he fucking brainwashed her. And he's still got a hold on her if she thinks what happened was her fault.

"I wanted it too badly."

"Your dream?"

"Yes."

"You're supposed to strive for what you want, Evie. You're supposed to fight to make your dreams come true. People like Brad, they take advantage of that need that exists in all of us. He made you think the only way to make it was through him. Like you had no other choice. Nothing he did is your fault."

"I could have walked away."

Everything I've learned about her tells me giving up isn't in her nature.

"We don't always see that option in the moment. He held your dream hostage."

"Was it worth giving up every part of me? My future? My self-respect? My virginity?"

The words rip out of her painfully—an almost violent explosion she can't stem. But they create a stillness in my body I haven't experienced in years. When all my emotions shut down so I can carry out a mission. So I can step forward despite the fear that wants to run rampant.

Fuck.

"Your virginity?" I can hardly get the words out through my clenched teeth. It's a wonder my molars are holding up under the pressure.

I don't think I've hated anyone more than I hate Brad Russell in this moment. I've dealt with lowlifes for years—both in and out of the military. I've dealt with ignorance and intolerance. But he takes the fucking cake.

"Y-yeah." She ducks her head.

"Evie, look at me."

"Why? So I can see the judgment written all over your face? Or pity?"

She pushes against my chest and tries to scramble up, but I lock my arms around her, unwilling to let her run away before she hears me out.

My thoughts couldn't be further from what she imagines.

"Evie."

"I can't. I don't want to see that. Not from you."

"Please."

With a deep breath, she finally looks at me, her expression shuttered like she's bracing for my reaction. But she won't see any judgment. Or pity.

What she'll find is admiration. She's endured hell. She had her dream stripped from her, but she never surrendered.

"You are the bravest person I've ever met," I tell her honestly.

She scoffs and rolls her eyes.

"You were in the Army. I doubt that."

Christ, this woman is going to be the death of me.

"God's honest truth. Do you know how much I admire your strength?"

"I—"

I cut her off with a finger pressed against her lips, ignoring the jolt of electricity at the small touch.

"You've been through more than anyone should have to go through to recognize a dream. You're still fighting. Maybe not for your dream anymore. But to escape the nightmare you endured. I've seen shit that would make lesser men fall, but I've never witnessed the strength I see in you. The way you've survived despite all the shit. Do you know how attractive that is?"

She cocks her head and gives me a dubious look.

"Fuck, I want to kiss you right now."

Another look. She wraps her hand around my wrist and tugs, removing my finger from her lips. Then she brings it so both of my hands are joined with both of hers on my chest.

"But he...after..."

"He's not what stopped me."

All the Brad Russells in the world couldn't dampen the desire I have for her.

"What is?"

She has no fucking clue how much power she wields. How I'd do anything I could to take away her hurt. To make her feel whole again.

"You."

"Me?" Her eyes go wide. "I'm not stopping you."

Her tongue peeks out to moisten her lips, proving her point. I don't bother to hide my groan. I'm only a man, and despite my best efforts, even I have limits.

"Fuck. I know *you're* not. But that's not what I meant."

"What did you mean?"

"You've only been with Brad." His name leaves a foul taste in my mouth, and I resist the urge to make a face.

"I know."

"And that experience was...not...I mean...fuck." I'm struggling to find the best way to describe it.

Sex should be pleasurable. But something tells me her experiences haven't been.

"No."

Neither of us has said it directly. But her time with him was hell. I've never wanted to murder Brad Russell more. No ifs, ands, or buts about it.

"What does he have to do with kissing me?" Her question brings me out of my dark thoughts.

If I didn't know better, I'd say she's coyly attempting to flirt with me. But she's not. Instead, there's a genuine curiosity I want to satisfy.

"Did you like kissing me?" I ask.

A pretty pink flushes her cheeks, but she doesn't break eye contact.

"Yes."

"Tell me."

She catches her lip between her teeth—fuck, I want to do that —and nibbles on the flesh for several moments while she formulates a response.

"Before...with him...that was darkness."

A red haze of rage encroaches on my vision. I breathe through it, willing it to subside so I can focus on her.

"I—I hate the dark," she continues.

I've noticed. There's always at least one light on in any room she's in. I figured it had to do with him, but hearing it confirmed makes me want to punch something.

"But you? You-you're like my own personal sun. My talisman against the boogeyman. When you kiss me, when you touch me—all I feel is light."

I cup her jaw, humbled by her explanation.

"Fuck, Evie. I—you're killing me, starling."

"How?"

"Your words have so much power."

"They do?"

I nod.

"Tell me what you want. You set the speed. Whatever you're comfortable with is what I'll hold to. If it means lying here all night, all day, and all night again, and simply holding you in my arms, then I'm in. Say the words, and it's done. If it's within my power, I will get it for you."

"I want..." She searches my face, her focus moving from my eyes to my lips and back again. "I want you to kiss me."

I tug her down until our lips are millimeters apart.

"Your wish is my command."

CHAPTER 13

EVIE

I can't remember the last time I slept so soundly through the night. But as consciousness spreads through my body, I realize I've done it. Covered in the thick blanket Sawyer gave me when we arrived, I'm spread along the couch while the fire blazes heat into the room. I'm warm.

Safe.

Comfortable.

Despite the well-rested sensation, I don't want to open my eyes. I'd much rather snuggle under the blankets. My only issue is that I'm alone. The man who held me all night has disappeared.

"Good morning."

My eyes pop open at the gravel-laced greeting. It takes me a moment to adjust to the bright light that streams through the windows while the storm still rages outside. Once I do, I can fully appreciate the man swaggering toward me with two coffee cups clutched in his hands. His dark blond hair is rumpled, and his face is shadowed by a layer of scruff I itch to feel against my skin again. It's rough, like fine sandpaper. But it's his expression that has my heart pounding and my lips tingling for more of his drugging kisses.

Instead of hiding his emotions, they're on display—interest, happiness, desire.

All for me.

"Morning." I sit up and make room for him on the couch.

Where will he choose to sit? At my side or on the opposite end?

"See something you like?" he asks with a smirk. He places one mug on the coffee table, then settles next to me.

Eek. Next to me!

"Mm-hmm. Coffee." I reach for the cup but squeal when his fingers find the ticklish spot on my side.

"Brat. Maybe neither of these cups is for you." He holds the second cup out, ready to set it next to the first, but I hold his arm.

"Neither?" I pout.

"I need both. Someone kept me up late last night." His lips twitch as he fights a smile.

In his defense, we did stay up late, making out on the couch until the first light of dawn lit the sky. My lips had burned, and my panties were more than damp, and he was just as turned on as I was. But true to his word, he didn't push for more.

"Oh really. Who was that?"

He presses his lips to one side, pretending to think for a moment.

"This amazing woman I met."

"Oh yeah?"

Warmth filters through me, and it isn't because of the fire that Sawyer must have stoked when he got up.

"Mmm. Maybe you know her. Gorgeous redhead with a smile that hits me here." He rubs at his chest.

"Hmm. Did you maybe bring her something warm to help her wake up since she was no doubt up late too?" I try to grab for the coffee mug again, but he holds it just out of reach. "Sawyer."

"Yes?"

"Please, may I have my coffee?"

"I don't know..." he teases. He holds the mug out finally, but he doesn't relinquish it when my fingers grip the handle.

"Sawyer," I whine.

"It's all yours...for the low price of a kiss."

I haven't experienced this playful side of him, but if possible, it makes him sexier than before. With an eye roll, I let go of the mug.

"I mean, it's a dirty job..." With that, I fasten my lips to his and press my tongue along the seam until he opens.

I'm only vaguely aware of the clink of the second cup on the table, too caught up in the way our tongues tangle to remember the coffee.

Our mouths shift together, finding the easy rhythm we established last night, and muscle memory takes over as I scoot closer. I rest one hand on his arm, but I can't get as close to him as I want. I can't touch him the way my fingers tingle with the need to when we're sitting the way are.

And without a word, like he can read my mind, he lifts me to straddle his lap. I moan and grind myself against his erection. He's just as turned on as I am. Just from this kiss. Same as we both were last night. I drape my arms around his neck and pull him closer while his hands drift to my hips, fingers flexing to move me faster against him and generating a friction that steals my breath.

I break the kiss, and he nips at my lips. Then he sits back and studies me. Lust simmers so fiercely in his eyes it creates an ache in my core. I squeeze my thighs to ease the bolt of desire and relish the way he moans.

"*Fuck*. Hi." His voice is raspier than before.

"Hi." Dropping my forehead against his chest, I take a deep breath while his warm hands sweep along my back.

I relax into the foreign sensation. In his arms, I feel safe.

Cherished.

Whole.

"How did you sleep?" His lips ghost the top of my head while the question rumbles in his chest.

I vaguely remember falling asleep as I lay on his chest, his heartbeat in my ear.

"Good, I think. You? I mean the second time around."

I can see the answer on his face before he says the words.

"No more nightmares."

Relief rushes through me. "Good."

"Can I tell you something?" The way he says it squelches that relief instantly and has my heart stuttering.

Does he regret what happened? He's not acting like it. Should we regret it?

I don't want to.

"Um, o-of course."

I brace myself for the letdown.

"I'm glad I had one last night."

My head shoots up at his admission.

"You are?"

He nods. "If not for the nightmare, you wouldn't have tried to wake me up..."

"And you wouldn't have kissed me," I add when he trails off.

The only sound now is the snap of the wood in the fire. It's an easy, comfortable type of silence.

"What would you be doing now if you weren't here?" he asks.

"*Here* here?" I wiggle in his lap to illustrate my point. "Or in Alaska here?"

He palms my hips and stops my movement, a muscle ticking in his jaw. "Either."

"If I was in LA, I'd be working on a schedule for Mia. For after her maternity leave."

"And if you weren't here here?" He flexes his fingers against my hips.

"Probably reading."

"You do that a lot."

I shrug. "I like to read. What about you?"

"Do I like to read?"

I giggle and shake my head. "No. If you weren't here."

"Working. Maybe hanging out with Benji."

"Do you spend a lot of time with him?" I ask, picturing him with his little nephew.

At Michaela and West's wedding, the sight of Sawyer with the baby, the way he tickled and teased him until he giggled, practically made my ovaries explode.

"When I can."

"Oh." It's not intended to be a reminder of the life he has outside of this. But it is.

Am I messing that up?

"At the moment, though, I'm enjoying being *here* here," he says, sliding his hands to my ass and squeezing.

"I still feel like I'm a burden," I admit. But it doesn't stop me from pressing back against his hands.

"You're not a fucking burden." Tension builds in his shoulders, and he leans back with a huff.

"It doesn't change how I feel."

"Does this?"

He claims my mouth in a hard kiss, and he doesn't pull away until we're both breathing heavily.

"Well?"

"Well what?" I ask dazedly, my concern all but forgotten.

His smirk melts my insides, along with what's left of my panties. "I want you here. I want you, period. I have since before Mikey and West's wedding."

Dropping my chin, I rub a hand up and down his chest. "What if this is all I can give you?"

With one finger under my chin, he tilts my head up so I'm forced to look at him. "What do you mean?"

"Kissing. Making out. This. What if...what if I'm not capable of more?"

It's my biggest fear. That even if I wanted to build something, I'd be incapable due to the damage my past has wreaked on my life.

"Then this is where we'll stay."

He says it like it's so easy. Like he isn't worried about it.

Maybe he's not. But I am.

"Sawyer."

"Evie," he mimics.

"You have to want more out of your life."

Even if it kills me that he won't have it with me.

"Don't sell yourself short," he tells me.

Huffing out a breath, I lean in again, inhaling his delicious scent. The bergamot and citrus may be his cologne, but I'll never associate it with anyone except him.

"Don't borrow trouble," he continues.

"Who's borrowing? I have more than enough."

"Right here, right now, it's just us, starling. The rest will be there when the storm lets up."

I press my lips to the thick muscle of his shoulder.

"Is it wrong to hope the storm lasts forever?" I whisper, resting my head on his chest.

Under my cheek, his chest vibrates with laughter. He pulls me in tighter.

"All storms have to end."

I'm not sure if he's talking about the actual storm outside or the storm that is my life.

"Then what?"

"We'll tackle that when it comes. For now"—he stands, taking me with him—"I want to try something."

My core throbs where it presses against his heat. I have no idea what he has in store, but I'm in.

"Like what?"

"Do you trust me?" he asks.

Completely.

"Yes."

"Oof." Sawyer grunts as his back connects with the floor in his home gym.

"Like that?" I ask, leaning over to look him in the eye.

He nods. "Better."

When he asked if I trusted him, I had no idea what he had in mind, even after he walked into this room with me still in his arms.

His hope, he said, was to teach me a few self-defense moves. When I told him I'd taken classes in the past, he asked me to show him what I remembered. Turned out, I had forgotten more than I retained. But it's coming back to me now.

Shifting off the floor, he wipes a hand down his face.

"Are you okay?" I ask.

"Starling, I promised you couldn't hurt me. I know how to land."

The first time he put me in a hold and told me to work my way out of it, I failed because I was worried I would hurt him. After promises from him that he would be fine, we tried it again.

And again.

And again.

Until I lost count.

"Flat on your back?" I ask sweetly. I can't hide my grin.

He brackets my sides with his hands and finds all the spots that make me squirm with laughter.

"Okay, okay, I give." I'm breathless with giggles and with the way my insides melt when he smiles like he is right now.

"You give, huh?"

He doesn't let up. Instead, he steps closer and wraps himself around me. Only when I'm close to falling over does he stop.

"I like your laugh," he says, hugging me close to him.

"I like your smile." I meet his gaze, waiting several breaths for him to lower his mouth to mine.

"We should keep practicing," he murmurs against my lips.

I sigh and squeeze my arms around him. When he returns the gesture, I swear my insides light up.

"I remember more than I thought I would," I tell him, content to stay exactly where we are.

"Repetition is important. It's better if you can defend yourself without thinking about it."

I nod.

I *did* freeze when Brad crowded me against my car. All those lessons were relegated to the corners of my mind, forced into hiding by the panic that ricocheted through my brain.

"So practice?" I let out a deep breath and drop my shoulders, then release him and step back.

"Practice," he agrees. "Let's try a few more moves before we call it quits. And we'll work on them every day. I want to know you can defend yourself when—if…"

When he's no longer around. When he goes back to his normal life and I go back to whatever my life is going to look like after all this.

"Evie?"

I blink, and Sawyer's face comes back into focus.

"You disappeared for a minute there. Where'd you go?" he asks.

I sigh. I'm not interested in getting into all that with him. "Just tired, I guess."

If he realizes I'm not being honest, he doesn't call me out on it.

"Okay. One more, and we'll call it a day," he says.

Taking a deep inhale, I let it out and square my shoulders again.

"Thatta girl."

His words shouldn't make me tingle.

But they do.

"Close your eyes," he tells me.

I hesitate. "Why?"

"I need you to be aware in every situation. We've talked through each scenario before we've acted it out. The bad guys out there—"

"Like Brad," I add.

"They won't give you that luxury. You won't know they're coming. They'll want the element of surprise."

"O-okay." Fear wells inside as memories from the afternoon Brad cornered me surface.

Sawyer isn't Brad.

He's doing this to help me, not hurt me.

"Close your eyes." This command is softer than before.

Without any more hesitation, I obey. "Now what?"

"You'll know when to open your eyes."

"How will I know?" I ask.

No response.

I try again. "Sawyer?"

I wait for several moments, straining for any sounds, but it's quiet. Too quiet. Peeking one eye open, I quickly scan the room, but there's no sign of him—only the elliptical and the weight bench. There's no way he left. I'd have heard him or felt him brush past me, so where—

"Surprise." One of his thick arms locks around my shoulders while the other secures around my waist, trapping my arms and rendering them useless.

"*Ahh!*"

My first instinct is to scream. My fight-or-flight mode immediately leans toward the latter option. Panic sets in, and an alarm blares in my head, making it a challenge to remember what he's taught me today.

Even through the trepidation, I force my muscles to relax, and I become dead weight. He said doing that might surprise Brad into dropping me. But it doesn't work on Sawyer, who merely shifts my weight and lifts me off the ground while I kick uselessly at empty air.

"What next?" he growls into my ear.

I struggle to keep the alarm from getting louder. "I don't know. I don't remember." My heart thunders in my ears, my breathing getting shallower the longer we're in this hold.

"You can do it. Remember," he tells me.

My feet touch the floor as I frantically flip through ideas like a slideshow on warp speed until it stops.

Turning into the hold, I wrap one leg behind his. I can't push with my trapped arms, so that leaves me with only one option. I lower my front knee so I'm in a semi-squat position, then I surge up and bounce against him.

It does the trick.

He totters back, tripped up by my leg behind his. Looking over my shoulder, I catch the glint of surprise on his face. Then he releases my arms and falls next to me.

"That's my girl." His eyes are filled with pride.

I'm not sure if it's the emotion I can read there or his words that create the warmth that washes through my body.

His girl.

I like being his girl. More than I should. He's still lying on the floor while I tower over him, and the difference in perspective is hard to ignore.

"Need a hand?" I hold one out to help him up.

His fingers slide against mine, tickling my palm before they feather along my wrist.

"I have a better idea."

He yanks me down, and I flop on top of the solid land mass

otherwise known as his chest.

"Hi," he says with a quirk to his lips.

"Hi. This is your better idea?"

"Mmm."

"Why?" I ask.

He molds his hands to my hips, shifting me until I straddle his waist, then he releases his grip and squeezes my ass.

I whimper, needing more. So much more. "Sawyer."

"Better." He brushes his lips along my jaw until his teeth sink softly into the flesh of my earlobe.

"Mmm."

I tilt my head to grant him better access, and he uses the opportunity to trace the column of my neck with his mouth, stopping when his lips rest against my pulse point.

My speed.

He's content with what we're doing. Where we're at right now. But I need him. I need—

"More," I beg and cover his lips with mine.

My tongue pushes forward to find his as I sink my fingers into the muscles of his neck. I grind down against him, consumed by the pleasure that kissing him brings. My breasts ache, and my nipples are hard where they press against his chest. They need more friction than I can give them at the moment.

It's not enough.

I break the kiss, drawing in a ragged breath.

"More," I repeat.

"Little starling."

The whisper of his voice is a call for me to open my eyes. The request is as clear as if he had said the words out loud.

He studies me closely, searching, his sapphire irises ablaze.

I'm on fire. One I can see reflected in his expression while his hands rest calmly against my lower back.

"How much more?" he asks.

"All of it." I hold his gaze. I want him to see the truth despite the warble in my voice.

Because it's not fear that's making me tremble.

"Are you sure? All of it?" he asks.

Those questions obliterate the last strains of doubt and leave me with only unfiltered need.

"Everything."

CHAPTER 14

EVIE

The word stretches between us, and he hardens further where I straddle his waist.

With other men, that word would have been the starting gun for a race to the bedroom—if they bothered to go that far.

But not Sawyer.

Why do I keep trying to force him into a box? When I'm with him, I'm overwhelmed with a sense of rightness. Like this is where I'm supposed to be.

Safety.

Not the physical kind. Although there's that too. But my heart feels safe with him. He treats me as if I'm fragile, valuable.

He rests his fingers against my skin with the force of a butterfly landing. "Are you sure?"

God, those eyes. I could drown in the stormy blue depths that study me so peacefully.

"I'm sure."

Again, I expect him to move to the next step instantly. To speed things along. But no. Instead, he pulls me down and glides his lips along mine. There's no frenzied rush of teeth and tongue. It's a leisurely exploration of the entire surface of my lips before a tangle of our tongues. The vibration of my moan stays trapped between us, the intensity building to an all-consuming fire that licks along my skin and settles in my core.

When my need for oxygen can't be ignored, I break the kiss and scramble up and off him.

"Ready?" I ask, holding out a hand.

My heart pounds in my chest as I wait for his response. He intertwines our fingers, but he doesn't need my help off the floor. He barely tugs on my arm as he stands with the grace and power of a jaguar.

The hum he gives me—along with the squeeze of his hand—is all the answer I need. I lead him from the gym to the doorway of the guest room, but he shakes his head and plants his feet. Doubt swirls with the lust that simmers in my blood.

Has he changed his mind?

Lifting our still joined hands to his lips, he brushes a kiss against the back of my hand, soothing the doubts almost as quickly as they formed.

"Not here," he murmurs, his lips tickling the skin on my hand.

"No?"

In silent answer, he tugs me toward the stairs and gestures for me to go first. He stays close behind me, his hand still locked around mine. The heat of his gaze locks on my ass as I take the steps one by one, despite the temptation to race up them.

When we reach the top, the ache in my core is unbearable and my breathing sounds like I ran the fifty-yard dash. It's not the physical exertion. It's the delay. This slow sinking into sensation. It's just as much an aphrodisiac as Sawyer's kisses. He doesn't stop in the living room, where the embers in the fireplace glow orange. Instead, he moves quietly to the staircase that leads to the second level. We take those stairs the same way we did the first, and I'm a puddle of unsatisfied sensation by the time we reach the top.

The chill in the air of his room tempers the heat I'm generating. He stops once we're standing next to his bed and turns to face me. Only then do I see the truth. He may seem calm and steady on the outside, but the lust firing through my blood blazes in his eyes.

"I—" His voice is more gravel-laced than usual, and he clears his throat. "Do you have any idea how many times I've imagined you here with me?"

My chest heaves with my breath. "No."

"I've lost count." He anchors one hand on my hip and cups my face with the other.

One step is all it takes to eliminate the sliver of space between us. My breasts brush his chest, and I clench my thighs together to stem the ache that has reached a fever-pitch.

"Sawyer."

I'm about to go up in flames, and he's barely touched me.

"We're only going to do what you feel comfortable with. Your speed," he reminds me.

I loop my arms around his neck and pull him closer. "Then we're going too slow."

Popping up on my toes, I sink my teeth into his lip and tug slightly. It's a quick caress, but it does the trick. His eyes darken, the deep blue akin to the water of the bay I've been fascinated with since we got here.

"You want me to speed up?"

"Yes."

The word still vibrates between us when his mouth descends on mine. His tongue teases the seam of my lips, and I open on a moan as I drag my fingers through the short hair at the back of his neck. It tickles my palms and adds another layer of sensation.

His hands drift under my sweater, his fingers feathering along the skin just above my pants. I gasp, but I don't shy away from the touch. I need him closer. He moves a hand to my lower back, pushing me against him and eliminating even the thought of space between us. His kisses are magic. They're a drug.

They're a current dragging me under. And all I can think of is *more*.

His lips leave mine, and I whimper at the loss. The sound turns to a moan as he finds a sensitive spot on my neck below my earlobe. A swift sting of teeth sends a zap of electricity through me, and the swipe of his tongue has my knees buckling. Not that he'd let me fall. I'm surprised my feet are on the floor since I've been practically levitating since he first kissed me.

"Are you ready for more, starling?" he growls against my damp skin.

I dig my fingers into his shoulders. *"Yes."*

"Can I?" He grips the hem of my sweater, his knuckles grazing the skin of my waist.

"Mmm."

"Is that a yes?" The laughter is clear in his voice.

"Mm-hmm."

He glides the fabric up slowly, making my stomach contract in the cool air. His finger brushes the valley between my breasts as he continues his mission. Once he's tugged it over my head, he lets the fabric drop without looking. His attention is locked solely on my newly exposed upper half. My plain white bra might as well be the sexiest lingerie from Victoria's Secret with the way his eyes heat.

The anticipation is agony. I need him to soothe at least a part of the intensity of the need I have. He lifts one hand, moving closer, but stops before he connects with my breast.

I don't think so.

Locking my fingers around his wrist, I drag him forward until his palm surrounds me. Only the ache doesn't lessen. His touch makes it almost unbearable. I tip my head back on a moan, my already hard nipple tightening further. He squeezes, tracing his hand over the fabric, and I strain to get closer to him.

"You like that?" he asks.

His thumb glides over the thin cotton again.

I mewl. "Yes."

Dropping his head, he continues to work magic with his fingers. His soft hair tickles my collarbone while his lips trace the edge of my bra. The roll of my hips against his is almost involuntary. His erection is iron between us, enticing me to find the friction I so desperately seek.

Leaning to the side, I fall to the bed and bring him with me. He settles into the cradle of my thighs without breaking his attention from my breasts. They're still clad in the bra equivalent of white granny panties, but that hasn't dulled his interest. Relief is short-lived with the shallow pulses of his hips through the layers of clothes between us.

I'm the only one who's lost clothing, and I'm already close to being consumed by the flames that dance between us. Desperate for his skin, I slide both hands under his shirt as far as the fabric will allow. But it's not enough.

I tug at the thermal, but in response, all he does is lift his head. Lips swollen and shiny from kisses quirk upward as he regards me.

The sight of him—scruffy, shadowed jaw and ocean blue eyes —has my heart racing and my legs quivering on either side of his hips.

"What's the matter?"

"I want to touch you," I pout. "But your shirt is in the way."

"Easily remedied."

He sits farther up and yanks the offending garment off. With a flick, he tosses it to the floor. I soak in the sight of his smooth skin and hard muscle. The soft chest hair and dark ink. Gently, I trace along the tattoo of a wish flower. The wishes blow in an unseen breeze. His heart slams against his chest under my palm, and he closes his eyes and leans into my touch.

"What is it for?"

Turbulent eyes open to meet mine. "I got it right after my last deployment."

"It's a wish tattoo."

He nods.

"It represents a wish for good fate. For a better future. Little did I know when I got it that I'd care to share its origin. But you're turning every thought I ever had on its head."

"I am?"

He nods. "I should be thinking about how to protect you, how to keep you safe. But instead, all I can concentrate on is how badly I want you."

"You have me. Now what?" I lift my hips against his.

Locking his gaze with mine, he traces the cups of my bra to the front closure nestled in the center. Forget breathing. All I can do is experience.

My slight nod is the answer he needs to flick the clasp. Then he shifts each cup slowly, his fingers caressing the skin he's exposing until I'm free of the fabric.

The air is more than cool in here, in complete juxtaposition to the fire burning through me as Sawyer reverently studies my body. Like he wants to worship me.

"Fuck." He presses his teeth into his lower lip, and his hips thrust more eagerly now.

I capture his hand and lift, ready to repeat my movements from earlier, but I don't need to. At my touch, Sawyer comes back to the present, shaking himself out of the spell he was under. Sure fingers explore the weight of my breast, then home in on the place that begs for his touch.

I cry out as white light snaps across my vision, and he drops his hand. The loss is instantaneous.

"Why'd you stop?"

"Are you okay?" He studies me, his brow furrowed.

I don't know whether to strangle him for stopping or kiss him for being so tuned in to what I want and need. It only takes a heartbeat to choose the latter. Then I'm gripping his shoulders and lifting myself up to press a kiss on his chin. I drag my lips along his jaw, tracing the hard line until I reach the soft skin of his ear, all the while relishing the delicious friction that tingles as my breasts rub against his chest hair.

"I'm more than okay," I whisper and rim his ear with my tongue.

The masculine moan he releases clenches around my insides. "Fuck."

"Don't stop," I beg, rubbing against him.

He finds my lips with his and caresses them in equal parts gentle and fierce. I have no idea what to call it, other than all-consuming.

With gentle hands, he guides me back against the pillows. Feathering my neck and collarbone with flirty nips and hot, open-mouthed kisses, he follows my body down until his lips hover above my nipple.

"Please." I run my hands through his hair, bowing off the bed in an attempt to close the distance.

Except Sawyer does things on his own time. I've witnessed it over and over in the weeks we've spent together. And he won't be rushed in this.

"I've dreamed of you like this. In my bed. Begging for my touch," he admits before flicking his tongue against my nipple.

I moan at the phantom-like contact, but it's gone as quickly as it came.

"Mmm. Better than my dreams." He closes his eyes and runs his tongue along his lips.

"Sawyer." My hands are in his hair again.

"Hmm?"

My body is coming apart kiss by tantalizing kiss, yet he sticks to the timeline he's created for himself. I need him as on the edge and as desperate to continue as I am.

"How would you know? You've barely tasted me."

His lids pop open. The blue of his irises churns, revealing the storm raging inside him. He's not as calm as he appears.

"Barely?" His voice is so thick it's hard to make out the word. But the flash in his eyes is hard to ignore.

"Y-yes." It's hard to breathe around the anticipation that fills me, let alone speak through it.

"Looks like I better do something about that." With that, he wraps his lips around the stiff peak, sucking with enough pressure to hollow out his cheeks.

"Oh god."

I arch off the bed, giving him access to tunnel an arm beneath me and pull me more tightly against his mouth. Lips, tongue, and teeth work together, pulling his name from my lips. Forcing a symphony of moans and gasps from me at the pleasure he's eliciting. Sinking his teeth into the tip, he tugs with enough force to create lightning that dances behind my eyes. In response, my pussy spasms. I wrap my legs around his waist, pressing my feet to his lower back. My thighs clench when he switches his attention to the other breast, repeating the almost rough caress immediately.

I whimper and hold his head in place while he soothes the bite with his tongue. His free hand plucks at the tip of my other breast. Wave after wave of pleasure laps at my ankles, building and hinting at a powerful torrent of ecstasy just out of reach. Lifting my hips against his, I seek more friction, desperate to drive the sensation higher. To realize what's beyond the horizon.

My legs fall from his waist, and I yank at my pajama pants, struggling to shimmy them down past my hips, given the string tied tight at the waistband. My movements catch Sawyer's attention, and he releases my breast with an audible pop.

Why is that sound so sexy?

"What are you up to?" he rasps.

I can't help the heat that rises from my chest to my cheeks at being found out.

"My pants are stuck," I mumble.

He chuckles, his breath blowing across my sensitive nipple.

"Stuck, huh? Need some help?"

"I can do it. I just couldn't reach the bow—"

"Allow me?"

I nod and drop my hands. I'd much rather he does it anyway.

With a wink, he sits up. The move sends cool air rushing between us. I shiver, having almost forgotten we're in the middle of a snowstorm in Alaska.

While he works, I give him a once-over, taking in the sculpted planes of his chest and only stopping my perusal at the impressive erection that tents his sweats.

Wow.

He smooths a hand down my stomach, pulling my attention back to what he's doing. Gripping one end of the ribbon between his thumb and forefinger, he pulls, loosening the knot. He quickly untangles both sides, and the pressure around my waist goes slack.

"Will you?" I ask, lifting my hips.

"Take them off?"

Wordlessly, I nod. It's all I can do.

"You're sure?" he asks, his nostrils flaring and his jaw clenched tight.

I'm long past any hesitation at this point.

"Please."

With a finger hooked in the waistband at either hip, he tugs them down, groaning as more and more skin is revealed.

"Jesus Christ. You're not wearing panties?"

"No." I bite my lip but can't hide my smile.

"You're killing me."

The change in temperature creates a shiver as he works my pants farther down my legs.

"In my defense, they wouldn't have been comfortable to work out in, given how wet they were—"

His mouth fuses to mine, stemming the words of my logical

but slightly diabolical response. My legs tangle in the forgotten pants, and I shimmy until I can kick them free.

"You're trying to make me lose control," he growls against my neck.

"Is that a bad thing?" My question ends on a gasp as he tweaks my nipple and stars flash behind my eyes.

"I *never* lose control. Except with you." He dips his head again, lips and tongue toying with my other breast.

I hold him there until I'm a writhing mess of pleasure and moans. "I like when you...lose...control," I pant when I can string together a coherent sentence.

"Well, little starling, you're definitely pushing that boundary."

He kisses the underside of my breasts and tongues my belly button before he shifts my legs farther apart and settles between them with my thighs braced on his shoulders.

"So do it already," I challenge.

His eyes glint at my words, revealing the true depth of the control he's exerting right now. He swipes his tongue along my folds from back to front, and I fall backward, directing every ounce of my focus to what Sawyer is doing.

He repeats the caress, and I grip the sheets and go rigid as passion overwhelms me.

"Oh my god." I release the sheets and rest both hands on his head.

With a growl, he swirls his tongue around my clit, rotating it until I almost have the pattern, can almost handle the intense pleasure. But then he switches it up, and absolute rapture drags me back down again.

No, not down.

Up.

My toes curl, and the orgasm crests higher, building in my core and radiating outward with the heat of the sun and its rays.

I'm falling and flying at once, held to the earth by the man between my legs as he drives me higher, tapping his tongue against the hard bundle of nerves and introducing a new sensation to the mix.

"*Sawyer.*"

There's nothing else to say. He is the epicenter of my pleasure, and I'm on the edge of an entirely new plane of existence. The flashes behind my eyes blend to create a solid beam of light. My body vibrates, stringing tighter and tighter as it hurls itself toward the finish line.

"Please."

He knows what I need. Pressing one finger inside, he continues using his tongue and teeth to fling me higher. A second finger joins the first, and he pumps once, twice, a third time, before sucking my clit with enough pressure to propel me higher than I've ever been. Into the sky. Into space. Into the heavens.

The luminous white shatters into millions of pieces that rain down—a waterfall of heat and pleasure. It shifts colors in the spectrum until the intensity recedes and leaves me centered on one thing.

Sawyer King.

CHAPTER 15

SAWYER

$\mathcal{E}$vie falling apart from pleasure—from the ecstasy I created in her body—is damn close to the sexiest fucking thing I've ever witnessed.

It's only beat out by the way my name breaks on her lips, the warm silk of her skin, the way she tastes—more potent than the strongest whiskey and more addictive than my favorite dessert.

She winds her legs around my hips and drapes her arms around my neck. Her cheeks are flushed pink, and her pouty lips beg for my mouth.

Who am I to deny their siren's call?

Dropping my head, I tease her, ghosting my lips over hers. Once. Twice. She tunnels her fingers into my hair to hold me in place, and her tongue pushes against the seam of my lips. I can cede control—for now—so I open for her. She moans when her tongue finds mine, and my dick jumps. It's already aching for more, screaming at me to finish what I started. To keep going until I'm buried inside her as we shatter together. But I refuse to rush this.

Her speed.

"Fuck." Ripping my mouth from hers, I growl the word against the damp skin of her neck.

Her hips lift against mine in silent demand.

"More," she begs.

Ignoring the way beads of sweat dot my temples and spine, I trail my hands down her sides, grazing along her breasts while she moves restlessly against me. My dick has one destination in mind, and her movements only encourage it to reach for the promise of her heat. It's taking *everything* to keep this torturous pace.

"*Sawyer.*"

"Patience, little starling."

I trace my lips and tongue along the line of her jaw to the soft skin below her earlobe and nip at the spot, then bite a little harder when her hands roam down my back to palm my ass.

Mewling, she squeezes the globes to pull me against her. As if there's any room to get closer.

"Do you like my teeth on you?" I ask.

"Yes."

"I fucking love your hands on me."

She flexes her fingers against my ass again, and I thrust my hips against hers.

"More. Please."

"Begging so nicely," I murmur against the pulse that flutters wildly beneath the skin at the base of her neck.

Rolling, I yank her with me until I'm on my back and gazing up at her slumberous hazel eyes. The heat of her pussy soaks through the fabric of my sweats to my dick.

"*Fuck.*"

She wriggles her hips, and stars pop in my vision. The movement drags her breasts across my chest, and she sinks her teeth into her lower lip, but she can't stem the moan of pleasure.

I did that. Me. It's a heady sensation that adds to what's building between us.

"I want you so fucking bad," I admit, rotating my thumbs along her hipbones. But I'm terrified of the intense emotion that swirls in me and how petite she is.

I could never hurt her intentionally. But if I lose control, I just might. That thought sobers me, even as I struggle to yank back the control untethering with each rotation of her hips against mine.

"Please."

She rubs back and forth across the front of my sweats. Her body is ready for the next step, but I need to ensure her mind is there too.

"Are you sure?" I ask.

Her nod is frantic.

"Give me your words, starling."

"Yes. Fuck me."

Confident in her response, I roll us again. Once she's settled on her back, I yank my sweats down and kick them off. Then I settle back into the cradle of her thighs. I'm ready, poised at her entrance, gritting my teeth as I fight for control.

But what we're about to do is more than just sex. So much more. And I need her to know that.

"Evie."

Long, red-tipped lashes flutter open, and her eyes lock with mine.

"This is more than fucking." I'm not ready to name the emotions that wrap around my heart, but this isn't just a simple physical release.

"Yes," she agrees with a nod. "I need you. Please."

I push forward and stop. My control snaps and snarls against the frayed leash. I'm barely hanging on. But there's something else I need to remember. For both of us.

"Fuck. Condom."

Something West said before we left made me pack a box. Just in case. And they're in my bag. Downstairs.

God dammit.

"They're in my bag." I push up and survey her. "I—I wasn't planning for this. But—they're downstairs—"

Her legs lock around my waist and halt my departure.

Eyes the color of sunlight filtered through a forest search mine while her teeth nibble the swollen flesh of her lip. Fuck, I want to kiss her. But kissing her means losing all sense again.

"I have an IUD. And I got tested after..." She trails off, reluctant to bring up Brad's name in this moment.

Good. That motherfucker has no place here.

I relax in the cradle of her thighs and take most of my weight on my elbows while my dick nestles against her folds. My lips graze hers in a chaste kiss.

"Are you sure?" I whisper.

If she says no, I can grab what I need and be back in under two minutes. Inside her in less than three. Guaranteed. My dick pulses against her heat, desperate to keep going. He's 100 percent on board with the thought of sinking into her with nothing between us. But he's not calling the shots here.

"I'm sure." The words are as clear as her eyes when they meet mine.

I clear my throat. "My last test was during my physical—"

"Sawyer." Her smile is worldly, indulgent, and sassy as fuck.

"Yeah?"

"Stop talking and kiss me."

"Yes, ma'am."

In a heartbeat, my lips are on hers again, and I shudder as her hands coast along my back until her fingernails dig into the muscles of my ass.

Inhaling a sharp breath, I try to reel in my body's need.

Slow down.

She needs to be in the driver's seat with this experience. I close my eyes, but without sight, every other sense centers on the beautiful woman beneath me.

The heady scent of her arousal. The slight moan she releases as our tongues tangle. The way her fingers grip my ass and pull me impossibly closer. It's an exercise in patience to take this slow. Her nails prick into my muscles and I moan.

"Fuck, woman. You're playing with fire."

There's nothing between us, and the heat of her pussy is calling to me like a damn siren.

"Maybe I like the heat." Her smile is impish as she watches me.

I've never experienced a playful side to sex before. But why doesn't it surprise me that I would with her?

"Maybe you…"

Fuck.

Pulling her with me, I roll until she straddles me and tunnel my fingers into her hair. With a gentle yank, I force her lips to mine again. Hard nipples rub against my chest, and I nip at her lip with a growl. Her slick heat rubs against my dick, and I hiss out a breath as our mouths fuse in a kiss that is all lips and tongue.

It's so much more than just passion.

God. I need her to hold still before I fucking embarrass myself. With my hands on her hips, I hold her in place, my dick at her entrance, demanding to move forward.

"Sawyer." She whimpers my name and rotates her hips to fulfill the promise of the friction she so desperately craves.

"I'm right here."

I don't need to say anything else. She knows.

Loosening my grip, I allow her to lower slightly. It's not enough. For either of us. But it's a start.

"Fuck."

"Mmm," she agrees, lowering herself further.

Stars flicker in my vision, and I grind my molars until I'm seated inside her.

"Starling."

I move my hands from her hips to her ass and grind her pelvis

BREANNA LYNN

against mine. She mewls, and I repeat the caress, thrusting at the same time.

"Gah. Please. More." Her words are breathy whispers against my ear.

I force my hands to release their plump treasure and tangle our fingers together.

She sits up, sending all my breath from my lungs. She's a fucking vision. Half-lidded hazel eyes burn into me, and her hair, turning more red than brown by the day, is a tangle around her face. This time when she rotates her hips, her pussy spasms around me. Fuck, it's amazing. I can't tell if this position is the best idea I've ever had or the worst. Her heat surrounds me, small pulses of her muscles driving my orgasm higher and higher.

"Set the pace," I grit out.

Her eyes flutter closed, and she nods, rocking back and forth. Her breathing shallows, and her fingers grip mine, mimicking what her pussy is doing to my cock right now. The beautiful bounce of her breasts draws my attention, tempting me to take them in my mouth again. Heaving up, I wrap my lips around the distended nipple and tug with my teeth, then soothe the pain with my tongue.

She cries out, her rhythm faltering.

"Sawyer."

"Are you close, little starling?"

"Mmm."

Her pussy grips me like a goddamn vise. She's right on the edge. I need her to come soon. Before my own orgasm batters at the last gate of my control.

"Tell me, baby." I thrust again.

"I'm so close, Sawyer." She throws her head back and moans. "I—I—" Her movements speed up, more erratic than before, and she drops against my chest.

From there, I take the lead, flexing my fingers against her hips, holding her steady as I piston into her. Faster. Harder.

Struggling to ignore the ever-tightening grip of her pussy around my cock. I'm fighting my own orgasm in an effort to drive her to hers first.

Every nerve ending, every ounce of my being, is focused on the place where our bodies connect.

"*Sawyer.*"

Fuck, I love the way my name crosses her lips.

"Come for me," I growl.

I increase my speed, and her thighs grip my waist, holding on for the ride. Until her muscles lock into place and her lips form an O. For a moment, her scream is silent, but then a cry shakes loose. Her pussy tightens so much that stars obliterate my vision. Only they're not fucking stars anymore. They're fireworks. Her muscles spasm around me, and I finally let go of my control. My orgasm rockets down my spine and ignites my entire body in a white-hot, explosive wash of a pleasure so intense I all but lose consciousness. Nothing exists except the woman who holds on to me as if I'm the only thing tethering her to this moment.

Just as she's tethering me.

CHAPTER 16

EVIE

*A*s I drift into the space between sleep and awake, a cozy sensation ebbs and flows through my body like waves crashing along the shore. The cotton beneath me is smooth and smells faintly like Sawyer. Bergamot, citrus, and something uniquely him.

I want to burrow beneath the blankets and hide from the storm outside. Pretend as if the reason we're here has nothing to do with the mess of my life. And right here, in my little scented cocoon, I can. As I stretch my legs, muscles twinge in places that remind me of what happened last night.

I had sex. With Sawyer.

This is more than just fucking.

Goosebumps shiver along my exposed arms, but not from the cold.

I'm naked. In Sawyer King's bed.

Except instead of being wrapped in Sawyer's arms with the steady thrum of his heart lulling me to sleep, I'm alone. What does he think about last night? Does he regret it? Should I? Where are my pajamas? Should I get up and leave?

And go where? You're in the middle of Alaska in a fucking snowstorm.

"I can hear your gears turning from here."

My eyes pop open at the sound of Sawyer's voice. It's thick with sleep. He's leaning against the frame of the bathroom door, watching me. After a long moment, he straightens and moves closer. His movements are more like a prowl. He's as naked as I am, and I can't help but take the opportunity to drink in his Adonis-like body. He's not ashamed of his nudity, but why should he be? Muscles line his shoulders and chest and taper to an eight pack of abs I've felt against the most intimate parts of my body.

A sensation I wouldn't mind experiencing again. My core throbs as I peruse the V-shape of muscles that lead down from his stomach to his hardening cock.

Fuck. He's beautiful.

And I want him. Again. Still. Whatever the case may be. My need is so strong I squeeze my thighs together. Only the ache intensifies at the masculine moan he releases.

"You're killing me, starling."

Starling. How has it only been a few days since he started calling me that? I've grown attached to the way he says it—the growl of the *R* as the word tugs on something deep inside me.

"I am?"

What could I possibly do to the warrior in front of me?

He sits on the bed, the mattress dipping with his weight.

"Licking your lips and staring at my cock like that? Yeah." The hum he releases is one of curiosity, making my nipples pebble under the blankets.

"I was?"

"Mm-hmm."

He glides his index finger along my jaw, then rests it against my lips. Desire unfurls in my belly. I want his touch. Everywhere. But he doesn't explore further. As if he's content to explore my lips only, running his finger along the seam.

That's all it takes, though. It's a flicker of flame when I need the all-consuming inferno.

I gasp, my lips parting. "Sawyer."

Pulling his finger into my mouth, I lick along the length. Given his naked state, the way his cock jumps snags my attention instantly.

He pulls his finger free, never taking his eyes off mine. "Know what else?" His voice is hoarse, raspy. It reminds me of how he sounds as he's close to orgasm.

I shake my head.

"I can see your breasts begging for my touch under this sheet." He plucks at the thin cotton. The move is close enough to my nipple to have my back bowing off the bed, but far enough away that I'm disappointed when he doesn't connect.

I didn't realize the blanket had fallen below my waist, leaving my upper half covered by only the thin sheet.

He lowers his head until his mouth is millimeters away from one straining tip that presses against the offending cotton.

I don't want anything between us. But Sawyer has other ideas.

"I promised myself we'd talk before any more happens," he murmurs, dragging his face back and forth.

"Talking is overrated." My words come out in gasps, and desire coats my thighs.

His gaze lifts to mine, the promise of his words clear. "We are going to talk about this."

"But—"

"Shh." His attention shifts back to my breast, and I squirm as he closes the distance. "Just a taste." Then he's sucking the cotton-covered tip into his mouth.

"God." I arch off the bed again, pressing myself against his mouth.

My body is already primed and begging for more. I lift my hands to his head, holding him in place while my legs part. The sting of his sharp teeth is muted a fraction by the fabric, but it's enough to pull a whimper from me.

"More," I beg.

He repeats the movement, harder than before, and stars pop behind my eyelids. The mattress dips again, and he lowers himself to the cradle of my thighs without releasing my breast.

Alternating sharp bites with hard suction, he presses his erection to me. God, I need him to touch me. I lift my hips, satisfied at the grunt he huffs out. He releases one nipple and sucks the other into his talented mouth. Cool air against damp cloth tightens the forgotten nipple further. The pleasure-pain builds and intensifies when he cups my breast, and fireworks spark when his thumb and forefinger pluck the hard peak.

I grind my hips against his, desperate to rid myself of the sheet and blanket between us. I want to wrap my legs around his waist. I need to be closer to him.

"Sawyer...please...I need..."

How he knows my body so well is a mystery. He doesn't stop as he grips the top of the sheet anchored at my breasts and tugs it down.

He stops as the sheet reaches the underside of my breast and delves his hand beneath it. His palm lands on my hip in a rough grip. Then he releases my nipple to claim my mouth. After last night, I thought I knew what it was like to be consumed. Only Sawyer has intensified the sensation. I wrap my arms around his neck and lightly scratch my nails along his scalp while he works his way up my chest and along my jaw to my ear.

"Do you have any idea how good you feel?" he growls. "How good you taste?"

I mewl as he rims my ear with his tongue to prove his point. But the damn blanket is still in the way, and I squirm to dislodge it. Sawyer pulls back and whips the blankets away. Free of the covers, I wrap my legs around his waist and lift my hips in a silent plea.

"God, you're fucking soaked." He dives back in, his words spoken against the skin of my throat.

"For you. Only for you."

I've never felt this level of pleasure before, never felt like I *had* to keep going or I'd break apart. The new experience is as exciting as it is terrifying. But I'm safe. With him.

And I need him with a ferocity that overrides every other desire.

"Fuck yes." He notches his dick at my opening.

I hold my breath and wait for him to push forward. The promise of pleasure tingles down my spine. But rather than move, he freezes and frowns down at me.

"What is it?"

"My phone." A muscle ticks in his jaw, and he squeezes his eyes shut with a sigh.

"Ignore it." I explore his chest, tracing my fingertips along the ink.

"It's Cole's ringtone."

In other words, he can't. He's already shifting away and pulling the blankets back into place. The apology is clear in his expression as he grabs the phone off the nightstand.

"There's only one reason he would call me," he explains.

"Brad." A shudder ripples through my body, and I grip the covers tighter around me.

He doesn't belong in this room with us. But yet again, he's forced himself into my life. I can't pretend he doesn't exist, even if I want to.

"Brad," he confirms.

The phone stops ringing as Sawyer continues to study me. What does he see?

"You should call him back," I tell him.

"I will. I—This, between us?" He waves a hand from himself to me and back again. "We're not done. Not by a fucking long shot.

After this conversation, I fully intend to pick up where we left off."

My body flushes at the heat simmering in his expression.

"O-okay."

My denied orgasm rears its head, more than ready for that moment. I don't bother to hide the whimper at the images his words conjure.

"Hold that thought, starling."

He unlocks his phone and presses a few buttons. A second later, the ringing echoes through the speaker.

Cole answers immediately.

"King."

The tone of his voice has dread curdling in my stomach. Sawyer must sense something too, because his shoulders tense and his muscles lock in place.

"Tell me."

"It's Mia. She's been attacked."

Mia's been attacked.

Mia's been attacked, and it's all my fault.

The words circle in my brain like a horrible broken record I can't ignore. They make it hard to focus on the conversation still going on between Sawyer and Cole.

I drop my chin, surprised to find Sawyer's fingers woven with mine.

"What happened?" Gone is the sensual man who kissed me brainless a few moments ago.

This is the warrior who promised to keep me safe.

"Mia had an OB appointment. From what I can figure, Brad followed her from her house, then cornered her in the parking lot."

Just like with me at the apartment complex. The memory of

the way he pressed me against the car is so real my hips throb like they did that day when he pushed me up against my car.

"According to Mia, Brad kept demanding she tell him where Evie is," Cole continues.

"Where the fuck were you?" Sawyer growls.

Startled, I jump. Instantly, he squeezes my hand in silent apology.

"*I* was doing my fucking job. I've been running all over LA looking for this weasel. Tracking leads all over the damn place. We never discussed putting a detail on Mia. We didn't think there was a credible threat to her or anyone other than Evie."

Brad went after Mia to get to me. He wanted information from her, or maybe he was trying to leverage her to get to me. But whatever the reason, her association with me is what got her hurt. Bile rises in my throat, and I swallow the bitter flavor with an unhealthy dose of guilt.

This is my fault. If I had quit working for Mia when I first tried to give her my notice, none of this would have happened.

"Is M-Mia okay? And the b-b-baby?" I clamp my teeth on my trembling lower lip.

"They're both fine. Mia's husband showed up, and Brad ran like the asshole he is. She's got a couple of bruises and was shaken up, but by the time I got off the phone with her, she was ready for war," Cole answers.

Sounds like Mia.

I've never seen anyone battle for her loved ones the way she does. Thank god Garrett showed up when he did.

"Have you talked to the two of them about security moving forward?" Sawyer asks.

Cole chuckles. "Mia didn't think that was necessary—"

"The fuck it isn't," Sawyer interrupts.

"Her husband said something along those same lines. I reached out to Eli at Vigilant to see if they can help us out. I figured you'd still want me focused on finding Brad."

"Yes."

"One of Eli's guys showed up before I was off the phone with Mia."

Sawyer glances at me, his forehead wrinkled in concern.

"Thanks for letting us know, Cole."

"Anytime, boss." With that, the line goes dead.

Sawyer drops his phone on the nightstand without looking at it. His eyes haven't left me for the last several minutes.

"Evie."

"It's my fault. He was after me. I ran away, so he attacked her." Panic, guilt, and fear swirl through my veins.

I shouldn't have run. Here I was pretending my life didn't exist, and Mia was paying the price.

"It's not your fault any more than it's mine."

I snort, but that doesn't stop him.

"If I had caught him by now, none of this would have happened."

He wraps his arms around me and lowers us both to the bed. Tugging the covers back into place, he leaves me locked in his arms while he draws patternless shapes on my back. With my head resting on his chest, I find the cadence of his heart and take a deep breath before releasing it.

"What if—what if something had happened to Mia? Or to the baby. I—"

"You can't think about life in terms of what if, starling. It's a lesson I learned a long time ago."

Tears burn the back of my nose, and I blink rapidly to try to keep them at bay.

"He wants me."

And that fact fills me with revulsion. And resignation.

I can't fight the tears anymore. They break loose and wind their way to the edge of my face before they drop to Sawyer's chest.

"It would be easier to give in. To give him what he wants," I say.

I survived five years with him before. He'll get bored and eventually leave me alone.

Maybe.

You spent five years with him when you didn't know better. When you thought that's what your life had *to be.*

"Evie." Sawyer's arms tighten around me.

"What?"

"Look at me."

With a sigh, I lift my head. The intensity that greets me is so forceful, I can't look away.

"He can't fucking have you, starling. I'm not giving you up. You're mine. And I'll kill him if he touches you again."

I shudder at the seriousness of Sawyer's words.

"Promise me something," he says.

"What?"

"No matter what happens, you won't give in."

What does that mean?

"What do you think is going to happen?" I ask.

"It's not about that. Just…promise me."

"I—" Exhaustion pushes at me. I'm so tired of fighting.

"Promise me," Sawyer demands.

"I…promise."

With a yawn, I nuzzle into him again, comforted by his strong heartbeat and the way his fingers skim along my back. My eyelids grow heavy, the adrenaline from Cole's call fading, being erased little by little with each glide of Sawyer's fingers.

"As long as there is breath in my body, starling, you're safe." His promise is a murmur, quiet in the stillness of the room.

That's what I'm worried about.

Sawyer won't back down from a fight, but Brad doesn't fight fair.

Those realizations follow me into a dreamless sleep.

CHAPTER 17

SAWYER

"This is the only way," I explain to Cole and Sydney an hour later.

It took Evie that long to drift off. For her body to finally relax, at least for the time being. In that hour, I mentally summarized what Brad had revealed to us so far.

First, he preys on women he thinks are weak. Michaela, Evie, and the other women he harassed. Now Mia. He's patient. He doesn't mind waiting to make his moves, so emotion isn't what's driving his behavior. Or is it? Because he went after Mia. Someone he has no interest in. Other than her connection to Evie. Is he escalating? Can we get him to? If emotion clouds his judgment, he'll get sloppy, and that's when we'll catch him.

Finally, he's smarter than I want to give him credit for. He knows we're looking for him and he knows how to hide. The bastard probably figures we'll chase our tails every time a random credit card charge pops up. Which is exactly what we've been doing for the last month.

Only I'm done playing his game.

"Are you going to tell Evie your plan?" Sydney asks.

Guilt pricks at me, but news of Mia's attack weighs so heavily on Evie. She's already dealing with more than she can handle.

"No."

"You're not?" Surprise is clear in Sydney's voice.

I didn't make this decision lightly, but I won't back down. Not now.

"It's better this way."

Bile rises in my throat, begging to differ.

Fuck.

"You're sure about this?" Cole asks.

Nope. Not even a little. But I'm done waiting for Brad. It's time to bring him to me.

And what if Evie is collateral damage?

Not going to happen. That's why we've crafted this plan.

"If you can do your part the way we discussed, yes."

"I don't like it," he responds.

"You said that already," I growl.

"I'm saying it again," he argues.

"We've tried everything else."

"There has to be—"

"Cole, if there was a better plan, we'd have come up with it by now."

His sigh speaks volumes. It's the best plan we have. The only one. He knows it. Even if he doesn't like it.

"Fine."

"Sydney?" I ask.

"It's your decision," she responds.

It's your funeral is what she means.

"Then it's settled. Let me know when it's done."

We hang up, but I don't leave my office. Instead, I scroll to another number in my phone—the one I could dial in my sleep—and bring the phone to my ear.

"It's about time you called," West lectures by way of greeting.

Ever the teacher. I roll my eyes but can't fight the smile that tugs at my lips. He worries about me, same as I worry about him and Michaela. And Benji.

"Jesus, *Mom*, it's only been a few days since we talked."

"That was before the snowstorm. Is it still going?"

Turning in my chair, I scan the sky. The gray clouds are still hovering low, but they're not as dark, and they're less dense than before.

"It's letting up."

"Good. Michaela can stop watching the Weather Channel now."

"I don't want either of you to worry."

"Tough shit. It's not about what you want," he fires back.

This is how it goes with family. It's why I'm calling him now versus when the storm stops.

"Yeah, yeah. As much as I like getting lectured by Professor Abbott, I called because I have a question."

"I thought your dad gave you the birds and bees talk already."

Heat pools in my stomach as an image of Evie, naked, head thrown back, flashes through my mind. Dammit.

My blue balls scream at me, and I clear my throat. "Fuck you."

West laughs. "Sorry, couldn't help myself. Seriously, though, what's up?"

"You guys notice anything strange recently? Cars following you? Anything like that?"

If Brad went after Mia, what would stop him from going after Michaela? What if he does, and Benji's with her?

"No, why?"

I breathe a sigh of relief and fill him in on Brad's attack on Mia.

"Motherfucker," he says when I finish.

"I don't think he'll go after Mikey, but I didn't think he'd go after Mia either."

It's too soon to tell if he's escalating. But West needs to be aware of the possibility. He had Michaela in his sights once

185

before, so it isn't a stretch to believe he'd try to come after her again. It kills me to be almost three thousand miles away from my family when all this shit is going down.

"Should I tell Michaela what's going on?" he asks.

"Your call, but keep an eye out. Keep her safe. And Benji."

"Daddy, we're home!" Benji yells in the background.

Fuck, I miss that boy. When my world is nothing but darkness and shadows, he's my reminder that innocence exists. That the world is not all corruption and psychos like Brad.

"Who are you talking to? Gramma?" His little voice gets closer. And damn if he doesn't sound older than he did the day I took him to the zoo. Impossible. It was only a month ago.

Even if it feels like a lifetime has passed.

"Uncle Sawyer," West says.

"Uncow? I wanna talk!" Benji yells.

"Okay, let me put it on speaker."

"No! Want to talk to Uncow myself."

"Oh, Jesus. He reminds me of Mikey," I say.

West snorts. He remembers how bossy my baby sister was when she was Benji's age. At least we know where he gets it.

"Who are you telling?" West asks.

"Daddy!"

"Okay, okay, here."

There's a shuffling noise before Benji's voice comes through loud and clear—incredibly loud and clear.

"Uncow!"

I wince and press the volume down button while I pray my hearing is intact.

"Hi, buddy."

"Where are you?"

"I'm working."

I haven't been gone this long since before he and I started spending Uncow-nephew days together.

"Working?" he asks.

"Yeah."

"Can you come over and play?"

My heart squeezes at his request.

"I can't today."

"Oh."

One word is filled with as much disappointment as he can muster. God dammit.

Yet another thing Brad is stealing.

"But when I'm not working, we'll spend another day together. How about that?"

"Can we go to the zoo again?"

"If that's where you want to go."

"In the car. No doors?" he asks.

I chuckle. Michaela's lecture after the last time still haunts me. But it was worth it—the look on Benji's face when he saw the Jeep was priceless.

"We'll have to ask your mom, okay?"

"Okay! Mommy!"

I have to pull the phone away this time, but quickly bring it back to my ear and redirect him.

"Buddy, how about we ask her when I come home?"

He sighs as if I've just asked him to wait an extra week for Christmas.

"Okay."

"I love you, Benji."

"Love you, Uncow."

"Hand the phone back to Daddy, okay?"

"'Kay. Bye."

"Bye, buddy."

Another shuffle, and West is back.

"The zoo and a car ride with no doors, huh?"

"Hey, what my nephew wants, my nephew gets."

"Plan on ice cream too."

"What else would we eat for breakfast?" I joke.

"Fuck," West groans.

"Kidding. Mostly."

"Yeah, right."

My family members claim I spoil Benji. And if that means ice cream for breakfast, then maybe I do. But in reality, I can typically steer him toward smarter breakfast choices. Not that he won't try that trick at some point.

"I need to get going, but I wanted to give you the heads-up."

"That asshole better hope I never see him near my family."

"Just be safe," I tell him.

"That's my line."

"I'm always safe."

Even when I can't tell him what's really going on. Because if I did, he'd know that response was a flat-out lie.

"Seriously, Sawyer, stay safe." West uses his standard goodbye.

"Safety is my middle name."

As I hang up the phone, I slump forward, bracing my elbows on the desktop.

When it chimes a minute later, I half expect to see a text from West.

It's Cole.

COLE

Something happened.

You're not going to like it.

What?

Brad broke into Evie's place again.

What? How?

The apartment complex called me. Evie's neighbor found the back window shattered.

I went over to take a look.

And?

The entire place is wrecked. TV on the floor, candles thrown against a wall. Bedding and clothes shredded.

Fuck.

Brad's always been a douchebag, but nothing like this. I need to get this latest information to Ed. Maybe he can make heads or tails of it, because my gut is telling me that the situation is becoming more dangerous.

Any surveillance footage? Witnesses?

Negative. It was during the day. Most of her neighbors were at work. And the surveillance cameras are only trained on the office and the pool.

Of fucking course.

Is anything salvageable?

Sydney said she'll help me sift through it all. It's going to take a while.

Are you going to tell Evie?

I don't want to. This is only going to add to her anxiety.

I don't know.

King, I'm having second thoughts about our plan.

He's not predictable at all.

It's the only one we've got.

Unless you've thought of something else?

No.

Something doesn't feel right.

> I know. But we can't keep. Playing hide and seek.

> Drop the bait.

Fuck.

Fine.

I want the record to reflect that I don't like this idea.

> Noted.

And I think we should tell Evie.

> I'll make sure she knows that.

If she asks.

"Fuck." I blow out a breath and toss my phone face down on the desk.

My gut is telling me two things. Our plan is still the only way to ensure Evie's safety. And I need to remind myself that she's safe. I need her in my arms. Right fucking now. Scrubbing a hand down my face, I stand and stride out of the room, leaving my phone where it is.

Instead of in bed where I left her, she's in her nook, watching as the storm fades. Her knees are drawn up to her chest, and her chin rests on top. The hunch of her shoulders shows how tired she is. She should still be sleeping. But if she was, I couldn't memorize the way she looks right now. And I know I'll have this image burned into my brain forever.

I'm falling in love with this woman. I can admit it. Even if it's the scariest thing that's happened to me since Amani. With Evie, though, the feelings are so much stronger. And that's much more terrifying.

She doesn't move as I approach. Does she hear me, or is she simply lost in thought?

"Hey," I murmur and wrap my arms around her while I brush a kiss against her hair.

She relaxes in my embrace, unwittingly easing the tension I'm carrying too. A month ago, she wouldn't have let me get this close. Two weeks ago, she would have stiffened, then forced herself to relax before pulling away as fast as she could.

Today, she's completely comfortable in my embrace, and this is the only place I want to be. In this moment. With her.

"May I sit with you?" I ask.

She nods.

After a little finagling, I lean against the wall, and she sits between my legs with her back to my chest.

"What are you thinking about?" I whisper, wrapping an arm around her shoulders to hold her closer to me.

The sigh she lets out speaks volumes.

"It's so pretty here."

"It is." And I'm not just talking about the view. She's made this place more beautiful than I could ever imagine.

"You like it here."

She nods. "Even when it was storming. It probably sounds crazy, but I feel like I can breathe here."

The deep breath she inhales and releases proves her point.

"It's not crazy. That same feeling brought me here to begin with."

And here she is, feeling the same way, even though I've never told her that.

My heart pounds in triple time.

This sense of rightness? This is it. And I can't do anything but kiss her in this moment.

Thumb and forefinger under her chin, I tilt her head back and slide my lips along hers until she opens for me. The way our breaths mingle, the electric sparks along my skin, and her moan as she tilts her head all relight the fire from earlier. My dick presses against my sweats, and she grinds her back against me. She rotates and presses her chest against mine. I break the kiss, watching her, waiting for her eyes to flutter open. The natural light streaming in highlights the strands of red in her hair, giving her a fiery halo.

"Do you know how beautiful you are?" I ask her.

"I know how beautiful you make me feel."

Before I can respond, she drops her hands to the hem of her shirt and yanks it up and off.

"Fuck," I grit out as it flutters to the floor.

Every thought not centered on the captivating woman in front of me evaporates. All I can see is the way her golden eyes shine, the smooth skin of her collarbone that flushes pink, her pert breasts with dusky pink nipples that beg for my hands. My lips.

"Make love to me, Sawyer."

My body hardens in a painful rush at her soft-spoken demand. Tightening the leash strangled around my control, I search her expression for any signs of hesitation, for any hint of emotion other than desire. Her blush pink lips are relaxed and parted slightly, shining from the moisture of my tongue. Her honey-colored eyes are clear and locked on mine with a fire behind them that glitters with a heat so intense I'm surprised it hasn't consumed us both.

Or maybe it has.

Her bare breasts quiver with her breath and her nipples pucker with my attention. At the sight, I squeeze my hands into fists at my thighs. They're itching to explore the soft globes. I lift them slowly, because speeding up means breaking this spell. My fingers tremble, and her breath catches and holds as she watches the movement. She wants the flash fire of pleasure that exists when we touch.

But I'm not going to give her that.

This experience will be a slow burn. Embers and coals. A flicker of flame that burns in both of us until all that exists is her and me and what we do to each other.

Make love to me, Sawyer.

That's what this is.

I love her.

That kind of emotion has been buried so deep for so long that it's foreign—a strange sensation that filters through my blood. But on the heels of that realization is another. *I can't tell her.* The universe has claimed the person I loved once before, and the fear that it will happen again is as embedded in my psyche as my love for her.

I can't tell her. But I can damn sure show her.

Ignoring the delicious offering of her breasts, I brush my hands along her biceps and curl my fingers around the muscle to tug her closer.

"Is that what this is to you?" I growl.

My voice is hardly recognizable. It's strangled by desire and emotion I can no longer fight.

"Yes."

Gone is the timid woman who hid from her monsters. The one in front of me is confident. Strong. And so fucking sexy I'm surprised my dick hasn't split the seam of my sweats. She coasts her palms along my thighs—it would almost tickle if I wasn't so turned on. A smile hovers at the corners of her lips, and her fingers wind in the hem of my T-shirt. I grit my teeth at the barely there brush of her fingers as she pushes the cotton up. A shiver racks my body, making her smile widen.

If it were up to me, she'd always wear that smile.

Your plan will cause her to lose that smile.

Guilt pinches my gut, but I shove it back in its box to deal with later. I failed to keep Amani safe. I will not fail Evie.

Once she pulls my shirt over my head, she drops it to the floor next to hers.

With a sigh, she rubs her hands along my chest, following the path with her eyes. She winds them around my neck and closes the distance until her breasts crush between us. Her lips against mine feel so natural. It's as if she was made for me. Like we've been kissing for years, not days. My tongue tangles with hers as I delve my fingers into her silky hair to grip the fiery strands and position her so I can deepen the kiss.

When my lungs scream for oxygen, I break the connection and gulp lungfuls of air, all the while tracing her jawline. She tilts her head, and I take her silent invitation and savor her sweetness as I trail my hands down her back to cup her ass and grind her against me.

I'm an addict desperate for his next hit, and she is my drug of choice. The skin of her throat is warm and supple against my lips, the beating of her heart at the base the next stop in my exploration.

"Sawyer."

The whimper of my name on her lips is a pleasure all its own. I shift my hands beneath the waistband of her pajama pants and panties to squeeze the firm muscles of her ass while I push the fabric down over her hips.

Flushed cheeks, swollen lips, and smooth skin are all bathed in the soft white light that filters through the windows. She is Aphrodite in human form. Temptation incarnate. And all mine.

"Fuck, starling. You're so goddamned gorgeous."

A rosy pink works its way from her chest and into her cheeks.

"Thank you. But you're overdressed."

"Easily fixed." I wink at her and surge off our makeshift bed so I can kick free of my sweats.

The fire is almost out, so I take the opportunity to toss another log on. I barely register the explosion of sparks before I turn my back on it, catching Evie ogling my ass in the process.

A smirk twitches at the corners of my mouth. "See something you like, starling?"

I know I do. She used the few seconds I was distracted to kick her pants and panties off and stretch her body along the blanket. An offering. My dick jumps, snagging her attention. I stand still and let her look her fill. After all, I'm doing the same thing. But when her tongue peeks out to moisten her lips, I'm done. I can't hold back anymore. Just a few steps, and I sink down next to her. She reaches out, ready to pull me in, but I have other ideas.

I grab one of her outstretched hands and bruise a kiss to her palm.

"If I could, I would trace every inch of your body with my tongue until I committed the entire masterpiece to memory. Every freckle, every muscle, every spot that drives you to heaven."

The smile that curls her lips is a mix of delightful and devious.

I'm in trouble.

"What's stopping you?"

Fuuuck.

"Nothing is stopping me. Absolutely nothing."

"Then do it." Her words break off on a gasp as I use my fingers to part her legs and find her clit like a heat-seeking missile.

"Some parts I've already memorized." I circle the small bundle of nerves.

"*Sawyer.*"

Her legs part and grant me more room.

"Do you like this?" I ask, pressing my thumb against her clit.

Involuntarily, she thrusts her hips, seeking more, claiming the pleasure she wants.

"Mmm. Mm-hmm."

Her eyes are closed, but ecstasy is clear in her expression.

"And what about this?" I ask. Spreading her thighs, I replace my fingers with my tongue.

"Gah." Her hips pulse, and she throws her arms out, scrambling for purchase.

Fuck, she tastes incredible. I circle my tongue in counterpoint

195

to her whimpers, and her fingers scrape along my scalp, creating goosebumps that ripple down my skin while my body continues to burn.

"Sawyer."

Her legs and hips move restlessly, and I place my hands in the crevice between her thigh and hip to hold her in place.

"Please," she begs.

I grunt, alternating my circles with light taps against her clit. She's so fucking close.

But I don't want her to come on my tongue. Not this time. It takes all my willpower to rip myself away, to straighten and climb onto the cushion with her. Her legs shake, and her moan is filled with longing. Gorgeous hazel eyes pop open to meet mine.

"Why did you stop?" Her question is practically a whimper.

Slamming my lips to hers, I push my tongue into her mouth the same way I want to drive my dick into her body.

"As much as I want you to come on my tongue, I need you wrapped around my cock more."

Her full-body shudder forces her breasts to rub against my chest and ratchets my need for her to another level.

"Are you ready for me, starling?" I glide my fingers between her legs and bite back most of a moan. "Fuck, you are."

"Stop teasing me."

I leave my hand where it is, my fingertips barely brushing her clit.

"Teasing you? Is that what I'm doing?"

"Yes!" She grips my face and pulls my lips back to hers in a kiss that conveys exactly how ready for me she is.

My control snarls and pulls against the fraying rope that holds it. My intent had been to worship her. To drive her up and over until we both shatter with pleasure. Instead, I'm losing control one intense kiss at a time. This overwhelming need to be with her, to connect on this level, is so powerful I can't fight it anymore.

Gripping her hands, I weave my fingers with hers and notch my dick with her pussy, swallowing hard and praying for just a little more control.

"Starling."

Long eyelashes flutter open, and slumberous eyes lock on mine as I push forward inch by agonizingly slow inch until my pelvis rests against hers.

"*Sawyer.*"

The emotions barreling down on both of us stoke the fire. My need is reflected in her eyes. In the way her fingers grip mine. The power of it sizzles in my blood and leaves no space safe from the way she makes me feel.

"I know. Me too."

I retreat until I'm almost fully out, then slowly thrust forward. She moans in response, and her muscles squeeze my dick until stars flicker in my vision.

"Fuck."

Down to my last thread of control, I grab her lips in another kiss, my tongue mimicking the motion of my hips with another slick retreat and deliberate thrust.

"I need you." She digs her nails into the muscles of my back and lifts her hips to meet me.

"I'm here."

Always.

Even if I don't say it out loud.

"Sawyer, I—I..." Her whispered words trail off, and her mouth forms an *O* as her muscles lock. Her gaze meets mine, frantic, overcome with lust. And something more.

It's the something more that does it. It sends me over the edge, and I can't hold back.

CHAPTER 18

EVIE

I love you.

The words are on the tip of my tongue. They beg to be set free while my orgasm curls my toes and crashes through my body. I want to close my eyes, to hide from every emotion Sawyer inspires, from every physical reaction that coalesces into the urge to confess my truth.

But I can't.

I bite my lips to stem the words that threaten to erupt.

It's too soon.

But it's not. It's been coming on since the first time we kissed. Physical attraction built and built. And now that I've discovered him, all of him, it's so much more.

I dig my fingers into his shoulders in an attempt to hold on to this moment as pleasure fizzes through my blood. When my hands slip against his sweat-slickened skin, he grunts and tunnels one arm under my neck so he can pull me closer. Close enough that his heart beats under my cheek, adding to the intense pleasure that lights my body on fire, one nerve ending at a time.

"Oh god," I murmur against his skin.

"Come with me." His words are forced through gritted teeth.

I'm trying to hold off my orgasm, but it's like using a sandbag to stop a tsunami—impossible in the face of an overwhelming power.

"I'm so close," I breathe, wrapping my legs tighter around him, but my whimper is lost in panted breaths and racing hearts.

He thrusts harder while his mouth finds my jaw. "Me too."

He rolls us, not stopping the rhythm, and this new position drives him deeper while his pelvis grinds against my clit.

"*Sawyer.*" Bright light washes through my vision, and the world around me shimmers before it disappears.

He's all I see. The pleasure he's wreaking on my body is all I feel.

I shouldn't love him. I fought the fall.

It's too dangerous.

But it's too late. And that realization unleashes the last thread I'm holding on to. Wave after wave crashes over me and breaks me into a million glittering stars. My hips falter, but he continues to move as a second orgasm rolls after the first. I cry out as the stars burst into flames.

He pulses once, twice, and stills as his own orgasm crests.

"Fuck, Evie."

The gravelly way he growls my name creates a shuddery aftershock, and I fall forward against his chest. So many emotions swirl through me, but the prominent one is happiness.

His hands roam my back, but otherwise, he is completely still. Recovering from the power of what just happened. Something has shifted between us. It's in his touch, the synchronicity of our heartbeats, and the way he keeps us where we are.

We don't say it out loud, but the difference is tangible. As I drift down from my state of euphoria, my mind and my heart discover two truths.

I love Sawyer King.

And there's no ignoring that.

But can I love him and keep him safe? Or will I have to let him go once our time here is up?

"I want to take you somewhere." Sawyer's chest rumbles under my cheek.

I'm not sure how much time has passed. We haven't moved in some time. No, we've lain together, soaking in the way we fit. Two puzzle pieces. Two halves of the same whole.

I rest my chin on my hand and survey him while he continues to gently glide his fingers along the bare skin of my back. It tickles. Almost.

"You already did."

"Heaven doesn't count, starling." One side of his mouth kicks up into a smirk.

I can't hold back a groan. "You're awful. But that wasn't what I meant."

He taps a finger to my nose, and his smile widens. Serious Sawyer is enough to make my panties damp. Smiling Sawyer? He incinerates said panties to nothing but ash.

I squirm against him and try to ignore the heat that builds in my core again. His semihard erection twitches against my leg, and my breath catches.

"What did you mean?" he asks.

How is it that I want him again? Is it again? Or is it still?

"Hmm?"

"What did you mean, starling?" His voice is full of humor.

I blink to break the sexual haze ready to take over my body. "You brought me here."

And this wild, majestic place has healed me in a way five years in the City of Angels couldn't. Or maybe it's the man holding me.

The realization that both have shared in my transformation is scary. It's a good thing I don't have to admit that out loud.

"It's like we've always been here," he murmurs.

"I don't want to leave," I whisper against his chest.

His hands still on my back for several breaths before he eventually resumes his lazy drawings.

"Where do you want to take me?" I ask.

"It's a surprise."

"Okay." I don't enjoy surprises. But from him? I'm in.

"Just like that?" he asks.

"I trust you."

That's been the hardest part of this. Trusting another person. With protecting me. With my body.

With my heart.

"What if I want to go outside?" he asks.

"Does that mean we have to get dressed?"

I've been enjoying cuddling with him under the blankets in my little nook. Only it's not just mine. It's ours.

He barks out a laugh and tightens his arms around me.

"We do. I may even have some cold weather gear you can borrow."

He's almost a foot taller than me. I can only imagine the way his gear will dwarf me.

"I don't think it'll fit."

"We'll figure it out."

An hour later, I'm bundled into one of his parkas while he tucks my hair under a fuzzy black beanie. I'm wearing my own sweater, a thermal that belongs to Sawyer—I only held it to my nose so I could inhale his spicy scent a handful of times—and a pair of leggings under my jeans.

"You need better boots," he grumbles.

"We just got these."

Before we left California, Sawyer took me to an outdoor supply store for actual boots instead of the dress boots I thought were fine for the trip. Now I needed more?

"Those are California boots. You need Alaska boots." He says it as if I should know what the difference is.

"What are 'Alaska' boots?"

"Something like these." He lifts his foot onto the bench in the entryway.

These have thick rubber soles and lined material instead of the soft but durable leather of my boots, which are built more for a hike than tromping through snow.

Despite the white stuff, I'm excited about going outside. Though I'm more excited to see where he wants to take me. Every day, aside from during the snowstorm, Sawyer has gone out on skis and returned an hour or two later. Is he taking me skiing?

Crap.

"I've never been skiing." The words rush out of my mouth.

"What?" He looks at me quizzically.

"I mean, if that's what we're doing. I've never been."

His fingers graze along my cheek as he tucks one last strand of hair up into the hat.

"We're not going skiing."

"Oh."

"I can teach you after..."

Neither of us acknowledges that no matter how close we've become, we've never talked about what happens after all of this ends.

What *does* come next?

"Ready?" he asks, yanking on a glove.

Mine are already on. Something else he lent me. My hands swim in them, but they're warm and tucked securely into my sleeves.

"Yeah."

The cool air bites into the exposed skin of my cheeks when we step out, though it's refreshing after so much time spent inside. Snow crunches under our feet as I trail him to the driveway and around the side of the house to a small shed built to blend in with the structure.

"I didn't notice this before," I tell him.

He shrugs. "I added it when I bought the place. I use it to store the snowmobile so the garage is open for stuff I may need when it storms. I built it so it didn't detract from the house—it's meant to blend in."

And it does. The wooden structure has been weathered to match the exterior of the house. It's just big enough to hold the single snowmobile that gleams in the shadows. He hands me a helmet from the hook on the wall before donning his.

"Two helmets?"

I can't stop the question before it comes out. He's already told me he hasn't brought anyone else here. Why am I suddenly jealous?

"I bought a second when West and Mikey came here. I have a four-wheeler in the garage. They used it the fall they were here on their honeymoon."

"Oh." A wave of relief hits me at his explanation, but it's immediately followed by embarrassment.

Pulling off his helmet, he presses a kiss to my forehead.

"You're the only one I've brought up here, starling. The only one I've wanted to share this place with."

"But Brad—"

"We could have gone to a different city or to any number of safe houses run by associates of mine. We didn't have to come here."

Warmth curls in my stomach at the implication. "Oh."

"Yeah, 'oh.'"

He takes my helmet from me and places it over my head. The padding around my ears and his full-face shield mutes his voice so I barely make out his directions once he puts his helmet on too.

"Stand right there. I'll get this out." He points to a spot just outside the shed door.

He swings gracefully onto the machine and cranks the engine. And before I can blink, he's next to me.

"Ever ridden on one of these?" he asks.

I shake my head. "No."

"Sit behind me."

With his help, I straddle the machine and scoot forward until I'm pressed against him.

"Hold on."

I wrap my arms around his waist, and he releases the throttle. Scenery blurs white around us as we speed away from the house and shoot along the pristine snow. I lean my head against his back while the wind rushes along my legs. My too-big jacket sleeves slap lightly in the breeze, but I'm not cold. Sawyer generates enough heat that it's impossible to be anything but warm. Only this heat starts from the inside and works its way out.

For the first time in years, genuine relief washes over me. The storm is lifting. The metaphorical sun thaws my body back to life. Because of Sawyer. My heart stutters in my chest at the reminder. I don't want our ride to stop. I need time.

Time to process all of this. To compartmentalize. To keep myself safe.

Despite what Sawyer thinks, it's *my* job to keep myself safe. To keep him safe. I just don't know how what we're doing plays into that. I'm still working through it all when we come to a stop. The sudden silence after the engine quiets is deafening.

Opening my eyes, I lift my head and take in our surroundings. We're as close to the bay as we can get. All that remains between it and us is snow and a rocky gray beach. Gentle waves lap against the shore, and farther out, a thin layer of ice sparkles when the sun peeks through the clouds.

Sawyer helps me dismount the snowmobile. A small smile hovers on his lips as he stands before me and gently removes my helmet. Once both helmets are situated on the seat, he reaches for my hand.

"Wow," I breathe as he leads me closer.

The one word isn't enough, but it's the only one I've got for now.

"You stare out the window in this direction a lot," he says.

I didn't realize I was so obvious about it. Or is he just that observant?

"There's...something about it. I can't help it," I say.

"I understand." He tugs me into his arms and presses his lips to the crown of my head. "I was the same way at first."

"At first?"

"Mmm."

"Does the view get old after a while? Did you get tired of it?"

I can't imagine that happening.

"Not tired exactly. I just...stopped looking." He studies my face, making butterflies swirl in my belly.

"What do you see when you do look?"

"Beauty."

His lips descend on mine, and the butterflies take flight. Their wings leave me breathlessly clinging to the man I never realized could be my missing half.

Is he?

Words aren't possible right now. So I kiss him instead, pouring every ounce of what he makes me feel into this kiss as that question swirls in my head.

CHAPTER 19

EVIE

*I*s it possible to rebuild walls around one's heart while simultaneously feeling closer to someone than ever?

Asking for a friend.

Okay, it's me. I'm the friend.

And I have no one to ask. Sure, I could call Mia again, but what exactly would I tell her?

I'm sorry my crazy stalker attacked you. Also, BT-dubs, I slept with the man who volunteered to be my bodyguard, and I might be in love with him, but I have no idea how he feels about me?

I snort a laugh.

"What's so funny?" Sawyer asks, stepping into the room dressed in dark gray ski pants and a black thermal shirt that molds to the muscles of his chest and arms.

Damn.

"Skiing?" I ask.

It's a stupid question. Since the storm has let up, he's been back at it every morning. But now he's added afternoon trips as well.

The insecure part of me wonders if he needs the breaks from

me. If he wishes I wasn't here anymore. He still touches me. He still kisses me.

But it's different.

"Yeah. I won't be gone long."

I want to ask him why. Why, when I think we're getting closer, when I stop fighting how I feel about him, does he choose to spend as little time around me as possible?

"Is it going to storm again?"

It's early afternoon, but with clouds that blot out the light, it looks closer to dusk.

He closes the distance and stares out at the swiftly moving clouds. "It doesn't look like it. The clouds are dark, but they're moving in the wrong direction to create another storm here."

"How do you know?"

He's moved close enough to touch me, but he doesn't. "I got caught in a storm once. Got smart about when to stay inside." One corner of his lips tilts up in a smile.

"You're sure?"

"Are you worried about me, starling?"

"Yes," I answer honestly.

His eyes soften, and he shifts close enough to press his lips to my forehead, resting his hands lightly on my shoulders.

"I'll be safe. Don't worry."

I want to wrap my fingers around his forearms and hold him here, but he pulls away before I can. He's almost to the door when I finally get the nerve to ask him the question on my mind.

"Is something wrong?"

"Wrong?" He turns toward me, his blue eyes studying me carefully.

"Have I done something to upset you?"

"No."

"Is there something else you're worried about?"

"Besides Brad?" he asks.

Brad is the ever-present thorn in our side. Still hiding despite how hard Cole and Sydney are working to find him.

"Yeah."

"Like what?" he asks, brows furrowed in confusion.

I blow out a breath.

"Do you regret what's happened between us? If so, that's fine, you can tell—"

One second, he's across the room, and in the next, his lips lay siege to mine like a Viking berserker intent on claiming me. He doesn't break the kiss until I'm tugging on his hair and my lungs burn for oxygen.

Fine by me. If he'd keep kissing me like that, I'd learn to survive without oxygen.

"Does that answer your question?"

"What question?" I ask.

All that's left of me is the tingling sensation in my lips and the throbbing in my core.

"I regret nothing that's happened between us, starling. Not a damn thing. Never doubt that."

With one more chaste press of his lips to mine, he's gone, and I'm left alone with my thoughts once again.

"I'm confused," Mia says almost an hour later.

That last kiss was the push I needed. I couldn't stay trapped in my own thoughts. Despite the massive amount of guilt I carry, I needed someone. I needed Mia. When I tried to apologize, she told me to quit being dumb and give her the dirt on Sawyer. Okay, then. But after I've spilled my guts, she's in the same boat I'm in.

"Now you know how I feel," I tell her, rocking in Sawyer's desk chair.

I can't sit still. The sensation that I'm doing something I shouldn't pricks at my stomach.

Should I be in here? Using Sawyer's phone? He told me to

make myself at home, and he gave me his passcode, but being in here without him feels like crossing a line.

"Obviously he likes you. And you like him," she says.

I more than like him, but I don't bother to correct her. I don't want to get into the more-than-like feelings right now.

"Yeah."

"Have you told him?"

"No."

"Why not?"

"I…what if…what if he doesn't feel the same way about me?"

There are so many other issues I should be concerned about right now. Like keeping him safe. But that's becoming harder to focus on in the wake of what's happening between us.

"Wasn't it you who knocked some sense into me when I was being an idiot about Garrett?" she asks.

I don't like where she's going with her question.

"Well, yeah, but that was—"

"Different? No, it's not."

"Neither of you was in danger," I argue.

"Do you think Sawyer is going to let anything happen to you?"

"No." I've never worried about that.

"What's the next argument?"

Damn her for knowing me so well.

"Mia, I'm serious," I say, circling back.

"So am I. Spill it."

"You and Garrett have known each other forever," I tell her.

"So?"

"I barely know Sawyer."

"But you know what matters."

I may not know the trivial stuff, but it's true. Amani. His time in the military. He's opened up about things I don't think he's mentioned to anyone else. But does that mean something, or am I making more of it than it actually is? He's never given me a reason to question. But I learned a long time ago to listen to my gut. And my gut is telling me something isn't quite right.

"You're not helping," I whine.

"I could add Kayla to the call. Maybe she could provide insight."

So we can tell his baby sister I might be in love with him?

No thanks.

"I realize she's your best friend, Mia, but...I'd rather keep this between us for now."

"That's fair. I wish I had a crystal ball so I could tell you what to do."

"I wish you did too. Maybe I just needed a sanity check. A reminder that I'm not going crazy."

"And it's not like you can talk to him about all this," she adds drily.

"Then he'd surely be running for the hills."

"He would not. He'd be lucky to have you, and I think he knows that."

I should already know this. I do. Or I used to. But now?

I'm not so sure.

"Thanks for the vote of confidence."

"Anytime. But I better go. We're heading to the parentals' for dinner tonight."

Mia's and Garrett's parents are still next-door neighbors. It's why they've known each other since childhood.

"Just be safe, okay?" I don't know what I would do if Brad found her again.

"That bodyguard will be around somewhere. So will Garrett."

She says it so nonchalantly. Like she isn't afraid of Brad.

"Mia."

"It'll be fine. If he gets anywhere near us, I think I might need to bail Garrett out of jail."

"Why are you bailing me out of jail?" Garrett's voice is muffled in the background.

"I'll explain later. Okay, Ev. I'll talk to you later. Keep me posted on how things are going."

"I will."

Once we've said our goodbyes, I set the phone on the desk and search the window for signs of Sawyer. He said he wouldn't be gone long, and it's been an hour. He's usually back by now. The darker clouds from earlier are gone, but it's getting later—closer to nightfall—and anxiety is a rock in the pit of my stomach.

Sawyer's phone buzzes against the desk, and I jump, then roll my eyes at my own foolishness.

"This isn't a movie with kidnappers calling and demanding ransom."

The device doesn't continue to buzz, so it's not even a phone call.

Brad?

"Right. Because he has Sawyer's number," I scoff.

The phone vibrates again, and I reach over to pick it up.

COLE: He took the bait.

COLE: It's not too late to change your mind.

Brad? And bait? Too late to change his mind about what? Why would Sawyer change his mind? My fingers hover over the keypad, ready to type in the code to text Cole back.

I shouldn't.

But maybe there's something I should know. Something Sawyer isn't telling me.

"Starling?"

The deep gravel of Sawyer's voice is so unexpected I shriek, and my flailing arms release the cell phone I've been so preoccupied by. Sawyer snags it and saves it from its certain collision course with the wall.

Because of course he does.

"Whoa there, slugger." He pockets his phone and gives me a

grin that's hard to return with the way my heart pounds in my chest.

"You're back." I wrap my arms around him as relief floods my body.

"Are you okay?" He puts his hands on my arms and tries to shift away, to find the danger he needs to protect me from.

But I cling tighter. Because there's no physical danger.

The only danger I face is having my heart broken.

"I didn't see you." My voice is muffled against his shirt.

"I came back a different way. There was a tree down across the trail I usually take. Are you okay?"

"Mm-hmm. I was getting worried about you, though." I bury my nose in the fabric of his shirt and breathe deeply.

"You don't need to worry about me. I know all the trails around here."

"I figured."

"But you were still worried." It's a statement more than a question.

"Yeah."

"Why?"

"Brad," I say.

"What about him?"

"What if he did something to you? He attacked Mia, and I—"

Gripping my chin softly, he tilts my head back so I'm forced to look at him.

"How many times do I have to tell you I'm not afraid of him?"

"What if he finds out we're here?"

He tenses.

"No one knows about this place unless I want them to know."

"Do you want Brad to know? Is that what Cole meant?"

He steps back, and cool air rushes between us, sending a shiver down my spine.

"Cole?" he asks.

"He texted you a few minutes ago. Just before you got back. What did he mean by bait?"

Do I really want to know?

No.

Yes.

Maybe.

"It's...complicated," he eventually says.

Complicated my ass.

"Try me."

"The team and I came up with a way to hopefully get Brad out of hiding."

"How?" I ask.

"Evie."

Evie. Not starling. What the hell is going on? What is he not telling me?

"Are you using Mia as bait?"

"What?" He reels back. "No."

"What about me?"

"What about you?"

"Am I the bait?" Nerves swirl in my stomach as I wait for his response.

"Do you trust me?" he asks, his eyes locked on mine.

"Yes, but—"

"I promised to protect you."

"I know."

"Please. Trust me then. I'm going to get Brad where I want him—away from you—and I'm going to protect you. Always."

"I'm not used to being protected," I tell him.

His eyes soften, and he cups my cheek. "Obviously."

His lips tilt in the semblance of a smile. It looks like all the others he's given me, but it doesn't feel the same.

"I care about you," he admits, ghosting his lips over the top of my head.

It's not an admission of love. But I don't expect one.

"I care about you too," I whisper.

But I can't shake the feeling that things between us have shifted again.

And I don't know if that's a good thing.

Or a bad one.

It's snowing again. Flakes whirl furiously outside the window, attacking the glass with violent taps, while the house groans at the intensity of the wind.

"Sawyer?" I call out, wandering through the house.

He should be here.

He knows when he needs to stay inside.

I'll be right back.

He wouldn't go skiing in this. Right?

The window ledge is icy under my shaky fingers as I lean against the glass and squint into the storm for any sign of him.

He has to be upstairs.

"Sawyer?" I call his name louder than before as I rush up the steps.

But there's no evidence of him in our bedroom or bathroom.

"Downstairs."

I race down until I can confirm he's not in the gym or the bedroom he slept in when we arrived. His office is empty, though his cell phone buzzes along the desk inside, barely audible above the wind.

Where is he?

The outer door draws me closer. My feet move like magnets along the tile until I clutch the frigid knob and pull. Wind howls into the entryway, and the snow smacks against my face.

"Sawyer!"

He promised he wouldn't go out in this.

But where is he?

I bolt upright in bed, gasping for warm air as the ice shards left over from my dream prick at my lungs. It was so real.

My feet are ice, even though I'm tucked under the blankets.

"Starling?"

I heave out a sigh of relief. Sawyer is beside me. His voice is muffled slightly by his pillow, and his words are thick with sleep.

He's safe.

My heart slows back to a normal rhythm, and the frozen sensation in my lungs ebbs as I take in another breath, then another.

"I'm sorry. I didn't mean to wake you."

My own voice is hoarse, like I was really screaming his name into the wind.

"Are you okay?" he asks.

"Mmm. Just a bad dream."

He tugs me down next to him and wraps his arm around me. His warmth is a shock against my cool skin, making me tense for a heartbeat, but I quickly settle closer into him, nestling my hips into the cradle of his thighs.

He groans. "Don't start something you can't finish, starling."

His dick hardens against my ass, and the adrenaline still coursing through me morphs into a different type of energy. Rotating in his arms, I bracket his hip with my leg.

"Who says I can't finish?"

CHAPTER 20

SAWYER

I've forgotten what it feels like to wake up slowly. That lazy reawakening of senses. It's been years since I've allowed myself this simple pleasure. Too often, sleep is a necessity. A job that needs to be done, like everything else.

Now, though, there's a silence outside that blankets the noise of the rest of the world. I'm cocooned in the warm blankets, wrapped in the sweet scent of a woman while my fingers tingle with the memory of the silk of her skin under my fingertips. Blinking my eyes open, I expect to find Evie still curled up next to me. But all that greets me is the navy-blue encased pillow with an indentation in the middle.

With a groan, I climb out of bed and pull my pants back on, and without bothering with a shirt, I head downstairs.

At the doorway to the kitchen, I freeze, and all the air leaves my lungs.

For the first time since Evie started staying with me, she's singing out in the open.

Not humming.

Not hidden by the shower and a closed door.

She stands at the sink, just a few steps away from the electric kettle, wearing my T-shirt and nothing else. The image is beautiful.

But the music?

It's heart-stopping. It reaches into my chest and tugs on pieces I thought I lost years ago. I recognize the song—"Iris" by the Goo Goo Dolls—but I've never heard it like this.

It's…haunting.

The kettle shuts off and the music stops. I want to beg her to keep going. Sit before her and listen all day. Instead, I move closer and wrap my arms around her middle.

"I didn't know you were awake," she says.

"I woke up and came looking for you," I say into the skin between her neck and shoulder.

She drops her head back against my chest. I could stay like this forever. The urge is so strong I want to hold on to it with both hands. Instead, I squeeze her a little tighter.

"Can I tell you something?" I murmur.

"Mm-hmm."

"You have an amazing voice."

I brace for her to stiffen or pull away, but she stays where she is, and her body remains pliant in my arms.

"I—I don't sing much anymore."

There's a pain in her voice so real it sends a mix of anger and sadness swirling through me. Anger at the man who took away her voice. Sadness because she believes it's still gone.

I'm going to convince her otherwise.

"I know." I clear my throat. "I have a confession."

She cranes her neck and surveys me. "What's that?"

I can't resist the urge to drop a small kiss on the end of her nose.

"I used to listen to you in the shower. I could hear you…"

"You listened to me in the shower?"

"Just singing," I amend, the tips of my ears burning in embarrassment.

Fuck, I sound like a creeper.

The corner of her mouth twists in a small smile.

"Can I tell you something?" she asks.

"Anything."

"I know."

"You know?"

She nods, and her face lights up.

"So when you sang in the shower…"

"I knew you were listening."

"That's diabolical," I tell her.

"I didn't know at first. But after a while, it became obvious. No matter where you were when I locked myself in the bathroom, when I was done, your bedroom door was always closed. I picked up on it." She shrugs.

"Would you sing for me without hiding in the shower?"

She nibbles on her lower lip and turns her gaze back toward the window.

"You don't have to," I tell her.

"I know," she says, turning those beautiful green eyes back on me. "I want to." She spins in my arms and locks her hands behind my back.

"Maybe I'll play guitar while you sing," I suggest.

"Maybe you'll sing with me," she counters.

"You know what, starling? I just might," I tell her and brush my lips against the crown of her head.

Anything for her.

Anything except losing at Trivial Pursuit.

"How on earth did you know that the Aral Sea has shrunk by 90 percent?" Evie asks incredulously.

I shrug.

"Starling, I tried to tell you—I've played this game a lot."

"By yourself?"

"Sometimes." I nod. "Other times I play online. I have another one of them in LA too."

"But it's pop culture. What the heck does the Aral Sea have to do with pop culture? I thought it would be questions about music or TV shows or—"

"Or something you thought you could win?" I arch an eyebrow.

Pink infuses her cheeks.

"Maybe," she admits.

"So you were trying to cheat?" I pick up the right color piece and drop it into my almost full token.

"No."

She might deny it, but the color in her cheeks gets deeper.

"I think so. I told you I'm a trivia nerd."

"That only explains why you have every edition ever made. Not how you knew that Leonardo da Vinci was the Renaissance artist who could bend a horseshoe with his bare hands or that video games are protected by freedom of speech." She crosses her arms, the last card still clutched in her fingers.

I fight back a cringe and shift forward so I can pull the card away before she mutilates it in her indignation.

"I'm sorry?"

She huffs a breath. "You hustled me. But instead of a pool shark, you're a trivia one."

"We tried playing Scrabble," I remind her.

Although her response when I played the word *Quizzical* was a lot like this.

"How are you so good at all these games?" she asks, her lower lip stuck out in a cute pout.

I fight to bite back my smile. "We'll find a game that puts us on even ground."

She glares at me, her eyes narrowing at the way my lips twitch.

"Like what?"

"Jenga? Dominoes? Poker? You like Poker?"

"I don't know how to play."

"Ahh. You'll have beginners' luck, then."

"Maybe."

"Never knew you were so competitive. You're quite…"

Sassy is the wrong word. If I say that, I'm liable to get punched.

"What?" she asks.

"Determined."

Her facial features relax slightly, and I breathe a sigh of relief.

"I've been this way for as long as I can remember. I got grounded once for hitting my brother on the head with the Monopoly board."

Finally, a smile blooms across her face, and I stop holding mine back.

"I haven't thought about that in years," she says.

"It's a good memory?"

"Oddly enough, one of my favorites."

"Violent, are you?"

She giggles. "Not normally."

"Just don't hit me with any Monopoly boards." I pull myself up and lean over so I can brush my lips to hers. "Are you done with games for the night?"

She nods. "It's probably for the best."

"I can think of one thing you do better than I do…" I trail off, then bark a laugh at how colorful her cheeks get.

"What are you thinking about, starling?"

"N-n-nothing."

"Uh-huh."

"What are you talking about?"

"Cooking. You're probably the best cook I've ever met."

"I just make basic food." She shrugs. "Nothing gourmet."

"Gourmet or not, it tastes good."

My stomach growls to back up my point.

"How about dinner?" I hold out a hand, and when she slides her palm against mine, I pull her to her feet.

We walk into the kitchen silently, and she quickly gets to work pulling out ingredients.

"Hey, Sawyer?" She looks up from the mixing bowl she's using.

"Yes?"

"Do you think after dinner you could teach me how to play poker?"

"Sure. I've got a deck of cards around here somewhere. We'll just have to find something for chips."

"Maybe we could play strip poker."

My dick hardens immediately at the thought, and my voice sounds strangled when I can finally answer her.

"I think that can be arranged."

But the big question is. Do I let her win? Or is there really a loser in that game?

CHAPTER 21

EVIE

"Concentrate," Sawyer demands, tightening his grip on my wrist.

The gentle lover who demands my pleasure is gone. This is the battle-hardened warrior who expects me to fight back.

"I'm trying." I pluck at his iron-like fingers where they press against my skin.

It doesn't hurt. It's not supposed to. We're training. But it's useless. I'm stuck. For the last two hours, we've practiced self-defense moves, and he's taught me a few new ones. My body is tired. My hair is half out of its ponytail, and my arms and legs are heavy. I want to give up. But this man is driven by some kind of invisible force. We've worked far longer today than we have in any of our other sessions.

"I need a break," I tell him. My shoulders droop and I sag against him.

"After you get loose."

I groan. "Sawyer."

"Come on, starling, I know you can do this."

Squaring my shoulders, I take a deep breath and yank my arm. He doesn't budge.

"Not even close," he taunts.

The moves he's taught me have become progressively more challenging, and with each one, he uses more strength. Because a real attacker won't take it easy on me. He's also discovered that if he gets me angry enough, my fight returns, no matter how tired I am.

The first time, I didn't expect it, and it took time—and an apology from him—for my anger to fade. By now I know what he's doing.

"This isn't funny," I whine.

"Who's laughing?" he counters, cocking a brow.

He's correct. Neither of us is. But the sneer on his face pisses me off. He reels me in closer, eliminating the little bit of headway I've made.

"Don't just stand there and let me win. Fight back."

Another inch eliminated despite the way I dig my feet into the carpet.

"A real attack won't move this slowly. You won't have time to fight," he says, but the tone of his voice has softened.

He's right. But it doesn't mean his newest technique doesn't make me want to either punch him in the face or stomp my foot like a two-year-old.

With a growl, I rotate my wrist toward his thumb and take a quick step to my left. The move works, and his grip loosens for the fraction of a second I need to tug my arm loose and put enough distance between us to keep him from immediately reaching out again.

I lost count of how many lessons he's subjected me to over the last few days.

Get away and stay away.

"Yes. Good." Pride shines in his gaze, and a genuine smile replaces the sneer.

He takes a step toward me, and I retreat, keeping my distance.

"Is your wrist okay?" He nods toward my arm.

Until now, I didn't realize I was cradling it so protectively.

Lowering my hands to my sides, I breathe out, willing the tension in my shoulders to subside.

"It's fine."

"Can I see?" He steps cautiously toward me.

"I guess." Holding my ground, I lift my arm.

Gentle fingers probe my wrist. But I was being honest. It doesn't hurt.

"I'm sorry," he murmurs, bringing his lips to my pulse point.

"You didn't hurt me," I tell him. "I'm fine."

"Fine? You're sure? Not still pissed off?"

"No. I know why you're doing it."

His eyes go wide, and a fleeting look of alarm flashes in them. It disappears so quickly, though, that I question whether I imagined it.

"Doing what?" His voice is calm despite the flash of panic.

"You want me angry enough to fight back," I explain.

The corner of his mouth kicks up in a half smile. "It works."

"Now that I know you're doing it."

He steps closer and envelops me in a hug. "I'm sorry I made you mad the other day. I was only trying to find a way to get you to fight back."

"I know."

"I need to make sure you know what to do when..."

"When what?" I ask.

"*If* something happens and I'm not here."

"Are you going somewhere?"

"Not planning on it."

"Then why do you keep saying things like that?"

"It's important," he says a little cryptically.

"Why?"

"Because it needs to be muscle memory. Instinct. Pure reflex," he explains.

"Why?"

"Fuck, you sound like Benji." He runs a hand down his face.

"Because I want to understand things that may affect me?" I ask, crossing my arms. "That's bullshit."

"I'll tell you something I don't tell him. Ready? I don't always have the answers. I operate on instinct more than anything else."

"And instinct is telling you I need to know all this?"

He grunts in response. His fingers find my hips, and my legs nearly buckle. Our double sessions have my muscles protesting more than usual. But he still has enough energy to go out twice a day to ski the trails around the cabin. The man is a machine.

"That feels good," I groan.

"You're tense," he murmurs.

"You try pleasing a drill sergeant and see how you feel."

He barks out a laugh. "Been there, done that. And something tells me mine was a hell of a lot harder on me than yours is on you."

"I'll be the judge of that," I tease.

"Take my word for it."

He spins me in his arms and kneads at the muscles in my shoulders until he finds a particularly sensitive spot on my neck. His thumbs work along either side of my spine from my neck to my tailbone, then he rests his hands on my hips and tugs me backward. His erection presses against my backside, and his lips find the sensitive spot below my ear.

"Sawyer." I tilt my head as he nibbles down to the tendon where my neck and shoulder meet.

He hooks his thumbs into the waistband of my leggings and pulls.

"We should eat lunch," I tell him, although food is the last thing on my mind.

"Are you hungry?" He sinks his teeth into my shoulder roughly.

I cry out at the pain mixed with pleasure that zaps through me. In response, he laves the spot with his tongue. His splayed fingers brush the edge of my panties and drive my need for him higher.

I whimper. "N-no. Are you?"

He plucks at the elastic band around my waist and lets it snap back into place.

"I'm hungry. But not for food."

This time my knees do buckle.

He loops an arm around my waist and pulls me to him, supporting my weight. It's not the first time we've foregone food to focus on each other. His *appetite* is almost insatiable. But mine is no better. If we're not working on self-defense or going through the motions of eating or sleeping, we're locked in each other's arms, exploring with our lips and hands. When he leaves, I have the house to myself to read, and we've even attempted Trivial Pursuit again.

I still didn't win. But it was fun trying to distract him.

"Neither am I—"

My words end on a gasp as he cups me over my panties.

He's a man possessed. But if possession equates to pleasure that leaves me boneless against him the way I am a little while later, I don't mind at all. It's dark by the time I can think beyond the pleasure.

"Sawyer?"

We're in bed, even though we really should head to the kitchen to scrounge up dinner.

"Hmm?"

I rest my chin on his chest and survey him. "What is—I mean, why all of a sudden..."

How do I phrase my question?

"All of a sudden what?" he asks.

"You seem very attracted to me."

"I *am* very attracted to you." He waggles his eyebrows.

I giggle. "Yes, I can tell. But for the last few days, we've done this more." I wave a hand between his naked body and mine.

Something flickers in his eyes—Regret? Hesitation? Guilt?—but it's gone before I can identify it.

"Is that a bad thing?" he asks.

"Well, no, but—"

He doesn't let me finish. His lips claim mine, and his tongue rekindles the flame I swear he just put out. Those flames scatter my questions in every direction until he breaks the kiss on a groan.

"Food. We need food," I tell him.

As if on cue, my stomach growls loudly.

"Yeah." He chuckles. "I guess we do."

CHAPTER 22

SAWYER

*M*y conscience gnaws at me, the acid eating away at my stomach until I want to puke.

Evie is sprawled across our bed on her stomach. The early morning sunlight peeks through the windows and adds a golden hue to everything in the room—including the highlights in her hair. I want nothing more than to crawl back into bed with her, to pull her into my arms and forget that, for a week, I've known it was only a matter of time before Brad would show up.

When I shared my plan with Ed, he cautioned me against it. After the break-in at Evie's, he was concerned that Brad was becoming obsessed as well as violent.

But the path was already set by then. Brad was coming.

The text from Cole this morning confirms it.

COLE

He's here.

Since Cole leaked our location, Sydney has been keeping an eye on flight confirmations. In the event that Brad used an alias to purchase an airline ticket, Cole posted himself at LAX, but it turns out that wasn't necessary. Unsurprisingly, the bastard booked the flight under his own name and using his own credit card. Now he's in Alaska. And so is Cole. He made sure he was on the same flight. One that landed last night. If he isn't here yet, he will be soon.

I've barely been able to look Evie in the eye. I'm responsible for bringing her worst nightmare to our bubble of happiness. And I didn't tell her.

You're protecting her.

But a voice that sounds a hell of a lot like Michaela keeps interjecting. Insisting I'm not protecting Evie. Reminding me that I've been lying to her. And the discomfort that settles in with that voice has my stomach in knots.

After the last week, she knows every self-defense technique I do. They'll be muscle memory if she needs them. Not that the knowledge lessens the pain in my gut.

No. I shake my head, clearing away the negative thoughts. The nagging voice.

She's not going to need them.

I'll fake out Brad by skiing toward Ed's, but I'll double back on foot and catch him before he gets anywhere near her. If I fail, Cole will be there.

She won't be alone.

Always.

I'll always be there to protect her. She doesn't have to face any more demons alone. She'll be free to live her life. Even if it means I'm not part of it. Because what woman, when faced with the freedom to pursue her dreams, would shackle herself to a man still haunted by his past?

I love her. But loving her means setting her free. Just like in the poem I recited to her. She's the starling, and I'm the man doing everything I can to set her free. Only I'm determined to succeed.

My phone beeps in my pocket, and Evie stirs in her sleep, her brows wrinkling with the disturbance.

Fuck.

I silence the device and check the screen.

COLE

In position.

It's my cue to leave, but my feet stay glued to the floor. She murmurs my name in her sleep and shifts positions so that one perfect breast peeks out of the covers.

Fuck.

My dick hardens in a painful rush. I palm the bulge and apply enough pressure to ease the ache. The dusky pink of her nipple hardens in the cool air, and she shifts again. Mustering all the self-control I have, I lean over and ease the covers into place to hide her beautiful body.

I ghost my lips along her temple and breathe in the faint traces of lavender that linger on her skin.

"I love you," I whisper.

Dragging myself away from her is an impossible feat. But I focus on the end goal and make my way down the stairs to the kitchen. I snag the notepad I left on the island and scribble a note so she doesn't worry.

Starling,
I've gone for a quick ski. I'll be home soon.
-Sawyer

I prop the note next to the coffee maker and square my shoulders. It's too late to stop things now. The pendulum is already in motion. All I can do is pray it goes as planned. The stairs to the basement are the hardest steps I take—the path to my personal execution.

Well, that's dramatic and morbid.

It's not that bad. But the guilt makes each step a slog through molasses. I change my mind with every step I take. *I need to stay here. I need to leave.* All the way to the bottom, where I grab my parka, hat, and gloves. Bright light filters through the window next to the door, at odds with the darkness that encroaches on my vision.

Dark equals safety.

Evie's light calls me back upstairs and demands I stay.

You have a mission.

Even so, it doesn't make stepping into the frozen air any easier. I've grabbed a pack I placed by the door so it looks like I'll be gone longer than I intend to be. There's no sign of Brad or of Cole, but the fine hairs on the back of my neck stand up. Proof that I'm being watched.

I pretend not to notice. Instead, I move leisurely to the storage closet where I keep my skis. Once they're strapped on, I set off in the direction of the trees. I go slower than I usually do and take a different path, one that goes farther into the hard woods, where the light barely breaks through the thick pines. It's colder here, and a shiver works its way down my spine, despite the exertion.

The gentle glide of my skis along the frozen snow is the only sound. The world around me is unnaturally still. As if something has disturbed the beauty of this place. My gut tells me he's close. I wait until I'm just past the halfway point through the forest before I stop and kneel to fidget with a ski. Nothing's wrong with it, but this provides me with an excuse to stop. Head down, I scan the area covertly. But there are no signs of him. Shit.

An uneasiness I haven't felt in years settles in my gut. The last time was in a desert instead of in a frozen tundra. He shouldn't be this hard to find. Surely, he's left a trace somewhere close by. I can't fiddle with my ski forever, so I straighten and lean back to stretch the muscles in my back.

"Make your move, asshole," I murmur, barely moving my lips.

Another quick survey of the trees surrounding me yields nothing, but the rock in my stomach grows bigger.

Screw this. I'm going home.

I've skied about ten feet when a sharp pain radiates through the back of my head. My vision tunnels, and I fall to my knees, fighting to stay conscious. He finally showed himself.

Find him.

But the darkness that presses down is too much, and I fall forward, landing face down in the cold powder. It tingles and burns where it touches my skin as I struggle to stand, to stay awake, to find him. But the buzzing in my head intensifies, and without my permission, my eyes drop closed.

CHAPTER 23

EVIE

*T*he sunlight that streams through the windows is bright enough to make me bury my head beneath the blankets.

"I want to sleep," I mumble.

If Sawyer has future plans to wake me up in the middle of the night like he did last night—head buried between my legs as he brings me to orgasm—he'll need to invest in curtains for this room. Though it would be a shame to cover up the views of the bay.

It takes a minute for it to dawn on me, but once it does, sleep is the last thing on my mind. This is home. I'm making a life with Sawyer, and it doesn't terrify me the way it should. I want this life with him. I want the future that hovers so clearly in my imagination.

"Sawyer?"

I reach out, not surprised when his side of the bed is empty and cool. He rarely sleeps.

Has he always been this way? Or was this something left over from his military days?

In order to ask him, I need to find him. My body aches deliciously as I move with slug-like speed from the bed and toss on my pajama pants and Sawyer's T-shirt before I stagger downstairs.

"Coffee first. Then Sawyer," I tell myself.

My stomach growls, a reminder of all the calories I've been burning—both in the gym and during my nocturnal activities with him. Warmth infuses my cheeks, and my body heats at the same time. Until Sawyer, I didn't know that was possible.

You didn't think a lot of things were possible.

I shake my head and continue downstairs, though the muscles in my legs protest the entire way. They may be tight from all the time I've spent in the gym, but the soreness between them is all Sawyer.

"Focus, Ev. Coffee. Sawyer. Breakfast. He's probably hungry too."

I'm hungry, but not for food.

How many times has he used that line on me? Regardless, it never fails to create an ache in my core. Even when it's only a memory.

I shuffle into the kitchen and find the coffee pot full and a notepad propped next to it.

Starling,
I've gone for a quick ski. I'll be home soon.
-Sawyer

It's not signed with love or any other type of closing endearment that would explain why my heart stutters in my chest. It's what he wrote.

Home.

Maybe I'm not alone when I picture a future together. One

with Sawyer and me here on weekend getaways. It would be even cozier with a few additional personal touches—colorful throw pillows on the couch, shelves with books and pictures scattered on them, and kitchen gadgets on the counter. It's so real that when I blink and it disappears, it leaves grief behind.

How can I grieve something when I've never even had it?

Our future hasn't happened yet. But I want it to.

I love him.

In this quiet moment, without lust to intensify the sensation, I can admit how in love with him I am. How a part of me is missing because he's not here.

The ache in my chest is real.

My stomach growls again. With a sigh, I open the cabinet and grab the toaster. I don't know why he keeps it up there, but we can debate about where to keep it later. Because suddenly, I know the exact place I would leave it out on the counter.

"I want it to be real," I whisper.

Long weekends, family vacations, a romantic getaway sprinkled in the mix. I want it all with Sawyer. Is that the home he envisions too?

Peanut butter toast finished and in hand, I eat as I stare out the window, lost in what could be. We're way past the client-professional relationship. And the friendship I promised myself would be enough.

He *is* my friend. He's also my protector. But he's so much more.

Does he love me? Could he?

I swore I would never risk another relationship, but how could I go back to barely living now that I've discovered what a full life could be? Does he think about what happens next—what life could look like after all of this?

I care about you.

Could he mean love? Is he just too afraid to say the words?

Aren't you?

I'm terrified. But what scares me more is the thought that if I don't speak up, I risk living in this weird space forever. One of us has to risk our current balance so we can either move forward or move on.

"I need to tell him."

I want a life with Sawyer. Nights on the couch. Saturday mornings in bed followed by Saturday morning cartoons. A little boy with bright blue eyes and red hair. A quiet, observant little girl who's a carbon copy of her daddy. A lifetime of memories. I want it all.

I have to tell him. I can't wait until this nightmare with Brad is over. Not even for him to return home. I need to tell him. Right now. If I wait, I may talk myself out of it. I'll convince myself I'm content to keep everything the way it is.

I don't want to settle for dreaming. I have to go for what I want. Abandoning my toast, I race for the stairs. I'll layer up with the gear he dug out for me, then follow his tracks. He's never gone too long, so surely, he hasn't gone far. He's probably already on his way back.

The shatter of glass takes a heartbeat to register. Small shards rain down and plink against the stone floor, scattering rays of sunlight through the space. It isn't until a gloved hand reaches through the window and twists the deadbolt that I understand. And by then, I'm stuck on the last stair, paralyzed by fear.

"S-S-Sawyer?" I croak as my heart threatens to pound out of my chest.

Maybe he forgot his key. Maybe he lost it in the snow.

I know better. He's too methodical and meticulous for that.

Run! My brain comes back online, and my flight response kicks in.

I turn to flee back upstairs.

Back to safety.

But it's too late.

Fingers wrapped in black leather grip my wrist and yank me backward. Bits of glass bite sharply into the soft soles of my bare feet, and the pain takes over.

"Hello, songbird."

CHAPTER 24

SAWYER

*T*he darkness is thick and sticky, holding me down while I struggle to break free.

God damnit.

With every ounce of strength I possess, I fight against it, cracking my eyelids just enough to be blinded by bright light. My head pounds, but I power through, forcing my eyes the rest of the way open. My vision swims, and my stomach rolls. A bitter flavor coats my mouth.

I lift my head just enough to shove a hand between my tingling cheek and the snow beneath it. The slight movement makes my vision blur, and I close my eyes and fight the throb in my temples so the darkness doesn't pull me back under.

Fuck. What happened?

"Sawyer! Sawyer!"

The voice is frantic and muffled. Like someone speaking underwater. Groaning, I roll over and come face to face with Cole, who's looming over me wearing a panicked expression.

What's he doing here? The sluggish question brings with it a litany of memories.

Cole.

Brad.

Evie.

"Fuck!" I rocket to a seated position and immediately scan my body for any other injuries. Except for the burning in my cheek and the pressure and fogginess in my head, I'm fine. But Evie isn't.

She's in danger.

I plant my hands in the snow and push, but Cole places his hands on my shoulders to keep me seated.

"Whoa."

"Where's Brad?" I grit out.

Speaking makes the throb in my head worse. But now isn't the time. We have to find Brad. Unless Cole subdued him. Maybe that's why we're here instead of racing back to the cabin to save Evie.

"He took off after he chucked this at the back of your head." He hefts a rock about the size of a potato.

I probe the back of my head until I find the spot where the rock connected. Pain lances down my spine, and the dizziness returns with a vengeance.

"Why aren't you following him? Where's Evie?"

The color that leeches from Cole's face is all the answer I need. Evie is still at home. Alone. Unprotected. Shit. What if she's still asleep? I'm not sure how much time has passed since I left.

Getting to my feet is a challenge, but I push past the physical struggle.

"Why aren't you following him?" I snap.

"I was worried about you. I saw you hit the ground—"

"I can take care of myself. The plan was to stay with him."

"I did," he argues. "I followed him while he was following you." He rubs a gloved hand over his face. "I was worried he killed you. Even after I confirmed that you were breathing, it took ten minutes to get you to come to. I was starting to worry—"

He cuts off, a muscle ticking in his jaw.

No soldier left behind.

On the battlefield, there are no exceptions. We brought every fallen brother home with us. The sights and sounds of battle after battle on hot desert nights swim along the edges of my memory, and I force them back.

He and I both bear the scars of too many friends gone too soon, but that doesn't alleviate the anger that burns in my gut. Cole was given orders to follow Brad. Our number one goal is to protect Evie. And he lost sight of the mission.

"What the fuck happened? First Mia. Now this. How does he go from a lazy asshole who assaults women to stalking you like a damn serial killer?" Cole asks.

I shrug. "Fuck if I know. Nothing that asshole has done has been predictable." Which is what's made him so hard to find.

"He's escalating."

Ed's word comes back to me. *Obsessed.*

And Evie is alone. Unprotected.

"He's unhinged," I correct. "He has nothing to lose at this point."

And that realization chills my blood.

"We can talk later. For now, we need to go."

My skis are scattered at odd angles, while my poles dangle from my wrists. Leaning over to right the skis increases the pressure in my head, and the throb quickens to the tempo of the *1812 Overture*. I close my eyes and swallow the nausea that rides shotgun alongside the sound.

"Can you move?" Cole asks. His look when I open my eyes again is dubious.

"Watch me."

This isn't the first time I've had to power through an injury, though never with one this severe. I grit my teeth and finish clipping back in while I box up the pain and shove it to the back of my mind. I don't have time for this shit right now. Evie's in trouble.

I failed Amani.

I won't fail her too.

"Skis?" I ask.

Cole nods.

"Left them in the trees. I'll grab them and be right behind you."

He rushes off, and I do the same. My balance is shit, but I pick up the pace anyway. Getting to Evie is my only goal. Despite Brad and Cole and me all being on skis, only two tracks are visible—mine coming out here earlier and Brad's heading back. My stomach clenches and my palms slip against the handles. I grip them tighter and drive them deep into the snow.

"I'm coming, starling," I murmur and push myself faster.

I didn't ask Cole how fast Brad was moving, but it doesn't matter. He's got a ten-minute head start, and I'd only been skiing for about twenty minutes when I stopped. Every curve in the trail has me straining to hear him and scanning my surroundings. All the while, my stomach grows tighter.

"This was a really bad fucking idea, King," I mumble to myself as guilt squeezes around my throat.

I should have told Evie what we had planned.

Too late now.

Fuck, I hope she's awake. My mind won't let me think about the worst-case scenario—Brad finding her naked in bed where I left her. My lungs burn, but I push myself faster.

"Hang on, starling."

I repeat it like a mantra—a soundtrack to my frantic race back. At some point, the hairs on the back of my neck lift. Cole must have caught up, but I don't stop. I don't look back. I press forward until the cabin comes into view.

From this distance, it looks like it always has. A picturesque structure within walking distance of the bay. Smoke curls lazily from the chimney, and for a split-second, hope builds in my chest. Maybe Brad hasn't made it here yet.

But the tracks overlapping mine tell a different story.

A sharp whistle rends the air, and I stop and turn back toward Cole with a glare.

"What the fuck is wrong with you?" I hiss.

"Think about this. If you go charging in there like a wounded bear, what do you think happens? What if he has a gun? What if he hurts Evie because we're not being smart and checking the situation out first?"

It's the advice that's saved our asses more times than I can count. It's saved a few clients too. Even if it does go against every one of my instincts. The adrenaline coursing through me is urging me to charge in there and murder that bastard. Because the difference between this scenario and those of the past is that the love of my life is at risk here.

"If he hurts Evie—" Every possible outcome flies through my imagination at lightning speed and makes it hard to breathe. "If something has happened, I'll kill him," I say.

"It's not going to come to that," he tries to assure me.

I shoot him a glare. "You can't promise that."

"No, but you can. Breathe. Let's think this out."

We're just out of sight of the cabin. Now is the perfect time to stop and plan out our next steps. But every minute that ticks by brings with it total agony and heavier guilt.

What if I can't save her?

What if this is Amani all over again?

CHAPTER 25

EVIE

"Hello, songbird."

Disgust fights with the fear that courses through my body. I hate that name. I hate the way it oozes out of his mouth like oil and brings all my deepest fears to the surface. I hate that despite locking my muscles, I'm being tugged closer to the man who haunts my nightmares as shards of glass from the broken window dig into my feet.

I cry out as one digs deep into the arch of my foot. The cruel smile that tilts his lips is proof that he enjoys my misery. I attempt to ignore the sharp pain and yank at my arm. It does little more than slow my progress toward him.

"Aren't you happy to see me?" he asks with an arched brow like a B-movie villain.

"How did you find me?"

I pluck at his gloved fingers, but it's no use. The leather is slick and hard to grip, and what little strength I have is lost in the flight-or-fight response with the needle firmly set to run.

"It wasn't hard."

"I doubt that. Sawyer and his team are good at what they do."

His grip tightens maliciously around my wrist.

"Not good enough," he snarls.

"Better than you," I retort.

Hatred flashes in his eyes. "Tell that to the man I left lying in the snow in the forest."

Sawyer.

No.

He promised me. Brad would never hurt him. I inhale sharply, and the pain that blossoms in my chest steals my strength. Brad uses my distraction to his advantage and pulls me next to him.

"Poor little songbird. You look so sad. Did you care about him?" The way he asks makes a mockery of my pain.

It's like one of these glass shards has punctured my heart.

"Did you love him? Did you spread your legs for him the way you did for me? Is that how you paid him to protect you?" He sneers.

Bile burns up my throat at the putrid smell of his breath. This close, his skin is sallow and drooping, and the broken blood vessels below it are visible.

"You were willing to do anything I wanted you to in order to realize your dream. It's too late for that dream now, but you will do as I say."

He cups my breast through Sawyer's T-shirt and squeezes until I cry out.

"Such a sweet little song for me. Should I tell you how I left him lying on the ground? If he isn't dead already, the cold will finish him off soon enough. I'll tell you about how he fell as I fuck him from your memory."

A shudder racks my body, the sobs stuck in my chest.

He's dead.

Despair and guilt take my breath away. Sawyer's death is my fault.

I should give up. I should have from the beginning. Then Sawyer might still be alive.

Fight back! Brad said he thought *Sawyer was dead. Maybe you can still save him, but you need to fight.*

Maybe there's hope. But it diminishes with every passing second. How far away is he? How long will it take me to find him? Can I even escape Brad so I can try?

Brad tugs me behind him as his boots crunch over the glass. I don't have the same protection as more shards slice through the soles of my feet.

"I've waited a long time for this, songbird."

He palms his crotch with his free hand as he drags me down the hallway. My stomach cramps at his vulgar gesture. I have to get free. Otherwise…I can't imagine the otherwise. That won't do Sawyer any good.

The bedroom Sawyer used early during our stay here is the last door on the left. Brad stops in the first doorway, and disgust colors his features at the sight of the big wooden desk and bookshelves lined with books and photographs. I scan the room in search of a weapon. But like every room here, nothing is out of place, and the books are too far to reach. Something rattles in the desk drawer, and I want to cry. It's his cell phone. Now I just need a way to get to it.

"Where the fuck is the bedroom in this place?" Brad mutters.

He steps back and tugs me farther down the hall, snorting a laugh when we reach the next door.

"A fucking gym? What good did that do him?"

His eyes glitter with malice as he scans my body in the mirror that reflects the two of us on the other side of the room.

"You could use a trip or two to the gym to get rid of your extra weight before we go back on tour."

"T-tour? Didn't Reverb fire you?"

His teeth click together, and his expression turns murderous.

"You cost me my job, cunt."

"You got yourself fired," I retort.

He digs his nails into the sensitive skin of my wrist. I wince and bite my lip to avoid crying out again, tasting the metallic tang of blood. He takes too much pleasure in my pain.

"That place was going down anyway. I'm starting my own label."

Without my permission, laughter bubbles up inside me. He's delusional.

Done with scrutinizing my appearance, he pulls us back into the hallway.

Laugh later. Think of a plan now.

"Fucking finally," he crows, slinging me into the room in front of him.

As the door slams shut behind him, my breathing goes ragged.

Never let an attacker trap you in a room.

Too late.

"Take off your clothes," Brad demands. He crosses his arms while he leans against the door.

"No."

It takes him a minute to register my refusal, but once he understands that I don't intend to give him anything, his bemused expression is replaced by anger.

"What did you say?" He straightens.

Fear is my companion right now, but I don't back down.

"No."

I clench my hands into fists and stand my ground.

He chuckles. "You're not going to fight me."

"The hell I'm not."

"You won't win. You're weak, songbird. I'm bigger and stronger." He shifts away from the wall and stalks toward me.

"I'm not weak."

He huffs a humorless laugh. "Of course you are. You always have been. Either you strip by the time I reach you, or I'll rip your clothes from your body."

The only move I make is to retreat against the wall.

"My, my. Aren't we full of fire." His grin doesn't reach his eyes. "I'm going to enjoy this."

He lunges toward me and grasps the front of my T-shirt. The fabric starts to give way with a small tearing sound. Without a second thought, I bring my forehead against his nose and head-butt him the way Sawyer taught me.

Blood spurts from his nostrils, and he releases the fabric so he can cover his nose.

"You broke my nose, bitch," he shouts.

He drops his hands. The blood on his face and mouth makes him look like a grotesque clown. The rage is there, but there's something more. A monster I never knew existed. I'm not only fighting for control over my body. Based on the violence in his eyes, I'm fighting for my life.

He leaps forward, and I bring my hands up to his chest and push him back. His fall propels him into the corner of the night-stand before he drops to the ground. His eyes are closed, and his chest moves up and down steadily. But other than that and the blood that continues to trickle from his nose, there's no other movement. The table managed to knock him out.

Relief washes over me momentarily. Until I remember the next phase of self-defense.

Get away from your attacker. Find Sawyer.

The cell phone.

I race from the room into the office. My fingers slip against the wood, and I waste several precious seconds as I try to open the drawer. Finally, I wrench it open, and the cell phone bounces out and against the carpeted floor at my feet.

I barely manage to grip the phone before Brad's rage-filled shout echoes through the house.

"Where are you, you fucking bitch? When I'm through with you, you're going to wish you were dead."

Fear pulses through my body and makes my movements uncoordinated. Like I'm moving in slow motion.

The snowmobile.

I can use it to find Sawyer and get us both to some level of safety. Then I can call the police. A loud boom echoes from the room I left him in and accompanies my sprint to the door. The glass is still sprinkled on the floor, but I don't notice the pain as I dart through it to Sawyer's slippers that sit innocently on the rug next to the door.

Get to the shed. Get the snowmobile.

Rushing blindly for my escape, I turn right and search frantically along the wall for the little shed. It blends in so well it's hard to find. Black dots swim in my vision—a combination of adrenaline and panic and the pain from headbutting Brad. Cold air burns the exposed skin of my arms, but I don't stop tracing the roughhewn exterior. I wince as a splinter catches my finger but shake it off quickly and continue.

"Please," I beg as snow works its way inside my borrowed shoes.

I'm not sure who I'm talking to at this point. Or am I praying?

"You're leaving tracks, songbird," Brad taunts behind me.

I turn the corner and come to the right side of the house and nearly sob in relief as the shed comes into view.

The inside is dark, but I close the door behind me anyway and move as far back as I can. I don't have time to start the snowmobile and leave, so I can only hope the darkness is enough to keep me hidden.

The door flies open and slams against the outside wall. Then Brad's there, his shadow eclipsing the bright light behind him as he steps inside.

"I know you're here."

I bite back the whimper that wants to escape and crouch low in the corner.

"Do you know how easy this would have been for you had you just given up? Instead, you ran away."

The door shuts, and now I'm trapped with him in almost

complete darkness. Panic rises within me, and I struggle to calm my breathing so I don't give away my position.

"It didn't have to be this way, songbird." His voice, closer now, is an oily poison that seeps around us.

I hunch further into myself and plant my hands on the floor below me to keep from falling over. My fingers brush against something cold and metallic. I grip whatever it is and lift it close to my body while Brad curses in the dark.

"Fucking phone. The damn light never works—aha."

The light blazes on, illuminating his face. He's much closer than I expected, and I nearly bobble the weapon in my hand.

"Fuck."

He squeezes his eyes shut, and I use the opportunity. Stepping toward him, I lift my arm and bring it down against his temple. His eyes focus on me for a heartbeat before they roll back into his head and he falls backward.

Run!

In two strides, I'm at the door and yanking it open. Between the effects of the headbutt, the adrenaline, and the hard wall of muscle that stops my escape, stars dance in my vision.

Strong hands grip my shoulders, and I struggle against the weight.

Fight.

I struggle against the grip and lift my injured feet to kick out. I connect with his shins several times before the voice registers.

"Starling, it's me. It's Sawyer. Stop. You're okay. It's okay. I'm here."

As his words wash over me, the adrenaline ebbs. I collapse against his chest and release the tears I've held back since the window first broke. Anxiety, love, fear, pain—they all war for dominance within me. The warmth of his hands on my back is a relief I don't have the strength for.

"He didn't kill you. He—he told me—"

"I'm fine. Especially now that I know you're okay. You are okay, right?"

He pulls back and drinks me in. His eyes darken, and he lifts his finger to the small tear along the collar of my shirt.

I cover his hand with mine and meet his gaze. "He didn't do anything. He tried."

"Motherfucker," he growls, looking past me into the shed where Brad is currently folded against the wall. "What happened?"

"Sawyer, it worked."

He turns to me again, brows furrowed. "What worked?"

"You kept saying how it needed to be automatic—"

"Fuck, Evie." He yanks me back against his chest and tightens his hold on me.

I squeeze him back just as hard.

"I saved myself," I tell him, propping my chin on his chest and meeting his concerned gaze.

"I knew you could." His lips quirk in a half smile, and he leans down and brushes a kiss against my forehead. It's gentle, but my forehead still throbs where I rammed it into Brad's nose.

"Um, King."

I jump at the unfamiliar voice, and Sawyer gently squeezes my arm.

"It's just Cole."

"Cole?"

I peek around Sawyer and take in the tall man with light brown hair who's wearing the same kind of gear Sawyer is.

"Nice to finally meet you, Evie." He clears his throat, and his attention moves back to his boss.

"King, you want me to…" He gestures toward Brad.

Sawyer shakes his head, tension radiating from his body. "Take Evie inside."

"Sir?"

"Stay with her."

I tighten my embrace once more, but it's no match for Sawyer's strength. He steps away easily and places himself in the doorway between Brad and me.

I move as well and wince as the cold registers against my injured feet.

"Starling?"

"I'll be okay. There was glass and then snow…"

I'm sure my feet are a mess inside the slippers that will probably need to be thrown out.

"Let Cole take a look at your feet when you get inside," he murmurs.

"What if you need help?"

"I won't."

"But what if you do?"

"Starling." He sighs.

"Sawyer."

He rolls his eyes and tucks a strand of hair behind my ear.

"Go." He points away from him. His tone brooks no argument.

With a huff, I spin, but I immediately slam my eyes shut and freeze. I can't move. I can't breathe.

"Evie?" Sawyer's voice comes from directly behind me, and his warmth travels along my back.

"She's probably in shock." This comes from Cole.

"Starling?" This time the warmth of Sawyer's palm connects with my hip.

He's safe. He's here.

"Yeah?" I croak out.

"Are you okay?"

Am I? Yes. Mostly. But for some reason, I can't make myself move. If I move, I'll crash to the ground.

"Evie, how about this? I'll walk in front of you." Cole's southern drawl is closer than it was before. "Follow me, and I'll count us off with every step we take."

I nod.

"Ready?" he asks.

I open my eyes and home in on him. He's only a few steps in front of me.

"Y-y-yeah." My teeth chatter in the cold air, and the adrenaline drains faster with every breath.

"Nice and slow. How about I tell you about Mistletoe Creek?"

"Mistletoe Creek?" I ask.

"Yes, ma'am. It's in Tennessee. In the foothills of the Smoky Mountains."

I take one step but turn back to look at Sawyer. He hasn't moved. My formidable sentry. My warrior.

His eyes soften when they meet mine, and he gives me a small smile. "It's okay. You're safe."

"I—"

I want to tell him how much I love him. I want to fall to my knees and thank God he's okay. But now isn't the time. I return his smile and turn to follow Cole, but a piece of me stays with the man who healed my soul before he stole my heart.

CHAPTER 26

SAWYER

I grip the back of my neck, hoping to ease the tension that throbs there. I'm about dead on my feet and desperate to lay eyes on Evie again. I need to check her over more thoroughly. But first I need to finish my statement to Owen Dean, Homer's Chief of Police.

When I bought the cabin, I made it a point to introduce myself to Owen. We've grabbed a beer here and there during my visits. I consider him as much of a friend as I do Ed. But right now, I need Tylenol and to pull Evie into my arms and make sure she's really okay.

The paramedics are checking her out now, and I don't like the way they continue to examine her wrist.

"And Mr. Russell was unconscious when you found him?" Owen asks.

I've answered this question at least twelve times.

It's procedure.

Fuck procedure.

"He was. But only for a minute or two. He came to pretty fast."

And he jumped up with a snarl, ready to fight with a woman he outweighed by close to eighty pounds.

A knuckle in my finger pops as I clench my hands into fists. If Owen sees, he doesn't say anything.

"Then what happened?"

Red rims the edges of my vision, and I have to take a couple of deep breaths before it recedes and leaves only the steady throb behind.

"Do I have to repeat what he said?" I ask with a furtive glance over my shoulder.

Evie doesn't need to hear the words.

Owen levels me with a look. *What do you think?*

I motion toward the kitchen and relish the heat of Evie's gaze on me as I follow the chief into the other room.

"He said he was going to make her wish she were dead. That he was going to"—I swallow down the bile that coats my throat—"fuck her until she was raw before he beat her to death."

Owen's eyes go round, and he whistles. "Motherfucker."

I grunt my agreement.

"I have to ask. He's saying you tried to kill him." Owen dips his chin and refers to his notes. "That you broke a couple of his ribs."

"I wanted to," I admit. I can think of seven different ways to kill him quickly, and a whole lot fucking more that would make it hurt.

"Did you?"

This is Owen the friend asking, not Owen the police officer.

"I didn't fucking touch him other than to yank his arms into the zip tie you found him in when you guys got here," I spit out.

Thank Christ Cole called the police as soon as he and Evie were inside. Because ignoring Brad's words was almost impossible. But I didn't want him in the house, and I didn't want to leave him by himself in the shed, so I waited with him.

I tried to tune out the vile shit he spewed, but it infiltrated my senses anyway. What he planned to do to her. Sexually. Physically.

"He's a fucking psychopath," I tell Owen.

"Is that Ed's official opinion or yours?"

Owen is plenty familiar with the retired FBI profiler.

"At this point? Both."

"How did he get the broken nose?"

A smirk curves my lips.

"Evie."

Owen leans around me to glance at Evie, who's practically swallowed up by the blankets on the couch. Cole sits nearby, close enough to provide safety but far enough to allow for her comfort. Though he's on her side, she doesn't know him, so keeping a little distance eases her anxiety.

"She did that? What about the bumps on his head?"

"She pushed him, and he hit it on the nightstand. Then she smacked him with a wrench when he came at her again."

Owen's eyebrows lift, his lips curling with admiration.

"Damn."

"She's protected, right? Self-defense?"

Owen nods. "Absolutely. He broke in and came after her." He nods toward the living room. "Looks like they're done with your girl."

The paramedics are packing up their equipment, and Evie is holding a disposable ice pack to her wrist.

I hate that the motherfucker touched her. But it could have been so much worse.

"You taught her the self-defense moves, I assume?" Owen asks, bringing my attention back to him.

I wince with the movement.

"Have they looked you over yet?" he asks.

"Yeah. Concussion. I'll live."

"Good thing you have a hard head."

"My mother says the same thing," I retort.

"What I don't get is how the fuck he knew where you were.

You're in security. You were special forces. You know how to cover your tracks."

I let out a loud sigh, prompting Owen to drop his pen and paper and lean against the island.

"Translation?" he asks.

"The bastard kept popping up and then hiding again like a damn whack-a-mole game. We—I—made the decision to leak our location in order to draw him out. I had my cyber expert tracking credit card charges and Cole staked out at the airport. He was right behind him when he boarded a flight."

The gasp from behind me comes a heartbeat before Owen peers over my shoulder.

With a steadying breath, I turn to face her.

"I-it was you? You brought him here?" Her voice cracks, and the betrayal in her eyes levels me.

On the other side of the kitchen, the ice pack drops to the ground in a slushy thud.

"Starling—" I step forward, but she holds up her uninjured hand.

"Don't. You should have told me. Instead, he...I...do you know what could have happened?" Anger quickly replaces the hurt.

Good. I deserve it.

"I should have. And I regret—"

"He could have killed you! He could have fulfilled his promise to rape me! Because that's what he wanted to do, Sawyer. He wanted to rape me."

Red creeps into my vision again. Fuck. If that had happened, I don't know what I would have done. The rage that fills me at that thought is all-consuming.

"I fucking know that!"

My voice rings through the house.

Owen clears his throat awkwardly. "I'll be in the living room."

He retreats with a vapor trail. Not that I blame him.

Evie shouldn't have found out this way. I planned to tell her, but I wanted to wait until we were alone. After I wasn't still hopped up on adrenaline in my race to save her.

I planned to confess everything. My plan. How much I love her. How I want to spend my life with her. How much I need her to forgive me so that maybe I can forgive myself.

I quiet my voice. She's not the focus of my anger.

"I know what he wanted to do to you. And if one of the cops hadn't already transported him to the hospital, I'd love to kick the shit out of him."

"You lied to me." She crosses her arms over her chest and winces when the move adds pressure to her injured wrist.

The purple bruises are clearly visible, despite the space between us.

"I was trying to protect you."

You spelled I'm sorry wrong, moron. Try again.

Fuck. "I—"

"Knowing the truth would have been better protection. I could have planned for him. Instead, he surprised me."

"You still kicked his ass, though."

I'm so fucking proud of her.

She closes her eyes, and her lips move, but no words come out, as if she's talking herself down.

"Starling—"

Her eyes flash open.

"Don't call me that."

Fuck.

"Evie."

I move across the kitchen cautiously and press my palm to her cheek.

"I'm sorry," I whisper and press my lips against her forehead.

"I know. And a part of me understands why you did it. But I just can't right now, Sawyer. I don't know which end is up anymore."

"It's been a rough day."

"It has. It's been a rough few weeks. It's been a crazy ten years. But now I know what I need to do."

"What do you mean?"

The dread that curdles in my gut is frozen by the cool air that swirls between us when she steps back.

"Brad's gone. Now I can go home. And…I need some time." She's rebuilding that wall between us we just obliterated.

But as hard as this is, she deserves what she's asking for. I should be grateful she's not calling it quits entirely.

She still could.

"Evie—"

"Please don't. This is hard enough as it is."

"I don't want to make this harder on you. If you need time, take it. But why can't it start when we get back to LA?"

Half her mouth quirks in a sad smile.

"Because I might chicken out. So I'm going to go to bed. Alone."

The second bedroom is a crime scene. Or was. I'm not sure whether Owen will need to do anything more with it. So it looks like it's sofa city for Cole and me.

Evie turns away, and all I want to do is beg her not to. When she stops, a glimmer of hope flutters to life in my stomach.

"The paramedics said someone should wake you periodically tonight. Maybe Cole can do that?"

The glimmer fades, and the ache in my chest grows with every step that takes her farther from me. No matter how much I try to remind myself that this isn't permanent.

I thought my heart shattered when I learned of Amani's death. But watching my other half walk away without a backward glance feels a whole hell of a lot worse.

Hell doesn't exist in the physical realm. It's not in the arid desert or in the icy solitude of isolation. Hell is lying awake on the couch as the woman I love sobs and screams in her sleep while she fights nightmares I can't protect her from.

"King, you awake?" Cole murmurs from the couch across the room.

"Yes."

Another sob, and my shoulders tighten further.

"Just checking."

I grunt and try to convince myself to stay where I am. All I want to do is run up the fucking stairs.

Don't do it.

Evie made her position abundantly clear. We're in limbo right now, and it's my fault. I fucked up because of my failure to communicate with her. My insane need to control the situation did the exact opposite of what I wanted. Physically, she's safe, but emotionally, she's reverted back to where she was probably years ago.

At the sound of another muffled scream, I sit upright, digging my nails into my palms as I try to hold myself in place.

"Have you slept at all?" Cole asks.

He didn't ask questions after Evie went upstairs. Just boarded up the broken window before coming back to study me with an all-knowing expression. Even if he hadn't overheard my conversation with Evie, he's an insightful man. His ability to read a situation has saved our asses more than once.

"No."

"So you've heard…"

The sobs started right after Owen left.

The screams came later.

"Yeah."

"Should I go check on her?"

"Cole, I love you like a brother. But if you go anywhere near those stairs right now, I will kick your ass and dump your body in the damn bay for fish food."

He barks out a laugh. "Then would you please quit being a coward and get your ass up there?"

I'm already on my feet.

"Grab some sleep. We need to head back to Anchorage in the morning."

Evie asked. And we have no reason to stay here any longer.

With a sigh, I tackle the stairs and breathe through the throb that still echoes in my skull. Bright lights shine from under the door and almost blind me when I open it.

She's curled in the center of the bed in the fetal position, covers twisted around her as she fights in her sleep. Anguish carves lines into her face, and her sprained wrist is at an awkward angle as she fights off the monster in her dreams.

I flip off the overhead light, then ease onto the edge of the mattress. The little shift is all it takes. She springs up and scans the room frantically before her gaze lands on me.

"Sawyer?"

"I'm sorry—"

She flings herself at me, sobbing as she wraps her arms around my neck. I lift her to my lap and stroke my hand down her back, whispering nonsensical reassurances. Each fresh sob is a knife in my chest. She's been strong for so long, held on to the fear and anxiety so tight, and now that it's spilling out, it's overwhelming.

"Shh, starling," I whisper as she gasps for breath. "You're okay. I promise. I'm here. I'll always be here."

I continue to rub her back while uselessness swamps me. The need to help her rages through my body. But the demons that torture her exist in her mind.

Slowly—so fucking slowly—her sobs turn to hiccups until she exhales one long breath across my chest. Her fingers coast over the short hair on my neck, and I shiver, but I don't stop the rhythm of my hand.

"Tired?" I murmur.

"Mm-mmm."

"You need sleep. I won't leave. Not if you don't want me to."

"Promise?"

"I swear."

She crawls off my lap and slumps onto the mattress face up. The soft light on the bedside table makes the red in her hair shimmer like firelight.

She's so goddamned beautiful it's hard to breathe.

"Light on?" I rasp.

"Do you mind?"

"Not at all."

I stretch out next to her and tunnel my arm under her pillow, unsure of what to do next. She takes the lead and shifts to her side so she can lay her head on my chest. Can she hear the way my heart rate speeds up under her cheek?

"Is this okay?" she asks.

I wrap my arm around her shoulder and squeeze her closer.

"Whatever you need is fine by me."

"Are you going to sleep?"

I attempt to ignore the way her fingers trace along my chest absentmindedly.

"No."

"What about your head?"

"Not the first time I've gone without sleep."

"You have a concussion."

"I'll be fine."

She's quiet then, and her finger slows before her hand stops and splays along my chest. But her body stays taut.

"You're not sleeping," I say.

"No."

"Sleep, baby. I'm here."

Despite a massive sigh, her body doesn't relax right away. I regulate my breathing, and hers eventually matches the tempo. Finally, the tension in her muscles ebbs slowly. I have no idea how much time has passed before she relaxes and her steady breaths blow across my chest.

"Evie?" I whisper.

No response.

She's finally asleep.

"I love you."

I can't stop myself from saying the words. I could have lost her today. I still could.

God, I fucking hope not.

Now that I've put it out into the universe, how much I love her, there's only one question left.

Is it enough to let her go?

What choice do I have?

CHAPTER 27

EVIE

*T*he sun is too bright. Or maybe it's too warm.

LA is different. It's changed.

You've changed.

A lifetime has gone by since the last time I was here. When I left, I was running from my nightmare. Now that I don't have to hide any longer, it's time to figure out who I am.

So what do I do now?

"Everything all right?" Sawyer steps behind me and places his hand on the small of my back.

It's the same as every other time he touches me. A Pavlovian response. If it was up to my body, I'd turn and kiss him senseless. But I can't. It wouldn't be fair to him, and it would only make the mess that exists between us more complicated.

I love him. But is it enough? He doesn't deserve the mixed signals, so I keep my lips to myself.

"Y-yeah."

"My Jeep is this way."

He guides me in the direction of one of the parking garages.

I hoped I would be less aware of him by now. What a foolish thought. The careful way we interact around each other only makes me more aware of how accustomed I've become to touching him and to being touched by him. Not that all the touches have ended. Now, though, they're frustratingly platonic.

It's what you want.

It is. I need time to sort out my feelings. Brad's gone. Sawyer lied to me. It might have been by omission, but the betrayal still stings. And my feelings for him are still very real and as intense as ever, which is a complication I didn't expect. My head wants time, and my heart—and my body—want Sawyer.

What happens now?

That's the question, right? I won't see him every day anymore. The space will allow me to get my head on straight. Will Sawyer be waiting for me when I figure things out? I never asked him to, so can I really expect it?

So many questions flash through my mind. One after another. And none of the answers are easy.

"West said he left it on the second level." Sawyer's raspy voice interrupts my spiral.

Despite carrying both of our bags and his backpack, he takes the stairs in front of us quickly.

Doesn't he ever get winded? A concussion can't even slow him down.

Enjoy the view.

The thick muscles of his shoulders stretch his black T-shirt, and his jeans hug his ass like a lover. Both vie for my attention, but I shift my gaze to the stairs in front of me to avoid the temptation.

Sadly, the stairs have more of a physical impact on me, and my heart pounds roughly by the time I reach the top of the second flight. The shape of Sawyer's behemoth Jeep gleams in the low lights of the garage. The wide-open space where the door should be is exactly how I remember it.

Does he even have doors for this thing?

"Oh, good. Another ride in the death trap with no doors," I mutter sarcastically.

Sawyer barks out a laugh and turns to me with a wide smile. "You know you love it."

Maybe a little.

I love the protective instincts that come out in him when I ride beside him. I've always been safe with him. From the first ride until now. He'd never let anything happen to me.

Except when he didn't tell you about Brad coming to Alaska.

He's already admitted he was wrong to not tell me.

This internal argument isn't new. And it's exactly why I need time. But it doesn't make it easier.

"I'll make sure you're strapped in tight," he says with a wink.

My breathing shallows at the innuendo, and I struggle with the impulse to respond in a similar manner. A week ago, I would have fired something back or closed the distance for a kiss.

"You ready?" he asks.

"Yeah."

He leads the way to the car and lifts the bags into the back. Once again, I'm preoccupied by the shift of his muscles under the soft cotton of his shirt. Luckily, I manage to make my way to the passenger "door" without tripping over myself.

"Need a hand?" Sawyer's voice is close by, sending a shiver through me.

I eye the distance between the concrete floor and the running board of the lifted SUV. I nearly fell the last time I tried to get in.

"Please."

He holds out a hand, and I take it. The electric zing still sparks at the connection, and I gasp. If he feels it, he doesn't react. He goes about his business, buckling the complicated seat belt with detached efficiency. I, on the other hand, am doing everything I can to ignore the connection we've discovered and the spicy bergamot scent that wraps around the two of us.

He's so close, but still outside my reach.

I get a reprieve when he finishes, but only long enough for him to walk around the car and lift himself into the driver's seat. We're silent as we make our way out of the garage. The echo of the rumbling engine makes speaking difficult until we're free of the structure.

"You're going to Mia's, right?" he asks.

When I called her yesterday to let her know we were coming home, the offer to stay with her was the first thing out of her mouth.

"Yeah. She said I could stay in her pool house for now. I don't..."

I don't want to go back to my apartment. Brad may be in jail, but the safety of my little one-bedroom evaporated the first time he broke in.

Sawyer's only response is a grunt. Without the radio on, the silence is unnerving, and my focus turns solely to the internal timer counting down on my final moments with him.

Stop being dramatic. You act like you're never going to see him again.

Will I?

Another question I don't have an answer for.

"Lots of traffic," I say in an effort to fill the void.

"More than Alaska."

Palm trees dot the horizon, but concrete and asphalt make up the majority of my view. That and the brake lights dotted all over the highway. A little red sports car zips in front of us and slams on his brakes. Sawyer is forced to do the same, and as he does, he stretches an arm across my chest like it will magically do what the seat belt can't.

"Motherfucker," he grits out.

He lowers his arm, but instead of putting his hand back on the wheel, he cups my thigh. The surge of adrenaline has my insides quaking. I'm not worked up because Sawyer's touch is reminiscent of other touches. Nope.

Sure.

His large hand wraps around my leg, his fingers almost brushing the inner seam of my jeans. It's enough to make me want to fidget in my seat. But I don't want his touch to end. Sawyer may take my movement as not wanting the touch, but nothing could be further from the truth. He may have slammed on his brakes, but my engine is definitely revved. My breathing is embarrassingly shallow, and my teeth are clamped on my lower lip as I hold back a moan.

In short, I'm a hot damn mess while he looks cool, calm, and collected. Well, almost. A muscle ticks in his jaw as he glares at the car in front of us. He glances down and lifts his brows when he realizes where his hand is. He moves it back to his lap, and I fight the urge to whimper in disappointment.

"Sorry."

I immediately miss the heat.

"I-it's okay."

"Are you?" He lifts his eyes to mine and doesn't look away.

"Sawyer, the traffic." I motion to the windshield, but he ignores what's in front of us.

Stubborn man.

"I'm fine," I tell him.

It's nowhere close to the truth, but I want to be. That has to count for something.

And I will be.

Once I figure out my life.

He nods and turns back to deal with the traffic that surrounds us all the way to Mia's. There's no sign of her in the driveway when we pull through the gate. Relief floods my body. I don't need an audience while I say goodbye to him.

The car is barely shut off before he's out of his seat. He grabs my bag from the back, and by the time he's finished and waiting at my door, I've managed to figure out the tricky seat belt.

"Here."

271

He grips my waist and lifts me just as easily as he lifted the suitcase. But when I'm out of the car, he doesn't let go. I close my eyes and lose myself in his nearness while I try to absorb as much of it as I can.

"What are you going to do now?" My voice is barely above a whisper.

"I'll go home. Unpack. Maybe take that camping trip I was going to before—"

Before this. Before us. He doesn't say it. He doesn't have to.

"Oh."

Strong fingers lift my chin until his gaze locks with mine.

"I'm sorry."

"Me too. I—"

I want to take it back. I want to go back. Back to Alaska. Back to the easy way things were between us. I want to tell him that he was the closest thing to home that I've had since I left my parents' house. That I can't picture my life without him.

But I asked him for time. And I need to make sure.

"You?"

"Er...thank you."

His confusion is clear on his face.

"Thank you?"

"For saving me," I tell him.

"You saved yourself."

"Sawyer." His name escapes my lips on a sigh.

He wraps his arms around me and pulls me against his chest. His heartbeat is strong, steady, familiar. I flex my fingers into the muscles of his back and breathe him in for the span of one breath and then another.

He pulls back and cups my shoulders. "I'm here when you're ready, starling."

When he presses his lips to my forehead, tears burn behind my eyes. This is goodbye. The goodbye I asked for.

So why is it this hard?

His steps don't falter as he rounds the hood. The way he climbs into the Jeep looks effortless. Confident.

Final.

Stop him.

But by the time my brain catches up with my heart, his tail-lights are on the other side of the gate and disappearing from view as he makes his turn.

He did what I couldn't—he walked away first. It's what I wanted. Isn't it?

"No, it's not what you want," Mia says with a frown, like she's questioning my intelligence.

She's got her feet propped up on the chaise at the end of her sectional and a glass of water balanced on her ever-expanding stomach. I've missed so much in the last month.

"I need time."

It's a lame explanation at best.

"Time for what?"

"To think."

"What's there to think about? You have your life back."

And that's scary. For the first time in years, my life is my own.

"I know that!" I snap.

"Then what's the issue?"

"I need to figure out what I'm going to do with my life," I tell her.

"With Sawyer," she adds.

"I'm not sure."

Her only response is to snort.

The fuck you aren't.

My heart is screaming at me to go find him. To explain that I want a life with him. That I want to be the woman strong enough to be his partner. My own person, not the hollowed-out shell I was for years.

"Yeah, okay," she says with a roll of her eyes.

"He lied to me."

Mia smirks at my weak justification and shrugs. "He didn't tell you something."

"And that's called a lie of omission," I retort.

"He thought he was protecting you."

"And how would you feel if Garrett did that to you?"

"Garrett and I had our own issues to work through. Ones you helped me realize I needed to get over."

"This is different."

Mia knew who she was. What she wanted out of her life. Even if it took Garrett leaving for her to come to terms with it.

You know what you want. Time to claim it.

"Are you really that upset about it?" she asks.

Her question hits way too close to home.

"What do you mean?"

"You've been hiding for the last few years. And before that, you were a prisoner. For the first time in a long time, you have your entire life in front of you."

"I know. That's what this time is for. To figure out what comes next."

"I think you already know what to do."

Well, shit. Am I that transparent?

"About what?" I ask.

"Everything. Your life. Sawyer. All of it."

"And what do I want, Ms. Smarty Pants?"

"To no longer live in the shadows."

Well, fuck.

"You're right," I whisper quietly, dropping my chin to my chest.

With a hand cupped to her ear, she teases, "What? What was that?"

SOLDIER FOR THE STARLING

"You're right," I say again, louder this time.

"So what now?"

This time, I'm the one who smirks.

"First things first, I quit."

Mia smiles a wide smile. "It's about damn time."

"Do you think I could get Michaela's number from you?"

Michaela's success with Arrhythmic Records is the inspiration I need. Especially because she dealt with Brad too.

"Yeah?" she asks, practically beaming.

I nod.

"Yeah."

Welcome back to the world, Evie McBride.

Brad stole my dream from me. He took my life from me. But now it's time I take them back.

CHAPTER 28

SAWYER

"So now what?" Michaela sets her wineglass on the table and looks expectantly at me.

Most of the talk at dinner has been about Alaska, my time with Evie, and its conclusion with Brad's arrest.

"He's being transferred to Anchorage. Owen said the DA is going to request Brad stay in jail, given that he's a flight risk and did a really good fu—" I glance at Benji, who's covered from hairline to belly in spaghetti. He watches me with adoration. "He did a really good job hiding."

"Did you ever find out how he did it?" West asks, leaning over and wiping Benji's face with a napkin.

In response, the little boy squirms out of reach, and West gives up with a sigh.

"Yeah. Sydney did eventually. He catfished some woman. She thought she was helping him avoid blackmail and knew how to cover his trail."

"That poor woman. Yet another victim of Brad's," Michaela says with a frown.

As Brad's last victim at Reverb, she surely has a heavy dose of compassion for the woman. And for Evie, who was one of his first. Michaela fought him off and came home. Only when West asked me to look into Brad did I find her.

My starling.

How is she? Is she settled at Mia's? Does she miss me half as much as I miss her? Is she still plagued by nightmares?

"Will you and Evie have to testify?" West drops his napkin and helps Michaela lift my energetic nephew from his booster chair.

I shrug. "The DA will let us know. It may be as easy as a deposition versus another trip to Alaska."

Just the thought of another trip makes my chest ache. The cabin—hell, the whole fucking state—is too intertwined with memories of her. And if she decides she doesn't want to be with me? It might be time to sell and find a new getaway spot where I can heal my broken heart. Walking away from her a few days ago was the hardest thing I've ever done. Worse than any mission. More painful than Amani. More difficult than hiding my feelings from Evie for as long as I did.

"Have you talked to Evie since you dropped her at Mia's?" Michaela tosses the question over her shoulder as she heads for the stairs with Benji.

"No. She said she needed time to think."

"I'd say she's already done thinking." Michaela is at the top of the stairs, her comment barely discernible over Benji's excited screams to go swimming in the tub.

What the fuck does that mean? If she's done thinking and I haven't heard from her, does that mean it's over? She's through with me?

West saves my chair from crashing to the floor when I stand and chase after my sister.

I stand in the doorway of the bathroom, hands braced on the frame. *"What?"*

"Uncow! Let's go swimming!" Benji reaches for me with sauce-stained hands.

I smile at his earnest expression. "I don't think I'll fit, buddy. But how about I take you to a real swimming pool this summer?"

"Yeah!"

Michaela winces at Benji's exuberant squirms.

"What did you say about Evie?" I ask her.

"Evie?"

For fuck's sake.

"Yes."

"Oh, she called me. Asked if I could set up a meeting with Jax and Nick."

Pride swells in my chest. Looks like my starling found her wings. Jax Bryant cofounded Arrhythmic Records with Nick Rhodes. He's also one of their bigger stars. Nick cowrites with virtually every one of their artists.

"Is she any good?" Michaela asks me.

The memory of her voice rushes through me. "She's phenomenal."

"I figured."

"So?"

"So what?" she asks.

"Did you set up the meeting?"

She nods. "Later this week."

I drag my sister—spaghetti-coated nephew and all—into my arms for a hug.

"Did I ever tell you that you're my favorite sister?" I ask her.

"I'm your only sister, you jerk." She lets out a laugh. "Now let us go so I can scrub dinner off this little turkey."

"I not a turkey!"

Michaela and I wince. Benji still hasn't grasped the idea of inside voice versus outside voice.

"No, you're a fish," I tell him, ignoring the dull ache in my head that's suddenly picked back up. "And where do fish belong?"

"In the bathtub!" Michaela answers.

Benji fidgets in her hold until he can stretch his arms toward me.

"Uncow do it."

"I should have known. You're his favorite person," Michaela says with a sigh. "I swear his first word should have been 'Uncow.'"

"I thought it was."

She levels me with a look. "I already told you the gibberish didn't count. His first word was *Mama*."

"Uncow," Benji corrects.

Michaela sighs.

"I'll give Benji his bath."

"You sure? These days, most of his bath water ends up on the floor."

I tickle Benji's tummy and smile at his giggle.

"I'm sure. I missed him."

Michaela hands Benji to me and heads for the stairs. "Good luck," she mumbles halfway down.

"I heard that."

"You were meant to."

With a chuckle, I head for Benji's bedroom for pajamas. He's gotten so much bigger since our trip to the zoo. How is that possible?

"Okay, bud, ready for your swim?"

"Bubbles!" he demands.

I nod. "Of course."

Bubble bath in hand, I adjust the water and toss in a generous amount. Then add a little more. If my nephew wants bubbles, I'll make sure he has the most bubbles he's ever seen.

"Ooh." Benji's eyes light up as they fill the tub and create soapy mountains on top of the water.

I make quick work of his spaghetti-covered shorts and shirt, and I have him in the tub when West shows up at the door.

"Michaela said you could probably use some help."

"You guys act like this is the first time I've given my nephew a bath."

"He's more…energetic than the last time."

The little guy is trying to shove a handful of bubbles into his mouth while spinning on his backside. He's got a tuft of suds on the top of his head already, and his smile is pure bliss. I can't disagree with West. The last time I bathed him, they were still using the baby bathtub.

"God, he's cute," I say.

"I'm biased, but, yeah, he is. For the most part."

I want this. The house, the wife, and the cute little kid who sloshes water precariously close to the edge of the tub while wearing a giant smile. I want it all. With Evie.

And I have no fucking clue whether she wants me.

"Do you know how lucky you are, man?"

West nods. "I do. I almost didn't have it, though."

"You came to your senses eventually," I remind him. "After I punched you."

"It wasn't because you decked me."

"Whatever you say."

"I'd already figured out I was a dick. I was just working on how to apologize to Michaela."

"I still say my fist helped you figure that out," I argue.

"I still owe you one."

"Anytime you're ready, Abbott, you take your best shot."

We both laugh, and Benji joins in, even though he has no idea what we're laughing about.

West sobers quickly, though. "Seriously. Are you okay? The concussion—"

I shrug. "I feel okay."

"Maybe physically. But you've been my best friend for almost all my life. I know when you're upset."

I grab the bottle of baby body wash and a washcloth from the basket beside the tub, then gently scrub the sauce from Benji's face to give myself a moment to process.

"What's that supposed to mean?" I ask. Not that I don't already know the answer.

"You were in love with Evie before you went to Alaska."

It's a statement. Not a question. He's right. I hadn't completely fallen for her before we left, but I was definitely more than halfway in love with her. No use in trying to deny it.

I keep my eyes trained on my nephew and get to work with the baby shampoo. "Yeah."

"What are you going to do about it?" he asks.

"What's there to do? She asked for time."

And the wait is killing me. Because the idea of loving her and losing her? It's a lot worse to imagine than never having her at all.

"Dude."

I rinse shampoo from Benji's hair, and he goes back to playing with the slowly disintegrating bubbles.

"What am I supposed to do? Beg her to stay in my life, to choose me?"

My best friend shrugs. "It's terrifying, isn't it?"

"What?"

"Realizing you need to win back the woman you love."

"It fu...dging sucks."

"Is she worth it?"

I nod without hesitation.

"So fight for her." He says it like it'll be the simplest thing in the world.

"I'm not sure how."

"Want to know what did the trick with Michaela?"

"No thanks. There are certain things a brother doesn't need to know."

"Whatever. If you don't want to talk about that, let's circle back to your love life."

Fuck.

"There's no love life to talk about," I tell him.

Once the bubbles are completely dissolved, I lift my slippery nephew from the tub so West can wrap a towel around him. Quietly, we work to get Benji dried off and in pajamas.

"You love her," West says once we're finished and Benji's snuggled close to me with his cheek pressed to my chest and his arms thrown around my neck.

I nod. "I do."

West cups a hand over Benji's ear. "Then fucking fight for her."

"What if she doesn't want me to fight for her?" I ask. The painful realization constricts my throat.

It's better to not know, right?

"What if she does?"

CHAPTER 29

EVIE

J twist the delicate silver bracelet around my wrist and follow Michaela along the path around Jax's house to a smaller building that looks like it might have been a pool house at one point in time.

"You got this," Mia says, tugging my hand away from the bracelet.

"I hope so. It's been a long time since I sang for anyone."

"True. But now you're a badass who's taking her life back, right?" she reminds me.

"You'll like Jax and Nick. I promise it couldn't be any more different from Reverb," Michaela says with a comforting smile.

My time with Reverb was a nightmare. Michaela knows exactly what it was like. And what having Brad as a label rep was like.

"Can I...can we stop for a second?" I ask just outside the door.

Without question, both friends pause and turn to me. I take a deep breath, release it, and try to quiet the negative voice that niggles at me.

What if you're not meant to do this?

Insecurity swirls in my stomach, amping up the desire to run

285

away and hide in Mia's pool house forever. But I haven't come this far to only come this far. If this doesn't happen, I'll find something else. I have options now.

No more hiding. My hair has returned to its natural auburn color, thanks to Mia's hairstylist. For the first time in two years, I'm not in baggy clothes. The stonewashed jeans and blue floral top are fitted and more my style than anything I've worn in too many years to count.

My outside projects confidence, and it's time for my inside to match. Time for me to fight the impostor syndrome that threatens to force me back into hiding.

After one more deep breath, I square my shoulders. "Okay, let's go."

The production room is both different and familiar. The recording and sound mixing equipment gleam in the low lights along the top of the desk. The studio lights are on, and Jax and Nick are both on guitars as they chat.

"You want to sit down? I'll grab them. Otherwise they'll be there for hours," Michaela says, pointing to a pair of comfortable couches along the back wall.

Michaela steps through the door separating the two rooms, and both men stop and turn toward us. Nerves flutter in my belly at the scrutiny.

As if she senses it, Mia squeezes my hand. "You got this, Ev."

I nod, more than a little afraid to open my mouth, given how close I feel to vomiting. I'd forgotten this part. Rejection is an everyday part of this industry. Very few people are offered record deals. I was. Then I wished I hadn't been.

"Evelyn?"

In front of me, a man with deep blue eyes and a warm smile holds out his hand.

"Evie, please. Evelyn is...someone else."

"Evie. Nice to meet you. I'm Nick."

We shake hands, and Nick introduces Jax Bryant. As if he needs an introduction. I've listened to his music for years.

"Michaela told us you were looking at getting back into music," Jax says after we're all seated.

"I am. It's been a while. Almost five years. I have no idea if—"

"It's like riding a bike," Nick says. "Trust me. I was out of the creative side for a long time."

"I hope so."

"Let's see, shall we?" Jax holds out a hand, gesturing to the booth.

I take it in—the stools, the equipment—and nerves jump in my stomach like kids in a bouncy house.

What's the worst that can happen?

Given enough time, I could probably name dozens of different worst-case scenarios. But I'm not here to do that. Swallowing around the nerves, I stand and follow Jax while Nick settles behind the recording equipment.

"You want a guitar?" Jax motions to the four that rest in stands along the wall.

"Er, no. Thank you. I only know enough to get by."

Jax nods. "No worries." He adjusts a microphone near me and hands me a pair of headphones. "You have a song in mind?"

"I do. Is it okay if it's not original?" I ask.

"Of course," he says with a genuine smile. "We've all messed around with covers before."

Some of the nerves settle. One less thing to worry about.

"I'm going to go join Nick in the recording booth," he says, pointing through the window where Nick waves and Michaela and Mia stand behind him.

"O-okay."

"Something tells me you've got this." He shoots me a wink.

The gesture and the veritable kindness behind it loosen the band constricting my lungs. "I'm going to try."

When he's settled in the booth, Nick speaks into the microphone.

"I'm going to hit record, then I want you to say your name and the song you're going to sing."

"Okay."

"You ready?"

A sense of rightness washes over me. This is who I am. It's what I was meant to do.

"I am."

Nick starts the recording, and I follow directions. Then, with a deep breath, I close my eyes, open my mouth, and remember what it's like to fly using only my voice.

"How does it feel to have a record contract?" Mia asks from where she's propped on Michaela's couch.

The words are so foreign, but they're true. I'm the newest signed artist at Arrhythmic Records. Nick and Jax have already given me the music for the first song they want me to record. It's amazing, and it's scary.

"It's surreal."

Michaela smiles from where she's kicked back in an oversized chair, and I'm cross-legged on the floor, still processing the latest twist my life has taken.

"You killed it," Michaela says. "The second you opened your mouth, the wheels were turning for both of them. I wouldn't be surprised if they have song number two for you soon."

"Really?"

She nods. "When inspiration hits, they've been known to crank—"

"Mama!" A little voice echoes through the room, followed by the sound of a door slamming. "Mama, we're home!"

"Hi, baby, we're in here," Michaela responds.

Footsteps race down the hall, and the little boy rushes into the room. But he screeches to a halt when he spots Mia and me.

"Did you have fun on the hike with Daddy?"

Curious green eyes shift from Mia to me before he turns his attention to his mom.

"Yep. I drove Uncow's Jeep."

Sawyer.

Is he here? Hope and nerves flutter in my tummy. I've missed him. More than I thought was possible. I want to share today with him. Not that he would have doubted it. But to have his arms around me and his voice in my ear would make this day perfect.

"You did *what?*" Michaela asks, her voice strained. "He did what?" she asks again. This time, she directs the question to her husband, who's propped up in the doorway.

"It's fine. We were in the parking lot at the trailhead, and Benji had his hands on the steering wheel."

"One day I'm going to end up murdering both you and my brother," Michaela grumbles.

"Who are you?" With his hands on his hips, Benji stands in front of me and studies me. Given my position, we're eye to eye.

"My name is Evie. Do you remember me? I visited you once before."

It's been a few weeks, so maybe not, but he nods anyway.

"Evie is my friend. And a friend of Uncow's," Michaela explains.

"Uncow?"

I nod. "Yeah."

"Oh. You having a baby too?"

Mia chokes on her water, and Michaela and West both chuckle.

"Umm..."

I'm not, but I'm lost as to how to answer his question or even if I should.

Michaela comes to the rescue. "Little man, not every woman you meet is going to have a baby."

Benji runs over to his mom and climbs into her lap.

"Can I have a brother?"

I attempt to hide my smile as both Michaela and West roll their eyes.

"Hey, buddy, how about we go scrub the trail off your face and let Mommy visit with her friends?" West holds out a hand.

That's all it takes for Benji to forget his question. In a heartbeat, he's wiggling off Michaela's lap and darting across the room toward his dad.

"He gets cuter every day, Kayla," Mia says, still wiping at the water she spit all over her shirt.

Michaela wears a soft smile. "He's been on this kick about wanting a baby brother. One of the kids at daycare just became a big brother, and Benji likes the sound of that."

"He reminds me of Sawyer." The words are out before I can stop them.

Both of my friends shift their gazes to me, and heat creeps up my cheeks.

"Have you talked to him since you got home?" Mia asks.

I shoot a glance at Michaela, who holds up her hands.

"Safe space. I can forget we're talking about my brother. Because I'm curious too. He misses you."

"I miss him too," I admit in a whisper. The pain of missing him is so acute it's like a knife to the chest.

"What are you going to do?" Mia asks.

Again, my gaze bounces to Michaela, but it's Mia who speaks.

"She's already said safe space. Please tell me you're not going to let him go."

"I—"

"And don't give me that crap about not knowing. You've grabbed the rest of your life by the balls. Tell me you don't want to do the same with Mr. Tall, Blond, and Silent."

"Er…can we maybe not talk about that particular activity?" Michaela asks.

I laugh. "Mia, you're crazy."

She just gives me a shrug. "I'm pregnant. I have an excuse."

"You were crazy before you got pregnant," I remind her.

"True, but you love me anyway. Now, what about Sawyer?"

"What about him?" I hedge.

What I want to do is find him and tell him I was wrong. That I need him in my life. Does he want the same thing?

Mia, clearly in rare form today, throws her hands in the air. "Ugh, Kayla, I'm done. Your turn."

Michaela sits up and looks at Mia before turning her attention to me.

"He'd probably kill me if he knew I told you this, but he knew about your meeting today."

"He did?"

She nods. "I've never seen someone look so happy but so miserable at the same time. He misses you, Evie. And I know he wanted to be there. But you said you needed time, and he respects that."

Pain pricks at my chest.

"What are you waiting for?" Mia asks.

On our way home from Alaska, I was convinced I needed to figure out my life before I was enough for him.

Haven't you finished?

I'm on my way.

Isn't that enough?

"Do you love my brother?" Michaela asks.

"She does," Mia answers for me.

"Mia—"

"Tell us you don't," she challenges.

I can't.

"It's written on your face, Ev."

"What if—"

"Enough with the what-ifs. You've been letting them rule your life. What if you didn't have to hide anymore? What if you tried to sing again? Seems to me those are working out for you."

"Yeah."

"So I'll ask again, what exactly are you waiting for?"

She's right.

I won't admit it out loud, because Mia doesn't need any more ammunition.

"I'm done waiting," I tell them both.

It's time to go reclaim my warrior.

CHAPTER 30

SAWYER

*M*y condo is the same as it's always been. Clean.

Efficient.

Devoid of emotion.

A silent reminder of how much I miss Evie's presence. Of how alone I am. Spending time with West and Benji yesterday helped, but the nights are the hardest. Lying in bed without her curled next to me. Hours spent in darkness, waiting for the sun.

West let a comment about Evie's meeting with Arrhythmic slip—or maybe it was on purpose—while we hiked an easy trail and Benji kicked rocks a few paces ahead of us. Evie was shy about singing when she came to stay with me, but even then, when the only time she'd let loose was when the water from the shower shrouded her and the sound of her voice, I knew. She has talent. And Jax and Nick would be fools not to sign her to a contract.

But what would that mean for us?

Call her.

I pick up the phone and smile at my lock screen. Benji holding out a rock. He's wearing a goofy expression, and there's a smear of dirt on his cheek.

Uncow, it's special. See how shiny it is?

The little flecks of sparkle had intrigued the almost three-year-old, and I get it. With only glimpses of Evie's true self, I knew she was special. What would she have said if I'd sent her flowers yesterday like I wanted to? Or if I called her and told her I missed her?

Or how about that you love her, you idiot?

That too.

I'm trying to give her the space and time she asked for, but every minute that ticks over into the next is killing me—death by a thousand cuts.

My phone lights up in my hand. It's a text from an old contact with Featherlight Studios, a movie production company I free-lanced for before starting Sentinel.

TOM

Heard you've had a hell of a few months.

How did you know?

I have ways. A friend of a friend.

Do I get any other details?

Need to know only.

Fair enough.

You have a job for me?

I don't freelance anymore, but I won't turn down another job for Sentinel.

Maybe.

What's that mean?

Featherlight is looking for new security.

I thought you guys were using Simply Secure.

Not anymore.

I've spent the last four hours clearing out a horde
of paparazzi who managed to break past their
barricades.

Aren't they under contract?

Again, not anymore.

We're taking it out to bid, but I wanted to
personally let you know.

I want Sentinel to bid on it.

It's a big contract for a three-person firm.

So you'll need to hire more people.

I'll be in touch next week.

Well, damn. Is Sentinel ready for the next level? It would be a lot of work for all of us. And while Sentinel is my company, I want Cole and Sydney to weigh in before I make any decisions.

I just got a call from the facility operations guy at
Featherlight.

They're going out to bid on their security.

They want us to submit a proposal.

SYDNEY

Really?

That would be a massive jump.

295

I don't know if I can handle all the cyber for that.

> It would mean hiring more people. Personal
> security, cyber teams, not to mention guards.

SYDNEY

Can I pick my team?

COLE

Cocky little shit, aren't you?

How do you know it's going to be your team?

SYDNEY

If there was someone out there better than me,
don't you think Sawyer would have hired them
rather than me part time?

She has a point. Cole must realize as well because he stops needling her.

COLE

Are we going to?

> I want to know what you two think.

SYDNEY

Why wouldn't we?

COLE

What do you want to do, King?

> What's the harm in trying?

As soon as I hit send, the words hit me.

What is *the harm in trying?*

Evie said she needed time. And I didn't fight for her. I didn't tell her how she makes me feel more alive than I've ever felt. I didn't pull her into my arms and kiss the shit out of her to show her how much I love her. I just...agreed. Walked away like an idiot. Like she isn't the other half of my heart. I acted as though it didn't kill me to walk away. Like I didn't care.

What the fuck is wrong with me?

No wonder I haven't heard from her yet. Given the message I sent the day I dropped her off at Mia's, I'll be surprised if I ever hear from her.

So go get her.

Thanking God I actually got dressed this morning versus staying in pajamas—like maybe, deep down, I knew I would need to move quickly—I haul myself to my feet. I pat my pockets to make sure I have my keys and stride for the door. The second my flip-flops are on my feet, I pull the door open, ready to barrel out and go get my girl.

But I rear back when the sight in front of me registers. It's Evie. She's standing at my doorstep with a large bag gripped in one hand. Her other hand is in midair, poised to knock. Her eyes round in surprise and a flash of something else. Regret? Disappointment?

"What are you doing here?"

"You're going out?"

We speak at the same time and smile awkwardly at each other.

"Please." I motion for her to go first.

She fidgets and nibbles at the plump lower lip I'm dying to taste again.

"I—sorry. I didn't realize you were going out. I can come back."

"I'm not going out. Well, I was, but not like that."

She scans my face, brow furrowed, like she's working through a puzzle.

"Do you want to come in?" I take a step back to give her room to pass if, by some miracle, she takes me up on my offer.

"Umm. Okay?"

As she brushes past, I drag her lavender and chocolate scent in, desperate for a hit of her.

"Do you want me to take that?" I reach for her bag.

She shifts it in front of her. It's big, awkward, and hides her toned legs. "No. I'll hang on to it."

"Do you want to sit?"

She nods and heads to the couch.

I follow, unable to stop the question that's eating away at me. "What are you doing here?"

The hope in my chest fizzles a bit given our positions on the couch—she's at one end, still gripping the bag, and I'm at the other. We're separated by one cushion, but there are miles of words between us.

Her gaze meets mine before it skitters away again. It's obvious her mind is working overtime as her attention bounces from object to object around the room.

"Evie, is everything okay?"

Gorgeous hazel eyes train on me. Then she pulls in a deep breath and squares her shoulders.

"Sorry. I guess I'm more nervous than I thought I would be."

Her statement tells me nothing. My future with her could go one of two ways, and the idea of living without her permanently has nerves knotting my stomach.

"Nervous about what?"

"I-I got a record contract. With Arrhythmic."

"I heard. I'm so proud of you. I never doubted for a second you could do it."

She dips her chin and fiddles with the strap of her bag. "I had my doubts. But it was time I reclaimed my life."

"You deserve it."

"I—thank you."

She doesn't say anything else, and the words trapped behind my lips don't want to be held back anymore.

"Evie—"

"I told you I needed time," she blurts out.

"I remember."

Pain slices through my chest at the memory. At the potential that we're at the conclusion of that time, and she's choosing not to come back to me.

"I lied to you," she tells me. Her fingers twist in the handle of the bag with her confession.

"You did?"

"I didn't need time."

Confusion joins the nerves that swirl in my stomach.

"What did you need?" I ask, bracing myself for her response.

"I-I needed to feel like I was a whole person. Like I wasn't a damsel in distress, but rather a woman worthy enough to be your partner. A real person instead of a shadow."

"Fuck, is that what you thought? That you were a shadow?"

Damn the cushion between us. I slide over, closing the distance between us, and search her eyes.

They tell me all I need to know—she really fucking believed it.

"Starling. You were never a shadow. You were the woman you thought you needed to be. A survivor. You're a fucking badass. I'm in awe of how strong you were—are—through all you've been through. Through everything I wish I could have protected you from. But you didn't need me—"

"I did. I do need you. You're the first person I wanted to call after my meeting with Jax and Nick. You're my first thought in the morning and my last wish as I fall asleep. Once I figured out what all that meant, I knew I had to come here and try. I hope I'm not too late. And I hope you want me as much as I want you."

I yank her into my lap, bag and all, and claim her lips. She melts against me, tangling her tongue with mine while I re-map her curves with my hands. She grinds against my dick, pulling an involuntary groan from me. I flex my fingers against her hips, searching within myself for a little control. We're wearing too many clothes. I want to remedy that so badly, but I have more to say. With all the control I can muster, I break the kiss. I trace either side of her jaw with my thumbs as her eyes flutter open.

Her lips are pink and swollen, shiny from my kisses, tempting me to claim them again. She grasps my wrists and holds me in place. Like I'm going any-fucking-where.

"Does that answer your question?" My voice is husky. I'd rather use my lips for more kisses than for words. My dick jumps, on board with the idea, but I fight back the urge.

"What was the question?" she teases with a sly smile.

I pulse my hips up once, and she drops her head back on a moan. It's gasoline on the fire. I'm desperate to be inside her.

Not yet. Tell her.

"There should have never been a question. And that's my fault. I didn't have the words to make sure you never doubted me. Never doubted us. But being without you, trying to go about my life when I was dying to have you next to me, made it clear. I've been a goner since our kiss at Michaela and West's wedding. I love you. And if that meant letting you go, I was prepared to do it. No matter how fucking bad it hurt. But then I realized I couldn't let you go without fighting for you, without telling you how I don't want to let you go, how I want to love you for the rest of my life."

Tears line her lashes, and one slips over and finds my thumb where it still rests against her jaw.

"I'm not giving you up, starling. Not unless it's what you want. It might kill me, but I'll—"

Her lips stop the rest of my words, her tongue seeking and finding entry to deepen the kiss. My heart races. Not only at having her this close, but because of my confession. I laid it all out there for her. Cut myself wide open. Regardless of what comes next, I couldn't let her go without telling her.

She breaks the kiss and rests her forehead against mine.

"Well, now it's going to sound stupid when I say I love you," she grumbles, her breath mingling with mine.

I jostle her in my arms and trail my lips along her jaw.

"What was that? What did you say?" I murmur against her skin.

"Mmm. I love you."

I nip at her earlobe in response.

Her breathing catches, and she whispers, "I was scared too. I couldn't help it. And by the time I realized, it was too late. I'd already fallen."

"Scared? Why were you scared?" I pull back enough to meet her gaze.

"I didn't want how I felt about you to put a target on your back. Brad—"

"I've already told you I was never afraid of him. The only thing I'm terrified of is the thought of losing you."

"You're not going to lose me," she says.

I pull her even closer. "Oh really?"

Her lips find mine again, and she drags her fingers along the hair on the back of my neck.

"Make love to me, Sawyer."

I surge off the couch, tightening my grip on her hips while her arms wind around my neck.

"Yes, ma'am."

The sun is setting, the light nothing but orange glow in my room when I wake up. I reach out, expecting to find Evie, only to encounter an empty bed.

Was it a dream?

If it was, I never want to wake up.

"Starling?"

I lift my head and scan my room. I'm alone, and the bathroom is dark. With no sign of her, I sit up, intent on finding her. But she walks through the doorway before I can move. The bag from earlier is gripped in her hands while my T-shirt skims her thighs.

"You're awake." She smiles and sits on the bed, holding the bag between us.

"I meant to ask you about this earlier." I hook one of the handles with a finger. "What's in the bag?"

Her cheeks pinken, and the hint of a shy smile tips her lips.

"I didn't want to be presumptuous, but this was going to be my gesture."

"You on my doorstep was all the gesture I needed, starling." I tug her back into my arms and groan when she wiggles her hips against my hardening dick.

"I didn't want to come empty-handed."

She opens the bag, revealing a soft blanket and pillows poking through the folds of fabric.

"A blanket?"

She looks over her shoulder at me with a nod.

"And pillows. When we were at the cabin, I had this image, and it reinforced what I knew even then. That I'm absolutely crazy in love with you."

"Oh yeah? What was this image?" I ask, snaking my hand under the hem of my T-shirt to find her naked hip.

Her breath hitches, and she stretches against me.

"A long, romantic getaway at the cabin I decorated. Throw pillows and a blanket and—"

"And all the things that would make it our home," I finish for her.

"I-I thought this could be a symbol of what our future together could be."

"What about here?" I ask. I drag my hand along her side to cup her breast and tweak her nipple with my thumb.

Her legs scissor open, and she mewls.

"Here?" she whispers.

"Will you make this house our home too?" I nuzzle aside the collar of the T-shirt, finding the tendon where her neck joins her shoulder, and press a kiss there.

"Mmm. If that's what you want."

She reaches back and wraps her fingers around my dick.

"I want you, starling. Right now. Fifty years from now. Always."

"I want that too."

"Good. Because tomorrow, we're packing. But for tonight, don't plan on leaving this bed."

I yank the shirt over her head and sling it across the room.

She spins in my lap and wraps her legs around my waist. "Where are we going?"

Her nipples are beaded and beg for my attention. Unable to deny their call, I tug at one distended tip, relishing the way my touch makes her cry out in pleasure.

"Alaska," I tell her, lining my dick up at her entrance so I can slide slowly home. "We have a house to make a home."

EPILOGUE

EVIE

*T*he notes fade into the darkness, and the silence envelops me for the span of a breath before the applause starts.

Holy shit.

I did it.

My first concert as a recording artist. Granted, I was one of the openers for the Arrhythmic showcase at the Coliseum—a sold out show thanks to names like Jax, Michaela, and Dylan Graves. It's not a bad place to experience my first concert, even if I hit the stage while people were still arriving and milling around as they waited for the bigger acts to perform.

I allow myself a deep breath before I smile. The nerves in my belly are finally at ease now that my part is over.

As the emcee of the event, Nick hops onto the stage and gives me a hug before he turns to the crowd.

"Evie McBride, everyone. One of Arrhythmic Records' newest additions. Isn't she fantastic?"

The crowd cheers again. God. What a high.

"Before Evie leaves the stage, I want to share something with her, and I want all of you to be a part of it."

What is he up to?

Whatever it is, I know it'll be positive. Michaela was right when she told me Arrhythmic was nothing like Reverb. With Jax and Nick at the helm, I'm surrounded by artists who share a pure love of music. Artists who have become my family. And if Jax and Nick are my big brothers, Michaela is my big sister. She's helped me navigate this world as a female artist in so many ways. I couldn't imagine doing this without her. Or her brother.

I squint into the darkness offstage, but there's no sign of him. Not like I expected one. He's good at what he does—guarding me from the dark.

My sexy soldier is hiding in the shadows, doing what he does best—keeping an eye on our surroundings, ensuring the night goes smoothly. While most of the time, he's busy as hell with the security contract at Featherlight, he never turns down an opportunity to support me and Arrhythmic. I like to tease him that it's because he's so protective of me. But in reality, it's because we can't bear to be apart for long. Even after living together for six months, an overnight trip for either of us is torture.

"How did y'all like 'Set Free'?" Nick's voice draws me back to the present.

The cheers grow louder, and warmth fills my stomach. In the words of Sally Field, they liked me. They really, really liked me. "Set Free" is my first single. A ballad about how love holds the power to set a person free—if they let it.

"What's going on?" I mouth to Nick.

His smile only grows wider.

"Earlier today, I got some news. News I've been dying to share with Ms. McBride. But I've been holding on to it. What better way is there to break the news that Evie's song certified gold than in front of almost 80,000 fans?"

The crowd noise surges again at the announcement.

Gold? I hit gold. The single has only been out for a few months—hell, we're still several months away from releasing the full album—so for one song to hit a million downloads already?

No. Way.

This can't be happening.

Nick turns to me with a nod and ducks close. "Congratulations, Evie," he says quietly. "You did it."

Tears blur my vision, but they're the happy kind. The only kind I cry anymore.

"That'll do it for Evie tonight. But hang tight for our next performers. They recently signed with Arrhythmic, and I think you'll enjoy them."

The lights dim, and he and I make our way offstage.

"I need to pinch myself," I tell him once we reach the side of the stage.

"He might have something to say about that." Nick nods toward Sawyer, who's emerging from the darkness.

I'm vaguely aware of Nick's departure, but like always, when Sawyer is near, the world around us fades.

He's dressed in black pants and a black button-down shirt. If he had a pair of aviators, he'd look just like he did the day I met him in Mia's driveway.

"Gold, huh?" A smile quirks his lips, and his eyes shine with pride.

"I can't believe it!" I launch myself into his embrace. "How is this my life?"

A recording contract. A dream fulfilled. A man who has made himself the biggest part of my heart.

"I feel so lucky," I whisper and find his lips with mine.

As far as kisses go, it's relatively chaste. But it heats my blood all the same. Will I ever get enough of this man?

Nope.

Not in this lifetime anyway. Not if I had a hundred others with him.

"Take a walk with me?" he asks.

"Of course."

We wander one small hallway after another until we reach a service elevator. Sawyer produces a key, and the heavy metal doors open.

"Where are we going?" I ask.

He pushes the upper most button, and we begin a slow ascent. With his arms looped around me from behind, he tugs me against his chest.

"Do you know how beautiful you looked up there tonight?" he murmurs, his lips grazing the delicate skin behind my earlobe.

I shiver at the contact. "I couldn't have done this without you."

"That's where you're wrong, starling. I always knew you would get here. With or without me."

"It's better with you," I tell him and run my hands along his forearms.

Once the elevator doors open, he tugs me out until we're back on the public side of the building—the abandoned sky deck.

"I thought Nick said they turned this into a VIP experience?" I ask.

"They did. A very private VIP experience. Just you and me."

The Edison bulbs are so dim, even the lights from the concert offer more visibility than they do. Downtown Los Angeles looks like a million fireflies in the background.

"Just us?" I ask as I step toe to toe with him and wrap my arms around his neck.

"Mmm."

The second our lips meet, he takes control of the kiss, mastering my mouth in a way that leaves me breathless.

"Have I told you how beautiful you look tonight?" he whispers against my throat. With one more gentle kiss, he steps back enough to meet my gaze.

My hair is curled and hangs down my back, and my makeup has been done to account for the bright lights. With Mia and Michaela's help, I found a black top with three-quarter length lace sleeves and a pair of black pants that make me feel incredible.

"It's just hair and makeup," I tell him.

He shakes his head. "When you were up on stage tonight, I couldn't take my eyes off you. You're beautiful first thing in the morning—"

"I highly doubt that," I say, quirking my lips.

He freezes me with a look. "As I was saying. You're beautiful to me every day. Any day. But tonight? Tonight, you were breathtaking. And all I could think about was how lucky I am to call you mine. That I get to love you. That you chose me."

My nose burns with unshed tears. Sawyer may be the silent type, but when he speaks, he's so full of love that it overwhelms me.

"Funny. I think I mentioned something earlier about being lucky," I tell him.

"A year ago, I didn't think I was lucky. I didn't believe in fate. I thought the universe had played a cruel joke on me when it took a person I cared about, only to put another in my path who wouldn't give me the time of day."

"I didn't want—"

He holds up a hand. "I know why you did it. But it's funny how fast things changed. Maybe I should be grateful you needed my protection. Because it's what finally brought us together. But then again, I still think we would have found our way here eventually.

"And now, I can't imagine not being here with you, exactly as we are. Having gone through all the pain and heartache we have. Because it all led to this moment. The moment where I confess exactly how much I love you. How you're so deeply ingrained in my heart and in my soul that I can't imagine not having you by my side. Always."

"Sawyer." I squeeze his hand and lean forward for a kiss, only to have him retreat.

What the hell?

"Our pasts led us to tonight. To right here. To me standing in front of you and asking you to be mine forever. To become my wife. To be my home, no matter where we are."

He pulls out a small ring box from his pants pocket, and it hits me. I don't need to pinch myself. Or rub my eyes. Because this isn't a dream.

My soldier is here, standing in front of me, holding a box where a glittering pear-shaped diamond engagement ring is nestled. As if that's not enough, he slowly kneels.

Dumbstruck, I search his face. And what I see there almost brings me to my knees along with him.

Hope.

Love.

My future.

All reflected back at me.

"Marry me, starling."

I don't need to think about my answer.

"Oh my god, yes. Yes, I'll marry you." I launch myself at him. And like always, he catches me. He never lets me fall.

My lips find his, and my fingers grip his biceps. He holds me tight, keeping me grounded when I feel like I could fly. But I'm already flying. Because of him.

"I love you. I never thought it was possible to let myself love someone this much. But the universe picked you for me before I could even think about finding love," I tell him as he slides the ring onto my left hand.

"Perfect fit," he murmurs.

"Just like you are for me."

His lips cover mine, and our tongues tangle in a kiss that has need throbbing in my core.

"Is it really just the two of us up here?" I ask.

"For now."

"For now?"

"Everyone else will join us later. After the concert. I thought we might have something to celebrate."

"Pretty sure of yourself, aren't you?"

"With you? No. But I hoped."

"I'm not going anywhere."

"That's good to know." He stands and pulls me to my feet, then leads me to a couch on the deck.

"What time will everyone be here?" I ask.

"After the last act."

"Good. That's plenty of time." Without another word, I yank off my top, revealing my lacy black bra.

His eyes darken, and he moves closer.

"Plenty of time for what?" he asks. He lifts his hand and drags his index finger along the satin edge of the bra where it cups my breast.

My breath catches, and I close my eyes to absorb the sensations he evokes.

"Well, you feel lucky—"

"Damn straight," he agrees.

I can't hold back my smile. "And I feel lucky."

I press my breasts against his chest and nuzzle his jaw until my lips find the pulse point in his throat.

"I-is that so?"

"Mmm. I was thinking that since we both feel so lucky, maybe we should spend some time *getting* lucky."

He palms my ass and drags me closer to his erection, grinding our lower halves together.

"I'd say yes. But I'd rather make love to my fiancée."

His sure fingers find the button on my pants and undo them

before he slides his hands back around, cupping my ass over my satin panties.

I moan at the contact, desperate to lose the rest of our clothes.

"I like the sound of that," I tell him.

"So do I, starling. So do I."

THE END

Thank you so much for reading!

LOVE THE MIX OF COLE'S VOICE OF REASON AND PROMISE OF STORIES FROM MISTLETOE CREEK? You can binge his second chance happily ever after with the woman he promised to marry on KU or keep reading for a sneak peek of Book 2 in the SAFE Haven series, Bodyguard for the Beauty Queen.

WANT A GLIMPSE OF SAWYER AND EVIE'S BIG DAY? Turn the page for your exclusive wedding bonus content!

BONUS EPILOGUE

10 MONTHS LATER

SAWYER

*W*est squeezes my shoulder as I shift my weight. He and Cole stand on one side of me. Benji's there too, rocking on his heels. His four-and-a-half-year-old attention has been captured by all the excitement around us. I, on the other hand, keep my gaze locked on the aisle Mia and Michaela have just walked down.

It's almost time.

I'm ready. More than ready.

I saw Evie earlier this morning—tradition be damned—but even so, we've set up the outdoor wedding with living screens covered with greenery and flowers so no one will see her until she starts her walk. The one I've waited forever for.

It's been less than a year since you proposed. And neither of you wanted to get married in the snow.

There was no doubt we'd get married here at the cabin, so that meant a summer wedding. Which gave us time to plan, despite our busy schedules. Between Featherlight and our normal security jobs, Sentinel is growing by leaps and bounds—enough that I made Cole a partner. Not only to help with the behind-the-scenes work, but also so I can travel with Evie when she tours. There's no way in hell I'd lose a month with her, even if it means living on a cramped tour bus with Michaela, West, and Benji.

"Deep breaths," West whispers as the music changes.

He acts as if I'm nervous.

Nothing could be further from the truth.

I've waited a lifetime for this woman. I'd wait forever if I had to. But I don't. Because under the arch, on the arm of her dad, Eric, she's there. My world shifts on its axis yet again. My heart races, and my breath stalls until my eyes lock with hers through the veil that covers her face. Her hair is pulled up and back, a braid creating a natural crown on her head while small pieces of hair flutter in the soft breeze that whispers off the bay. Her dress is simple. The ivory color highlights the gold in her eyes. The style is a mix of demure with lace shoulders and sexy with the deep plunging V of the wrap top. It shows off her breasts in a way that makes my hands itch and my thoughts anything but pure.

"I felt the same way about Michaela," West says.

Asshole.

I do not need to hear about what he thought of my sister as she walked down the aisle. I'm sure this is his revenge for the hard time I gave them for disappearing as the officiant finished the ceremony. I'd glare at him, but I don't want to look away, even for a moment, as the love of my life moves toward me.

The small smile that curves her lips creates one of my own in response.

My fiancée. My soon-to-be wife.

Fuck.

She and her dad stop next to me, and he lifts her veil to

kiss her softly on the cheek. It took her a while to tell her family about the Brad saga—guilt and embarrassment had kept her quiet for too long—but once she did, her family was instantly close knit, like they had been before she distanced herself. It was another thing Evie had lost because of Brad, but now that he's in prison, he holds no more power over her.

"Who gives this woman to be married to this man?" The officiant's voice is clear in the quiet that surrounds us.

Eric clears his throat.

"She gives herself, but with her family's blessing."

Evie's gaze slips to him. During the rehearsal last night, we didn't talk about what he would say, only the cue for it. But I don't think a more perfect response exists. She may be my starling, but she's the hero of her own story. I'm just the lucky son of a bitch who gets to love her.

With his piece done, Eric moves next to Evie's mom, Leah, across the aisle from my parents and older brother and his family. Faces of friends and family dot both sides, and the photographers we hired move silently through the crowd. I'm amazed we've managed to keep this event as private as we have.

"Be seated," the officiant says.

The crowd does as they're instructed, and Evie's attention comes back to me. Tears line her lower lashes, and she blinks quickly to dispel the moisture.

I lift my hand carefully and cup her cheek to brush my thumb under her lashes. "You look beautiful," I murmur.

If it's possible, her smile gets brighter.

"Thank you. You look good yourself."

My tux is tan to fit the outdoor scheme, the tie a light blue that Evie says makes my eyes glow. Whatever that means.

"I want to kiss you." My attention strays to her softly painted lips.

Now that I've said it, it's the only thing I can think about.

"There's a place for that," the officiant tells me with a wink. "But for now, how about we get started?"

We both nod and turn our attention forward.

"Dearly beloved, you've all been invited here today…"

Evie squeezes my hand, and the universe ceases to exist. It's simply her and me in this moment. Repeating our vows and sliding rings onto one another's fingers. Fucking finally we get to the part where the officiant directs me to kiss my bride.

With pleasure.

She twines her arms around my neck, and I hook her around the waist with one of mine to draw her closer. The other rests against her cheek.

"I love you," I tell her.

"I love you."

The words are barely past her lips when I claim them. She tastes of mint and something more familiar—uniquely her. Like home. Like forever.

And I'll never get enough.

I could kiss her for the rest of the day, but we have an audience, and they're cheering loudly. When I pull back, Evie's eyes are dilated, and her lips are swollen as her breaths come in pants.

"Keep that thought, starling," I murmur.

She nods.

"Ladies and gentlemen, let me be the first to introduce you to Mr. and Mrs. Sawyer King," the officiant concludes.

The cheering continues as we make our way down the aisle. I'd drag her back to the cabin right now, but today isn't about that—not entirely. And I'll behave.

For now.

EVIE

The sun hangs low in the sky by the time we say goodnight and head to the cabin. It's nine, and the wedding reception is winding down. The majority of our guests are staying in Homer for the night before returning to Anchorage to catch flights home.

Meanwhile, my husband and I have the cabin to ourselves for the next ten days.

Husband. Eek!

Two years ago, this was unimaginable—walking hand in hand with the sexiest man alive. Now, he wears my ring. Just like I wear his. I brush my thumb over the simple white gold band under my engagement ring, but I don't have to pinch myself.

This is real.

"Tired?" Sawyer asks.

"A little."

Sleep was elusive last night. I'd drift off but wake up and check the time before drifting off again. The pattern repeated itself all night.

"It's been a long day," he murmurs.

"It's been a good day—"

He sweeps me up into his arms at the threshold and carries me up the stairs to the main level. But he doesn't stop there. As I hold tight to his shoulders, he takes the next set of stairs as if I weigh as much as Benji. The door to our bedroom is closed, and since his hands are occupied, he gestures for me to open it.

Candles burn on every surface, and a bottle of champagne and two flutes sit on a nightstand. The room-darkening shades are pulled most of the way, so although they grant us privacy, the bay still comes into view.

"Oh."

"Do you like it?"

He studies me cautiously, nerves visible in the lines that deepen around cobalt blue eyes.

317

"I love it. But when did you do this? You've been by my side the whole day."

He shrugs. "I have my ways."

His lips are strong and sure as he brushes a teasing kiss against mine once, then again, while he lets me slide down his body slowly. I gasp as I graze his erection.

"Still tired?" His tone is filled with mirth.

"I think I found my second wind," I tease.

I stand on my tiptoes and pull him in for another kiss. But this one isn't teasing. It's lips and tongue and roaming hands as I push his suit jacket off his shoulders. He grips my ass and presses my lower body against his, forcing a whimper from me.

"We're wearing too many clothes," I breathe.

He trails hot, open-mouthed kisses along my jaw and nips at my earlobe.

"Easily fixed," he growls.

I've already made quick work of the buttons on his dress shirt and have moved on to running my hands over the smooth cotton of his undershirt. Hairs have come loose from my up-do and tickle along my neck, making me shiver at the light contact.

"Can you help me with my dress?" I ask him.

"It's been at the top of my to-do list all day."

I spin in his arms so he can undo the buttons. With the open back, there aren't many, but most of them are hard to reach.

For a man of his size, he's gentle as he undoes each one with expert precision. His fingers graze along the skin of my back, teasing me and creating goosebumps along my skin.

"Did I tell you how beautiful you look today?" he asks as he places a kiss on the side of my neck.

"You did. Many times."

"I'm so fucking lucky to call you mine."

Once the last button is undone, he pushes the shoulders down to free my arms. The only thing holding the dress up is the swell of my hip. It hangs there for a heartbeat before it drops to the ground. Clad only in my panties, I shiver again, but not because I'm cold. If anything, the heat in his gaze is enough to set me on fire.

"*Fuck,*" he groans.

A moment later, he pulls me back against him, the soft hair of his chest tickling along my back.

He's already shed his unbuttoned dress shirt and undershirt.

"That was fast," I tell him.

"I need to touch you, starling."

"I'm all yours."

"Yes, you are. My wife."

My core pulses at the possession in his voice.

"Say it again."

"My wife." He lifts his hands, cupping my breasts, and brings his mouth to my shoulder.

I tilt my head, granting him better access, and cry out when he sinks his teeth into the tendon at the same time he plucks at my nipples.

My knees buckle, but he bands one arm around my waist to hold me up.

"Do you know how long I've wanted to do this?" He guides me forward until we're next to the bed and lowers me slowly down to my knees.

"H-how long?"

He slides two fingers into the elastic of my panties and tugs them down my quivering thighs.

"Since the minister pronounced us man and wife."

He brings a hand between my legs and finds my swollen clit with his fingers, circling it quickly.

"Sawyer." I moan, falling forward until my elbows and knees are all that hold me up.

The slide of his zipper is loud in the room, the sound making my core throb. God. I've been dying for this since the moment we first kissed as husband and wife.

"I need you," I tell him. "Now, please."

His naked body covers mine, but he shifts us until I straddle him. His eyes shine with love and desire as he plays with my breasts until I lift my hips against him. Only then does he line himself up at my entrance and slowly pull my hips down until I'm seated fully on his cock. I mewl at the fullness, at the number of overwhelming sensations that buffet my body all at once, at the orgasm that shimmers at the edges.

Need.

Love.

His hands twine with mine, and he holds our arms out until my breasts barely graze his chest and create friction as he lifts his hips, increasing his pace until I'm balanced on the edge. Fluttering my eyes open, I meet his gaze. His tendons strain while a muscle ticks in his jaw—he's as close as I am. That thought alone ratchets my orgasm up one more level.

"Fuck. I'm close. I need you to come with me, starling."

"Me...too," I pant.

His hips piston faster, and starbursts flash in my vision. If I didn't know better, I'd swear it was the northern lights. But it's Sawyer. It always has been.

"I love you," he groans.

His words are all it takes for my orgasm to take over. The starbursts shift to a white light as pleasure fires through my blood—a fire that leaves nothing untouched as it burns us both.

"I love you, my husband."

His body stills as he finds his own orgasm, growling into my ear when I collapse against him. With both hands, he traces nonsensical patterns along the skin of my back. The pattern shifts until he's drawing letters on my back.

F-o-r-e-v-e-r-l-o-v-e.

Forever love.

"Forever," I murmur, capturing his lips as the fire burns once more.

It may be just long enough to love him. But as he rolls me under him for round two, I highly doubt it.

———

Now that Sawyer & Evie have found their happily ever after, who's next?

Keep reading for sneak peek of Bodyguard for the Beauty Queen!

BODYGUARD FOR THE BEAUTY QUEEN

COLE

7 YEARS AGO

"What's the matter, Honey Girl?" I glance away from the windshield to spy my girlfriend curled up on the opposite side of the truck seat, clutching the door handle and looking like third runner-up in the Miss Mistletoe Creek County Fair Pageant.

But even me using a nickname for her that ordinarily makes her smile only creates a sigh.

Fuck.

I flip on the radio, tuning in to our favorite station as we wind the back roads through the foothills of the Smokies that surround our hometown of Mistletoe Creek, Tennessee. The reception is spotty the farther up we drive, but it fills the silence as I rack my brain and try to figure out how to make our last night together a happy memory rather than a sad one.

I'm going to need that memory to keep me going until I can see her again. Hopefully ten weeks from now when I'm finishing up basic. That's if she can make it out to South Carolina for my graduation.

She's still waiting on the information on when her freshmen move-in date is. I'm so fucking proud of my girl for getting into Vanderbilt.

"I'm fine," she says.

But the normal lyrical cadence to her voice is flat. Robotic.

"Sweetheart, it's been a long time since you weren't snuggled against my side. And the last time you were this quiet was the time you lost your voice at the football game we won against Devil Falls."

I find the turn that's little more than a gap between two of the trees. The path is clear, but only barely fits my old truck. Between the bumps and the trees I've skimmed with my fingers when my window is down, I can't watch for her response.

The trees finally spread out more until they're in my rearview and all that's left in front of us is a vista of Mistletoe Creek. The high school is on the edge of town, quiet now that school is out for the summer, and the rest of the little town nestles around it. It's idyllic and it's charming, but it's too small for what I want in my life. I've grown up here, but I'm not willing to just settle down and be a Volunteer before coming back to work in Dad's distillery. That plan might make sense for Justin and Jared, but I am not like my older brothers.

It's what makes the military so exciting—because it wasn't planned out for me.

I put the truck in park and reach for Hannah Grace's hand to tug her toward me.

"Han."

"Don't."

Fuck. Her voice is thick with tears, and proof of one drops on my hands.

"Sweetheart."

I pull her against my chest, rubbing my hand along her back while she sobs into the cotton of my T-shirt.

The scent of her citrus shampoo tickles my nose, and I take a deep breath.

"It's our last night together, baby. I don't want you to cry."

I don't want this memory.

Already the guilt is enough to have me second-guessing my choice.

"I don't want you to go," she mumbles, the words hard to understand through the tears and hiccuping breaths.

"I know." I drop my lips to her hair and keep the steady rhythm of my hand on her back.

She leans up, those cornflower-blue eyes shiny with tears.

"It didn't feel real before, Cole. I want this to be a dream. To wake up tomorrow and not have to say goodbye." Her lower lip trembles, and she sinks her teeth into it to stop the vibration.

I lift my hand and glide my thumb along the swollen flesh.

"It's not forever," I tell her.

More tears slide under my palm that rests against her cheek.

"I can call you…and write. And it's only ten weeks until graduation."

"It's not the same. I've seen you every day for as long as I can remember. I won't be able to do this"—she runs her hands up my chest— "when you're four hours away."

I try to ignore my body's natural reaction to her touch, but my dick jumps. And since she's almost on top of me, I can't hide it.

"Fuck, Hannah Grace, I'm sorry. I didn't bring you up here for this." I groan and lean my head back against the seat.

Even though *this* is something I've thought about since I hit puberty.

"I know. You've never…"

"No."

I respected Hannah Grace too much to push her to do something she wasn't ready for. I respected my own mama's hand upside the back of my head too. I didn't need any other reason to make her want to use it. Between five kids, she has plenty of her own reasons.

Her expression shifts, the tears only salty trails on her cheeks, while mischief tilts her lips.

"What's that look, Hannah Grace Whittaker?"

It's one that's never boded well for me.

In fact it normally results in one or both of us getting grounded.

It's not like Mom can ground me, since I'm leaving tomorrow morning.

It's an accurate statement, but I'm still hesitant to go along with anything involved in that particular expression on Hannah's face.

The last time had resulted in us launching over a thousand bouncy balls in the high school's auditorium during the county's beauty pageant that Hannah hadn't wanted to participate in. Turns out, it didn't stop the pageant. However, it did end up getting back to both our mamas.

Being grounded and voluntold into helping with the high school's locker clean-out day was a consequence I never wanted to live again. Several lockers hadn't been cleaned out all year—and the lunch bag/science experiments inside had proven it.

"Why did you bring me up here?"

"This is our spot, sweetheart. I couldn't imagine our last date happening anywhere else. My favorite view in this world is this view with you in it."

Reaching forward, I grab my phone off the dash and shake it toward her.

"Come with me," I tell her and open my door.

"No pictures. I'm a mess. I'm all splotchy." She tries to stay in the car, but our connected hands make it easy to tug her out.

"You're not splotchy; you'll always be beautiful to me," I murmur and brush a kiss on the tip of her nose.

Her hands come up and rest against my biceps, her fingers skimming the underside of my arms and coming close to my ticklish spot.

I shy away.

"No, you don't."

"It pays to have known you forever," she tells me and sneaks past my defenses to run her fingers up my side.

I giggle and clear my throat as I wrap my arms around her and hold her to my chest with her hands trapped between us.

"Gotcha," I say.

She moves to her tiptoes and puckers her lips in my direction, and I oblige by covering her mouth with mine.

"Would you please take a picture with me?" My lips tease hers with my question. "I want to have one with me that's recent. That's us. Not made-up for prom. But the real us."

"How do you always know what to say that makes me want to say yes?"

Her question is innocent enough, but I hope there's more truth to it since I have another question to ask her. One more important than to take a picture with me.

I position us so that she's still wrapped in one arm, the vista behind us, and lift the camera to capture one selfie of the two of us smiling.

"How about one with a kiss?" she suggests.

"Hannah Grace!" I hold my phone against my chest, pretending an affront that the older generation in our town has down pat.

Something I will never say to the leaders of that generation—Fern, Fawn, and Merry. Although deep down, I think they enjoy watching young couples in love.

"Stop pretending like you don't want to kiss me, Cole Strickland." She smacks my chest playfully.

I oblige her request for a kiss and lift my camera at just the right time to capture the two of us locked together. I manage to separate us before my hormones take over then pocket my phone.

My fingers brush the velvet box in my pocket, and I suck in a deep breath as Hannah turns in my arms to focus on the view at our feet.

I clear my throat again, swallowing the lump of nerves that wants to take up residence on my vocal cords.

"I'm going to miss you, sweetheart," I whisper.

She rotates in my arms and squeezes her arms around me.

"I'm going to miss you too."

"I love you."

It's not the first time I've said the words, but this is the moment when they take on the most meaning they've ever had.

"I love you," she murmurs and presses her lips against my heart.

"Hannah Grace, I've loved you for forever, and I'm going to love you for the rest of my life. Maybe even longer."

"Cole?" She looks up, her brows furrowed as she studies my expression.

I take advantage and drop my lips to hers again. She's where I find my strength and my peace. And I doubt she even realizes it.

"I've known I was going to marry you from the time I was ten years old. You walked into the community center Christmas dance in that red party dress with white lace—the one you told me you hated—and all I could think about was how soft it looked. And how nice you were to wear it because your mama wanted you to match the dress she had."

"What are you saying, Cole?"

"I won't ask you to marry me now, Hannah Grace. Partly because I haven't talked to your daddy for his permission, but mostly because I want to see you finish school, sweetheart. I'm so fucking proud of you for getting into Vanderbilt. And I refuse to let you give that up to follow me. You're going to be something, baby. And I'm going to be cheering you on. But until then, I won't ask you the question I really want and instead, I want to make you a promise. Someday, Hannah Grace, someday I'm going to ask you to marry me. With your daddy's blessing and when we're ready. Nothing is going to stop me." I pull the box from my pocket and flip up the lid. "It's not a ring, not yet. I want you to have one—the one you deserve—but I also wanted you to have something that sealed my promise."

I lift out the chain where a key rests next to a small heart with the initials C and H engraved in it.

"What I'm asking is if you'll accept my promise? If you'll let me love you forever and wait for me, for us, for the right time. To someday be my wife."

She nods furiously, throwing her arms around me as soon as I'm done with the speech I've rehearsed a thousand times.

"Yes!"

My arms tighten around her and I hold her to me, burying my head in her neck and breathing in her sweet citrus scent.

She said yes.

Her lips find mine, and she bounces in my arms until we break the kiss with a laugh.

"Put it on me, please?"

She spins again, and I lift the necklace over her head and wait for her to move her hair out of the way.

"There." Closing the clasp, I kiss the back of her neck and relish the shiver that works its way down her spine.

"Cold, sweetheart?" I ask, already knowing that even in the mountains, our June weather is hard to be cold in.

"Can we get back in the truck?" Her question catches me off guard.

"Sure. Sorry. I didn't think. It is colder up here..." I boost her into the truck and climb in behind her.

The door snicks shut and she straddles me, her mouth

claiming mine while her hands grip the hem of my T-shirt and tug. My dick hardens in a rush, pushing against the zipper of my shorts.

"Whoa, whoa, whoa, what's all this?" I ask, pulling away and holding her at arm's length when she appears ready to dive back in again.

"I want to, Cole. I—"

"I didn't make my promise for anything like this from you, Hannah Grace. We can wait."

"*I* can't wait. I want you. Right now."

She grinds her pelvis against my dick, and I can't hold back the moan that works its way out of my throat. Every part of my self-control is focused on being a gentleman even though she's telling me that's not what she wants.

Her lips find the pulse point in my neck and her tongue laves the spot, pleasure overwhelming every other conscious thought.

"Please. We just have tonight."

Apparently done fighting my shirt, she sits up and lifts hers over her head, displaying a perfect pair of tits clad in a light-pink lace bra.

I squeeze my eyes shut and fist my hands into the cotton of her shorts. She wiggles some more before grabbing my hands and lifting them to her now bare chest, and my eyes fly open to find my traitorous palms grazing the soft skin of her breasts, her nipples poking into the center of my palms.

"*Please.*"

Any chance I had of fighting against her temptation evaporates. With more strength than I think I have, I lift one hand and cup her nape to bring her lips back to mine and give in to the fire that burns us both until all that's left is the two of us...no longer two, but one.

What happens after Cole leaves Mistletoe Creek and Hannah Grace? You can binge his second chance, forced proximity happily ever after, BODYGUARD FOR THE BEAUTY QUEEN, on KU by scanning the QR code!

ARE YOU READY FOR DETECTIVE FOR THE DEBUTANTE?

He swore he'd never fall in love...until she became the only thing worth falling for...

Coming September 30, 2025

Scan the QR code to pre-order this first responder, age gap, romantic suspense happily ever after on Amazon!

PLAYLIST

Sawyer and Evie's playlist is a compilation of heartbreaking songs like Imagine Dragon's "Wrecked" and anthems like Concrete Castles' "Porcelain." The songs that inspired Evie and Sawyer's love story are a mix of the powerful and the heartfelt—exactly like the two of them.

Want to listen to the music that inspired *Soldier for the Starling*? Check out the playlist on Spotify by searching for the "Soldier for the Starling" playlist or scan the QR code below.

 You can both the playlist and the bonus tracks on my website:

https://www.breannalynnauthor.com

ACKNOWLEDGMENTS

To you. Yes, you. The one who just read Sawyer and Evie's story! Thank you for taking the chance on the two of them. I hope you enjoyed reading *Soldier for the Starling* as much I enjoyed writing it!

For my family—thank you. This dream was almost unreachable lately and I couldn't have done it without all of your support! I love you!

Claire and Alina—Thank you for continuing to push me and encourage me into finishing Sawyer and Evie's story. There were times I doubted I could do it, days where I didn't touch this manuscript, and yet you were always there.

Beth—For reminding me that taking my time was okay!

For Lori—whose support of this story—and life in general—has been a part of what I needed to keep going.

To my Alpha Readers, my Betas, and my ARC team—your excitement as you anticipated reading Sawyer and Evie's story kept the words flowing! Thank you for being patient! I hope you enjoy this story!!

I can't imagine this journey without any of you! XOXO

ALSO BY BREANNA LYNN

HEART BEATS SERIES

Written in the Beat

In The Beat of the Moment

Keeping the Beat

Betting on the Beat

Embracing the Beat

Falling for the Beat

SAFE HAVEN SECURITY

Soldier for the Starling

Bodyguard for the Beauty Queen

Detective for the Debutante

STAND ALONE NOVELLAS

Rockin' Around the Christmas Tree

Midnight in Mistletoe

Hating Mr. Write

One Weekend in Vegas

ABOUT THE AUTHOR

Breanna Lynn lives in Colorado with her two sets of twins (affectionately referred to as the Twinx), her boyfriend, his son, their two dogs, and three cats. A classy connoisseur of all things coffee, Breanna spends her free time keeping the Twinx from taking over the world. When not coordinating chaos, Breanna can be found binge reading, listening to music, or watching rom-coms with a giant bowl of popcorn.

Want to follow Breanna? Scan the QR code for all the ways to stay caught up!